What the critics are saying about...

Bad In Boots: Colt's Choice

4 Stars! "...Lust, passion, deep desire and tender feelings all play a part in setting the course for a happy future in this second story in Michelle's Bad in Boots series. If you enjoy hot and spicy romance, and strong sexy cowboys, then don't miss Colt's Choice." - *Leigh, Romantic Times Bookclub*

5+ Stars! "...If I could have given this more than a 5 star rating, I would have. This was such a well-written and well thought out story that it will be hard for any reader to put it down once they start." - *Christine, eCataRomance Reviews*

5 Ribbons! "...You don't find many writers that can make you want to live the story, but Patrice makes me want to go back to Texas. This book is a scorcher..." - *Phyllis, Romance Junkies Reviews*

5 Rating! "...Ms Michelle writes a powerful story, just the kind I like. The ending gave me some major emotional tinges and I will definitely be looking out for her next cowboy book." - *Valerie, Mon-Boudoir.de Reviews*

5 Stars! "...These Tanner men make me wanna be a cowgirl, baby! Excellent story, I highly recommend it." ~ *Patrice Storie, Just Erotic Romance Reviews*

4 Stars! "...Fans of Ms. Michelle's work will not be disappointed as she provides steamy sex, witty dialogue, and an interesting plot. For those who love their Westerns spicy, this is the perfect book." ~ *J.B. DuBose, Just Erotic Romance Reviews*

Bad in Boots: Harm's Hunger

"Author Patrice Michelle certainly packs a lot of heat and passion with her debut romantica, HARM'S HUNGER. Her characters were refreshing and passionate, and their storyline perfect for them. I can't wait to read more by this new author..." - *Jordan Moon, The Word on Romance*

5 Roses! "Patrice Michelle takes you where you want to be and desire to be. Pick up this book when you can for a great read with a cowboy touch and a great ending!!" - *Alma, Love Romances*

"...This first book in the Bad in Boots series is electrifyingly hot, sensual and marvelous. Patrice Michelle writes this tale with strength and knows how to please her readers." - *Tracey West, The Road to Romance*

Hearts Afire
(from the Hearts Are Wild anthology)

5 Stars! "...Saddle up ladies! You're in for the ride of your life when you read how this sexy cowboy teaches his lady to ride a horse. This thrilling and scorchingly sexy cowboy story, penned by the magnificently talented Patrice Michelle will set your "Hearts Afire" - *Christine, eCataromance Reviews*

"...Patrice Michelle has another winner with Hearts Afire. Well-written and thought-provoking, it might even make some readers cry..." - *Angela Camp, Romance Reviews Today.*

4 Stars! "...I enjoy a story by Patrice Michelle and <u>Hearts Afire</u> is no exception. I like Sabrina's sensual but discriminating nature and Josh is a hot, intense alpha who is able to tap into Sabrina's latent sexual desires. He is so sexy that he gave me the shivers..." - *J.B. DuBose, Just Erotic Romance Reviews*

COLT'S CHOICE
BAD IN BOOTS 2

Patrice Michelle

COLT'S CHOICE
An Ellora's Cave Publication, April 2005

Ellora's Cave Publishing, Inc.
1337 Commerce Drive, #13
Stow, OH 44224

ISBN #1419951440

Colt's Choice © 2004 Patrice Michelle
ISBN MS Reader (LIT) ISBN # 1419900522
Other available formats (no ISBNs are assigned):
Adobe (PDF), Rocketbook (RB), Mobipocket (PRC) & HTML

ALL RIGHTS RESERVED. This book may not be reproduced in whole or in part without permission.

This book is a work of fiction and any resemblance to persons, living or dead, or places, events or locales is purely coincidental. They are productions of the authors' imagination and used fictitiously.

Edited by *Martha Punches*.
Cover art by *Syneca*.

Warning:

The following material contains graphic sexual content meant for mature readers. Colt's Choice has been rated S-ensuous by a minimum of three independent reviewers.

Ellora's Cave Publishing offers three levels of Romantica™ reading entertainment: S (S-ensuous), E (E-rotic), and X (X-treme).

S-ensuous love scenes are explicit and leave nothing to the imagination.

E-rotic love scenes are explicit, leave nothing to the imagination, and are high in volume per the overall word count. In addition, some E-rated titles might contain fantasy material that some readers find objectionable, such as bondage, submission, same sex encounters, forced seductions, and so forth. E-rated titles are the most graphic titles we carry; it is common, for instance, for an author to use words such as "fucking", "cock", "pussy", and such within their work of literature.

X-treme titles differ from E-rated titles only in plot premise and storyline execution. Unlike E-rated titles, stories designated with the letter X tend to contain controversial subject matter not for the faint of heart.

Also by Patrice Michelle:

A Taste for Passion
A Taste for Revenge
Bad in Boots: Harm's Hunger
Cajun Nights anthology
Dragon's Heart
Ellora's Cavemen: Tales from the Temple II anthology

COLT'S CHOICE
BAD IN BOOTS 2

Patrice Michelle

Dedication

To Martha Punches…my calm editor with a keen eye. Thank you for always letting me keep my voice while making sure I write the best story I can.

Chapter One

"Woo-hoo! Ride 'em, cowboy!"

Colt turned in his chair at the very feminine voice. *Wonder if her body matches that sexy voice?* he thought as he bent the blinds to peer out the window. She stood on the bottom board of the fence and leaned over the top rail to cheer his brother on. The position made her faded jeans fit her rear end perfectly, displaying all her feminine curves. His gaze traveled up her body to the glossy, jet-black hair that swung against her fitted pink tank top as she watched Mace ride their newest bronco. She had to be Mace's bunny of the week. He always had one or two going at a time.

"Damn," he muttered to himself as he shoved away from the desk, grabbed his hat and headed outside. "Mason!" Colt called out. His brother landed in the dirt and quickly rolled away from the bucking horse's hooves while Sam, his best wrangler, grabbed hold of the reins and pulled the stallion back to the stables.

"It's one thing to break in a horse when needed, but what have I told you about riding the broncs just for kicks?" He directed his anger at his brother while he walked up to the fence. "If Cade wants to risk his neck riding in the rodeos, so be it, but I need at least one brother to keep a head on his shoulders in order to help me run this place."

Colt didn't give a shit if he came off sounding like a dad, for the truth was, he'd been responsible for his brothers since he was twenty. He might only be five years older than Cade and seven years older than Mace, but fifteen years and two grown brothers later, he found old habits died hard.

Colt's brother picked up his hat, dusted himself off and

casually headed toward him. Mace flashed him a quick smile before he settled his hat on his head and turned his green eyes to the lady standing next to him. "Nothin' I like better than an audience," he said, while his appreciative gaze roamed over her form.

Colt focused his attention on the woman, now that he had a full view of her face. She couldn't be more than a year or two older than Mace. Lust slammed him hard in the gut as he took in her exquisite features. For once in his life he experienced outright jealousy for something Mace possessed. And it was all wrapped up in a five-foot six-inch, nicely shaped package of sultry green eyes, rosy cheeks, pouty lips and soft, sun-kissed skin. He smiled and the woman returned his smile as she put her hand over the fence toward Mace.

"Nice to meet you," she said as she turned to face his brother, "Mason."

Mace, never one to pass up an opportunity, clasped her hand in his and instead of shaking it, leaned over and kissed her fingers. He touched the brim of his hat. "Actually, I go by Mace." Grinning, he continued. "Pleasure's all mine, Miss…?" He paused, his eyes carrying a hopeful look.

She gave a throaty laugh at his obvious attempt to find out if she was single. "*Miss* Elise Hamilton."

Colt stiffened at the woman's name. His brother cut his gaze over to him before he straightened and released her hand. "Good to meet you, Elise." He smiled and winked at her. "I'm sure you and my brother have a lot to talk about, so it's off to work for me." He gave Colt a quick salute and headed for the stables.

He put out his hand. "Colt Tanner." He knew his tone was brusque, but the woman showing up in Texas totally threw him.

"Nice to meet you, Colt." She put her small hand in his larger one and gave him a firm handshake before she released his hand.

He never expected his 'partner' to come to Texas.

"You didn't have to come all the way to Texas to sell your half of the ranch to me, Miss Hamilton." He needed to keep the formality. The feel of her hand in his felt somehow…right, way too damn right.

She gave a melodious laugh and looked him straight in the eyes. Her chin jutted up just a little higher as she said, "You're right, it would be ridiculous for me to come all the way to Texas just to sell my half of the ranch to you. But that's not why I'm here. I'm here because I plan to keep it."

* * * * *

Elise chuckled inwardly. Her new partner couldn't have been more floored by her statement if she had hit him upside the head with a two-by-four. She knew by the gimme-a-fuckin'-break expression on Colt's face that he didn't think she knew her way around a horse, let alone a ranch. She'd been on a ranch before, but one thing was true—she knew absolutely nothing about rodeos. That was why she came here. She wanted to learn. She needed to learn. Coming to Boone, Texas was about starting out fresh.

She'd noticed the heated look in his steel blue eyes before he knew who she was. He was attracted to her and, heaven help her, the feeling was definitely mutual. Her gaze traveled up his six-foot two-inch frame as she took in the scuffed leather boots, the soft worn blue jeans, and *oh my*, the thick bulge at his crotch.

As much as she wanted to linger on that spot, she shifted her gaze upward. His white western shirt, a stark contrast to his tanned skin, fit his muscular upper body only too well. Dark hair peeked out from underneath the black Stetson perched on his head. What would it feel like to run her fingers through that hair? Was it wavy or straight?

She lowered her gaze to his face once more. With a square jaw and late afternoon stubble already showing, his features were more rugged than chiseled, but in her mind those rugged edges made him even sexier. The sensual combination of a thin upper lip with a fuller bottom one caused her stomach to drop to her knees.

Unfortunately, right now that mouth had compressed into a thin line and his left jaw muscle jumped with what seemed to be suppressed anger. She wondered if his jaw always did that when he was angry. When her gaze finally settled on his, the deep blue pools, fringed with thick dark lashes, stared back at her, narrowed in obvious irritation.

Elise moved around him and started toward the stables. She glanced over her shoulder and gave him a winning smile. "Come on, Cowboy, show me around the ranch."

As she entered the stables and the fresh smells of leather, hay, dirt, horseflesh and open outdoors assailed her senses, Elise knew she'd made the right decision to come to Texas. Inheriting the other half of the Lonestar ranch from her Aunt Marie had given her an opportunity she just couldn't pass up—one she desperately needed.

So she quit her job—to her father's delight—and then booked a flight to Texas—to her father's outrage—telling her parents she'd be in Texas for the rest of the summer. Her father was livid. Like that was new. He'd always expected her to come to work for Hamilton Enterprises, Inc.

She'd shipped some of her things and driven to Texas where she'd rented an apartment in town for now, but soon she would rent a house closer to the ranch. First, she had to figure out how to convince the other owner of the Lonestar, and her partner, that she was serious. She had no intention of going back to Virginia. She just hadn't told her parents that yet.

* * * * *

Colt watched Elise walk away, her slim hips swaying in her fitted jeans. His body immediately reacted to the rhythmic movement as the stirrings of desire slammed into his crotch. He clamped his jaw tighter to keep a rein on his growing attraction to the woman.

Last month he'd been furious when his Uncle James' will

was read and he discovered he hadn't inherited the other half of the Lonestar rodeo ranch, as had been agreed upon for the last fifteen years.

Five years ago, his uncle had married and since then had left the running of the Lonestar completely to Colt, which suited him just fine. But instead of keeping his end of the agreement, upon his death, his uncle willed his half of the Lonestar to his wife, Marie, "to do with as she saw fit". Marie, Lord love her, decided to give her half of the Lonestar ownership to her niece, Elise Hamilton.

Colt didn't hold anything against Marie. He just wanted the ranch. The sooner the better. He'd hoped the knowledge that his uncle hadn't left him the ranch had stayed within the family. If Riley learned the news, the man would definitely up the ante on Colt's ability to buy his land back. What a freakin' mess that would be, having his neighbor finally get his hands on part of the land he'd always felt was rightfully his.

Throughout the years, Riley had often times tried to pit his father and uncle against each other. But blood meant a lot in Texas and even though the two brothers argued from time to time, they'd never wavered in their mutual love or protection of their land.

Once Colt learned the contents of his uncle's will, he'd immediately sought backers to put together a fair offer to Miss Hamilton. Seeking financial help stretched him thin, but would be worth it if he could own the ranch outright. Owning one hundred percent of the property would go a long way in locking his hold on the Lonestar ranch and surrounding land.

Colt had his attorney draft papers for Ms. Hamilton to sign, selling her half of the ranch to him and he'd overnighted the package to her. He'd never expected her to show up here. She was from Northern Virginia—an elitist society type, from money, *old* money.

Her curved backside drew his attention like a magnet, pulling him out of his reverie. The memory of the way her soft hand felt against his a minute ago, a hand that had apparently never known a day of hard work, both aroused and irritated the shit out of him.

Annoyed with himself for being drawn in by her looks, he dropped his gaze to less arousing territory. Dust had just started to form on the heels of her boots. Yep, they were new as a baby colt and just as shiny. She stopped outside the stables and shook Sam's hand before following him inside the building.

Why was she here?

Maybe she just wanted to have a look-see at her inheritance to make sure it seemed to be run properly, Colt rationalized. What could showing her around the Lonestar hurt? The sooner he did that, the sooner she could feel the ranch was in capable hands and then be on her way back to Virginia. He'd figure a way to talk her into selling her half of the ranch to him.

By the time Colt entered the stables, Elise was already mounted on Sam's horse. She looked down at him after she'd cast a warm smile at Sam who stood there holding the horse's reins.

"Sam said I could ride Jack, for now, and he would saddle up a suitable horse for next time."

Colt turned accusing eyes to his wrangler. Sam was too busy staring up into Elise's face. His smile was so broad his black mustache was bent at a strange angle. Colt gave a loud sigh and moved to saddle his horse. Great, just what he needed, a ranch full of star-struck cowboys who wouldn't get a lick of work done because they were too busy ogling the new half-owner of the Lonestar. Make that the soon-to-be ex-half-owner of the Lonestar, he corrected as he swung his leg up on his horse. And the sooner he got rid of her, the better.

As he pulled his horse up next to hers, Colt reached over, lifted a spare hat off of a hook on the wall and plunked it down on her head none-too-gently. "Here, it'll help keep the heat off," he said in gruff tone, before he kicked his heels into Scout's sides and took off ahead of her. He didn't want to think about the fact that it also helped hide her beautiful face and ebony hair from the curious cowboys they would meet during their tour.

Colt intentionally took off at a gallop. He needed to blow off steam. Heading in the direction of the open pastures, he figured he'd have to stop and wait for Elise to catch up. He didn't even think to ask her if she knew how to ride a horse. It would serve the "princess" right if she fell off once or twice to show her that ranch life was not easy.

As he started to slow Scout down, Elise came flying past him in a full gallop, the cowboy hat flying off her head. Her long black hair streamed behind her along with her laughter as she left him behind in a cloud of dust kicked up by her horse's hooves.

After stopping to pick up her hat, Colt remounted Scout and dug his heels in, taking off after her. He lowered his head and spoke to his horse, urging him on. Up ahead, Elise turned her horse to jump a fallen tree. His heart slammed in his chest at her reckless move, but relief and finally grudging respect dawned as he watched them clear the obstacle with ease.

Elise slowed her horse and waited for him to catch up. When she turned laughing eyes his way, Colt didn't want to like her sultry gaze. He didn't want to wonder if her silky hair felt as soft as it looked. He drew his horse up next to hers, his knee brushing against her thigh as he jammed the hat on her head. "That has got to be the stupidest thing I've ever seen someone do," he ground out.

Her smile faded and she stared back at him in surprise.

Colt rambled on, letting his anger override his libido—or hell, maybe it was because of his libido. "Don't you know better than to try to jump a horse you've never ridden before? How did you know Jack wouldn't have stopped short of that tree and sent you flying?"

Elise's cheeks flamed and her eyes narrowed at his words. "First of all, I'm very familiar with horses. Second of all, I did think to ask Sam particulars about his horse before I got on him. Third of all, you have no right to talk to me like that. None whatsoever."

He felt his neck go red at the truth of her last comment, but already he and Elise weren't starting off in the most normal of circumstances. He leaned closer to her.

"When you're on my ranch, your safety is my responsibility. So yes, Princess, I do have a right to make sure you don't break your lovely little neck."

She gave him a knowing smile and leaned close to him, her nose almost touching his. "I guess it's a good thing the Lonestar is half my property then, isn't it?"

A challenge had been laid and he'd be damned if he'd pass it up. Colt ignored her cry of surprise as he cupped his hand behind her neck and pulled her mouth to his. Their horses neighed while he explored her lush mouth with his tongue. His kiss was dominant and hard, just as he meant it to be.

When her resistance melted and she started to respond, his kiss instinctively gentled. He wanted to pull her against him, feel her breasts against his chest, her arms around his neck. He pulled back, angry with himself for wanting to continue, for wanting to know what she'd feel like underneath him as he drove into her sweet flesh, his hips cradled against hers.

"What the hell was that for?" Her eyes flashed, a mixture of anger and desire reflected in their green depths.

Colt sat up straight in his saddle, putting much needed distance between them.

"Just getting that out of the way, darlin'," he said in a rough voice.

He didn't say another word, just turned his horse and trotted off toward the east side of the property. As far as he was concerned she could follow him or trot her way straight back to Virginia.

*****

By the time Elise caught up with him, Colt seemed to have

calmed down enough to give her a guided tour of the ranch. He acted as if he'd never clamped his mouth over hers or had his tongue down her throat. That kiss blew her away. He'd smelled unbelievably good, like leather and soap mixed with a dose of all male. Even though she knew his act was meant to put her in her place, to show her he could control her, she found the bull-headed, sexy cowboy a T-total turn-on, especially when his kiss had changed as if he couldn't help but respond. But she couldn't let him know that he affected her, at least not yet, she thought with a smile.

Elise pushed her musings about Colt to the back of her mind and focused on the breathtaking view. Texas hill country had never been more beautiful. Cedars and oaks covered the rolling hills bordering the Lonestar's vast acreage. Colt pointed to the green pastures, showing her the different areas where the cattle grazed and the horses roamed. Along the way he introduced her to Rick, his foreman, and many of the ranch hands.

She received more than one raised eyebrow at her half-ownership status, but the men were all very friendly and helpful in explaining their areas of expertise. Rick stayed with her while Colt went off to see to a newborn calf. She let her gaze follow Colt as he dismounted and helped the calf get moving on feeding for the first time.

"Are all chores shared equally among the cowboys?" she asked Rick, curious to see Colt so intimately involved in the workings of his ranch.

"If you're asking can any cowboy step in and do any job on this ranch, then the answer is yes. We all have jobs we're assigned to do, but—" He nodded his head toward Colt, his brown eyes crinkling in the corners. "Even the boss gets in there and does anything and everything to get the job done for his ranch."

A fissure of guilt washed over Elise at his words. No wonder Colt was resentful. He'd worked hard for this ranch and here she came waltzing in and telling him she planned to keep her half, which was nothing more than a piece of paper, not the hard-earned, sweat-rolling-down-your-back, aching-muscles kind of ownership Colt experienced. Hell, she'd be pissed, too. She squared her shoulders. Well, she'd just have to show him she could be a valuable asset to the Lonestar in her own way.

Rick pulled off his hat and wiped his brow with the back of his sleeve. He turned his weathered face toward her. "Yep, there's always a fence to be mended, vitamins to be dispensed to the livestock, or hay to be baled. The work is a joint effort of all the ranch hands."

Before he placed his hat back on his head, he squinted against the sun, making the wrinkles embed deeper around his eyes. Elise guessed him to be in his early fifties. "What do you know about ranching, Miss Hamilton?"

Elise cut her eyes over to Colt, thankful he was out of hearing range and answered honestly. "Very little." She smiled sheepishly. "But I'm a fast study and I'm eager to learn," she finished with sincerity.

"Well, then, that's half the battle, Miss Hamilton." Rick smiled. "How about a little ranching 101?"

Elise grinned back. "I'm all ears."

Rick's deep voice took on a proud inflection as he began the lesson. "The spring and fall are our calving, branding and roundup seasons, and summer is the time for baling hay."

He stopped talking and met her gaze. "Did you know a cattle rancher depends on the weather just as much as a farmer does for his crops?" When she shook her head, he continued, "The rancher needs the rain to water the land so the cattle will have good grazing grass." Rick swept his arm out across the pastures toward the livestock. "A good portion of the Lonestar's stock is bred right here, but Colt also attends auctions several times a year to purchase additional bucking stock for the rodeo."

When Rick delved deeper into the ranch lifestyle, Elise was amazed at how much she didn't know about ranching. And the information she learned from the foreman was all just normal routine ranch life. The rodeo part of the ranch added a whole new dimension.

Colt mounted his horse once more and trotted over to them. "Ready to go, Elise?"

Elise nodded and thanked Rick for his time. He winked at her conspiratorially saying, "Anytime, Miss Hamilton."

As Colt took her around to other areas of the ranch, they slipped into a more comfortable rhythm—Colt the teacher and she, the avid learner. The one thing that became evident as they traveled every area of the ranch was the love and pride he had for the Lonestar. She could appreciate that. She also loved the outdoors, always had.

Elise never really felt like she fit in with the rest of her family. Yeah, she could mingle with the best of them at the latest high society party or charity ball, but her heart wasn't really in it—well, maybe the raising money for charity part, but she could do that without all the other trimmings. She didn't want to become a society wife, even if that was what her father wanted and expected of her.

That world wasn't for her. She wanted to do something with her life. Run a business, put her heart and soul into it. Prove to herself she could be self-sufficient and successful as well. Okay, so inheriting a ranch that was already in working order, and apparently good working order, wasn't exactly running "her own" business. No, she didn't have a veterinarian degree nor did she grow up on a farm. But she was smart. She did have undergraduate degrees in business and computer science. And the rodeo portion of the Lonestar *was* a business. There were ways she could help out. She just needed to figure out the best way to prove to Colt she was valuable enough for him to want to keep her around.

As they neared the stables, a little devil on Elise's shoulder whispered, *Come on. You know you want to do it.* She slowed her horse and let Colt move ahead of her a good five feet or so as she reached for the rope on the front of Jack's saddle.

Colt turned in surprise when the rope landed over his shoulders to drop down around his arms. "Gotcha." Elise grinned as she pulled the trailing end of the rope taut, tightening the loop around him.

"What do you think you're doing?" Colt glowered at her.

Elise grinned at his expression. "Just trying to show you how handy I can be."

Just then, Mace walked by and let out a low whistle.

Colt sent him a look that would have withered a lesser man.

Mace winked at Elise and turned to his brother. "Now, why are you sitting there, glaring at me when you have a gorgeous woman who has you tied up in ropes and wants to show you how handy she can be?" He turned his suggestive gaze back to Elise. "I certainly know what my response would have been."

"Mace!" Colt barked.

His brother continued walking, his hands raised in the air. "I'm going, I'm going."

When Colt glanced at her, she had a hard time holding back her laughter. He pulled the rope up over his shoulders and let it drop to the ground. "Where'd you learn to do that?"

"I have a friend who grew up on a farm." She winked. "Let's just say, she showed me the ropes."

Colt turned his horse and walked him back toward her. His leg brushed up against hers, his knee touching the top of her thigh as his blue eyes penetrated hers. "What do you want, Elise? Why are you here?"

Heat spread from his leg to hers, making her heart pound at his blatant male virility and serious eyes. *You*, her body wanted her to say. Instead, logic dictated she rein in her revved-up libido. "I want to help you run the Lonestar ranch and rodeo."

Interest stirred in his eyes before it was quickly masked. "No."

"But you said yourself that you need help," she said,

keeping her tone light.

"No, I didn't," he countered, his expression turning hard.

"Yes, you did. You told Mace you needed at least one brother to help you run the Lonestar."

He narrowed his eyes on her. "You don't know the first thing about running a ranch, Princess."

"How would you know what I do and do not know? I'll bet you assumed I didn't even know how to ride a horse a couple of hours ago." *Okay, so she was bluffing about the ranch part, but she'd learned a lot today. That counted for something.* She noted the muscle ticcing in his jaw again. *Bam!* She'd pegged him. Sure enough, she had her answer—he always clenched his jaw when he was angry.

"I don't need your kind of help, Elise."

"What kind of help is that?" she asked, feeling slighted.

His eyes softened. "I can't afford you, Princess."

Why did she get the feeling he wasn't talking about the ranch anymore? "Listen, if you're worried about paying me, don't be."

"Why?" His eyes flashed in anger. "Because you're so pampered you can just fly on over to little ol' Texas and dabble at playing cowgirl until you get bored?"

Elise's spine stiffened. "Is that what your attitude is about, Colt? You think I'm playing until I get bored?"

"If the shoe fits, darlin'," he drawled.

She pulled on Jack's reins, backing the horse up. Lifting her foot out of the stirrup toward him, she said, "You see this? It's a boot, Colt, not a glass slipper. It may not be dusty and worn like yours, but I'm going to prove you wrong," she finished in a determined voice as she slipped her foot back in the stirrup and kicked her heels into Jack's sides, trotting him into the stables.

Chapter Two

Colt sat in an Adirondack chair on his deck, enjoying his morning cup of coffee. The sun had just begun to peek up over the horizon. Putting the cup to his lips, he surveyed his land. The fifteen acres of property his house resided on were not part of the Lonestar ranch. Situated on a hill along the edge of the Lonestar property, the house, a two-story rambling log cabin with a huge deck across the back and a stone fireplace lining one side, was his sanctuary. It belonged to him and him alone. He'd paid for it in blood, literally.

When his dad passed away fifteen years ago, Colt was a reigning rodeo champion. Calf roping and saddle bronc riding were his claim-to-fame events. He didn't mind giving up the circuit to raise his brothers. There was no way in hell he would have asked his mother for help since she saw fit to desert them when he was sixteen.

The rodeos had served their purpose. The winnings paid for his home and land. Mace lived at the ranch and Cade lived on the road, following the rodeos. The slant of the sun across the deck told him it was getting late. Time to go to work. Colt drained the rest of his coffee and headed for his truck.

He drove his silver Ford 250 pickup truck the mile from his house to the ranch office. Elise invaded his thoughts as he made the final turn into his parking space. She must have left the ranch after she took off yesterday because he hadn't seen her again. He was glad to see her gone. He didn't need her to try to prove him wrong. Her green eyes, infectious smile and sexy, throaty laugh were way too inviting.

He'd tossed and turned in his bed all night long, thinking about her lips and just how kissable they were. Setting his jaw, he pushed all thoughts of Elise Hamilton from his mind and hoped the next time he saw her would be when she handed him the papers selling her half of the ranch to him.

Colt entered the office and said his usual, "Good morning" to his secretary, Mabel, as he put his hat on the rack by the door.

"Good Morning, Colton," she responded with a smile. She tilted her gray head and gave him a concerned look. "You look a little tired, dear. Are you feeling well?"

"I'm fine." He didn't want to be reminded of his sleepless night. "Any messages?"

"Yes, there's a message from Jim Peterson. He wanted to meet to go over the proofs from the last rodeo." She handed him the pink slip of paper.

"Why didn't Mace take the call?"

She cut her eyes back to the half-closed door of Mace's office where the sound of laughter floated to the front of the office. "Well, he was otherwise occupied, so I just took the message. If you want, I can give this to Mace."

"No, that's okay. I'll tell him myself." Colt's boot heels dug into the carpet as he walked back to his brother's office and pushed open the door.

Elise sat in Mace's chair in front of the computer. Mace leaned behind her, his arm slung across the back of her chair in a casual manner. He looked at the computer and smiled at something she showed him.

"Colt," she looked up, her smile bright. "I just figured out how I could make myself useful."

I'll just bet you have. "Oh, really?" he said, trying to sound as bored as he possibly could when all he wanted was to tell Mace she was off limits. She was his. His gaze, as he flicked it to his brother, must have held some kind of territorial gleam, because his brother backed away and gave him a telling smile.

"Mace, Jim Peterson called. He wants to meet to go over the proofs from the latest rodeo. Seeing as how you've taken over PR duties, I thought you might want to call him back personally."

Taking the pink slip from Colt's hand, Mace said, "I think Elise might be on to something. Check it out while I go call Jim."

Elise beckoned Colt with a wave of her hand. "Come look at this."

He moved around the desk and stood behind the chair, looking at the computer screen. "It's the Lonestar's website," he stated the obvious.

Elise laughed as his stoic manner. "Well, give the cowboy a star! No, here's what I wanted to show you." She proceeded to pull up other rodeo ranches' websites, pointing out differences in them.

Colt put his hand on the desk and leaned forward as she pointed to the idea others had used of selling tickets to the rodeos right over the Internet. "Why doesn't the Lonestar do that?" She turned her face to look up at him.

"We have a person contracted to run our website," he replied. "To be honest, it wasn't something I thought much about."

"Well, you should," she admonished in a light tone and turned back to the computer screen.

As she clicked into the screen to show him how easy it was to buy a ticket online, he had to admit she was right. It would help to increase ticket sales by making advanced selling easier. He leaned closer. The smell of her shampoo mingled with her own natural scent was an enticing combination. The scent reached in and wrenched him right in the gut, well, in this case, right in the groin as the tightening of his pants could attest to.

She continued to talk about websites and webmasters and ticket sales and all he could think about was what her eyes would look like as he touched her. Would the green color change when she was aroused? Colt shook his head to clear his lustful thoughts when something she said did get his attention.

"You could save the outlay of cash to have your website revamped to include selling tickets online."

"How can I do that?"

Elise turned her gaze to him. "Haven't you been listening to me, Colt? I can do all this for you. I have a degree in computer science. All I did was work with web programming languages."

He looked into her sincere eyes. "You really want to do this, don't you?"

"If you're asking if I really want to help, be a part of the Lonestar and carry my weight, then the answer is yes."

Colt wondered about his sanity as he answered, "Okay, but only until the website is up and running. There are no other jobs here for you, Elise."

Elise glanced up at him. "We'll see about that," she said with an enigmatic smile before she turned her attention back to the computer screen and started taking notes on the pad of paper in front of her.

* * * * *

Elise rolled over in bed and groaned at the incessant ringing of the telephone. Lifting her head from the pillow, she opened her bleary eyes and glanced at the window. Still nighttime. Her head pounded from her late night vigil in Mace's office the night before as she finished up her notes for the revisions on the website.

Glaring at the annoying phone, her gaze shot to the alarm clock. 5:30! Who in the world would be calling her at 5:30 in the morning?

Leaning over, she picked up the phone from her nightstand. "Hello?"

"Elise?" It was Colt. "Get up and get a move on, woman."

"What?" she mumbled, her voice sounding raspy.

"As part owner of the Lonestar, you have responsibilities to attend to. I'll meet you at the ranch in half an hour." With that said, he hung up the phone.

Elise set the receiver in its cradle and clenched her teeth at his presumption. Counting to twenty, she had to remind herself...she did ask for this. This was her chance to prove to Colt she was serious about staying.

With a sudden burst of energy, Elise jumped out of bed and headed for the shower.

*****

As she pulled her red Audi coupe up beside his truck, Colt walked to her car in long, purposeful strides.

"You're late," he commented, irritation obvious in his tone when she opened her door.

Elise looked at her watch as she climbed out of her car and gave him a patient look.

"I'm one minute late."

He turned on his heel, calling over his shoulder, "Come on. There's a lot to do before the workday gets started. Every minute counts."

Elise followed him over to the stables. No one was around. Well, of course not! Who would be up at this ungodly hour?

Colt handed her a pitchfork. "Here, put some hay in the stalls for the horses."

Elise gave him an incredulous look.

His eyebrow shot up. "Not above doing a little hard work, are ya?"

She clamped her lips shut to keep the retort that sprang to mind from escaping. Turning on her heel, she headed for the broken up bale of hay. As she shoved the pitchfork into the straw, she imagined it was Colt's rear end. At least that brought a smile to her face.

Thankfully, someone had at least cleaned the stalls and that wasn't her assigned task for the day. While she shoveled hay, Colt fed and watered the horses. After an hour, she stopped and brushed her hand across her brow. The smell of the stables and the fresh hay assailed her nostrils, causing a smile to ride up her face. She forgot how much she loved the smells, well, minus the odor of manure, of course.

"Hey, get to work, slacker," Colt called out from over one of the stalls.

She stuck out her tongue before she started moving hay again.

Colt looked back down, but she thought she saw a smile before he turned his head.

Ten minutes later, Sam walked into the stables. A surprised look crossed his face when he looked at the pitchfork in her hand.

"Mornin' Miss Hamilton," he said respectfully as he turned questioning eyes to Colt.

"Mornin' Sam." Colt walked over and took the pitchfork from her hands.

He handed the tool to Sam and escorted her out of the stables. "I guess it's time for us to get to work."

Elise rubbed her sore hands on her jeans. "Anything else?"

He rubbed his jaw thoughtfully. "Not right now."

She saluted him and sauntered off toward the office.

* * * * *

Later that day, Elise smiled to herself while she opened another file on the computer. With Mace out of town for a couple of days, she had complete access to his computer and had already made good progress on the website. Glancing at her watch, she realized it was almost lunchtime. She rolled her shoulders and decided to work a little longer to get to a good stopping point. If she worked over, she could always go see Nan in the kitchen.

Before Mace left, he'd told her about Nan, "Not only does she fix the meals, but she helped raise us." He'd winked at Elise on his way out saying, "Yep, Nan's as much a fixture around the ranch as the horses."

After a half hour, she shut down her computer and started to pull her purse out of the drawer, ready to head out for lunch, when Colt walked into her office with an extra cowboy hat in hand.

"Where are you going?"

She looked up at him. "I'm going to lunch."

Colt reached over and put the hat on her head. "Not right now, Princess. We have a fence that needs mending. You can eat later."

"Now?" She gave him an exasperated look.

Colt turned on his heel, expecting her to follow. "Now. The cattle can't wait, Elise."

With a growling stomach, Elise gritted her teeth and followed him out of the office.

He didn't say a word as they made their way to the stables. When they got there, Colt handed her the reins to her horse.

"This is Bess. She'll be a good ride for you while you're here," he said in a no-nonsense manner before they saddled their horses and rode out.

When they reached the area of the fence that needed repairs, Colt got off his horse. As she followed suit, he said, "Fences are checked often, especially after a rain in case the fencepost loosens in the mud."

He handed her a pair of working gloves. "Here, put these on."

She complied and waited for Colt to give her further instructions. He moved over to the fence and pointed out the broken barbed wire. "See this, we constantly watch for broken wire or we could take a chance on having the cattle roam free."

He hunkered down and indicated for Elise to do the same. Colt pulled on another pair of gloves and used a tool he called a carpenter's wrecking bar—a crowbar—to hook a barb on the shorter broken strand and pull it taut using the post for leverage.

Nodding to his saddle he said, "Get the staple gun out of

my saddle bag and staple this side down."

Elise retrieved the staple gun and stapled the wire against the fence post.

Colt took the extra wire he'd brought and wound it around the broken wire several times until they were completely spliced. His quick, efficient movements showed his familiarity with even the most basic of chores. Once he'd stretched that wire in the same fashion, he had Elise staple it to the opposite post. When he finished, he stood on the wire saying, "It's done right if the new wire can withstand your weight without slipping." Once he stepped down, he turned to her and handed her the crowbar-like tool. "Now, it's your turn to repair the other snapped wire."

She arched an eyebrow but didn't say a word as she took the tool from him. Moving closer to the fence, she started to repair another section, employing the same methods she'd seen him use. After she and Colt had attached the first short wire and she moved on to tackle splicing a longer length to the broken wire, he stood behind her, watching her movements.

"No, Elise, like this," he said. He put his arms around her, manipulating her hands with the barbed wire.

Heat radiated from his body as he pressed against her back. He smelled of outdoors and leather and faintly of soap. She had to remind herself to concentrate on the task at hand while Colt showed her how to work with the barbed wire. The whole experience felt a little awkward with knowledgeable hands working with unknowledgeable ones. As they manipulated the wire, a spiked barb snapped around and caught Elise's wrist, causing her to bite back a cry of pain.

Colt dropped the tool and quickly turned her to face him. He pulled his gloves off, and threw them to the ground before he reached for her hand. As he slid her glove off, blood welled from the torn gash on her wrist. "I'm sorry, Elise," he said, his tone regretful as he pulled a handkerchief out of his back pocket and dabbed at her wrist.

She tried to pull her hand away. "It's okay, Colt. It was an accident."

Colt held fast to her hand and looked into her eyes, his blue ones full of concern. "When was the last time you had a tetanus shot?"

Tiny jolts of electricity moved up her arm at his touch. She returned his gaze. "Last year, so there's no need to worry."

He searched her gaze and then ordered in a gruff tone, "Keep that on your wrist until it stops bleeding." He picked up his gloves. "I'll finish up."

"Uh-uh. I started it, I'll finish it." Elise quickly wrapped the handkerchief around her wrist and used her teeth to secure it in a knot.

With swift movements, she pulled on her gloves and held her hand out for the tool, smiling up at him. Colt's gaze held grudging respect as he put the wrecking bar in her hand.

It was after 2:00 p.m. before Elise entered the kitchen at the ranch house. An older woman looked up from shucking corn, a questioning look in her chocolate brown eyes.

"Hi, I'm Elise Hamilton." She stuck out her hand.

The woman wiped her hands off on her apron and shook her hand. As she grinned, her dark skin only enhanced the white in her perfect, straight teeth. "I'm Nan. Heard all about you, child."

Elise laughed. "Good things, I hope?"

Nan returned to shucking her corn, a twinkle in her eye. "Yeah, Mace seems to think so."

"Mace mentioned you always have leftovers," Elise said with a hopeful look.

Nan nodded and pointed to the fridge. "There's some leftovers in the fridge if you want anything in there." She squinted at her. "Kind of a late lunch, isn't it?"

Elise smiled. "Yes, Colt had me mending fences, so I didn't get a chance to go anywhere."

Nan raised her eyebrow at her comment. "Showing you the ropes, is he?" she chuckled.

Elise sighed as she pulled luncheon meat and cheese out of the fridge. "Yes, but I suppose as half-owner, I need to learn to carry my weight around here."

Nan gave her a surprised look before she returned to her task.

* * * * *

The next two weeks were much of the same, Colt calling her in the wee hours of the morning. He always started the day with her pitching hay for the horses. Various jobs always needed tending to. Checking on the livestock, moving them to other land to graze, administering medicine and vitamins to the animals, etc. After two busy weeks, Elise once again found her way into Nan's kitchen.

"What can I get you, Elise?" Nan called out in her booming voice.

"How about some time to get work done in the office?" Elise quipped as she pulled open the fridge and poured herself a glass of lemonade.

"Colt's running you ragged, hmmm. Are you hiding out?" Nan teased.

Elise looked up from her glass and gave a conspiratorial smile. "Shh, don't tell anyone."

Nan winked at her. "Well, truth be told, I've had more ranch hands in here in the early morning time than usual myself."

"Oh, really?" Elise raised an eyebrow.

"Sure, since you're doing their work, they've decided to stop in for coffee these past couple of weeks."

Elise slowly lowered her glass. "*I'm* doing *their* work?" she spoke slowly so as not to scream in frustration.

Nan looked back down and began peeling potatoes once

more. "That's what I said."

Outrage filled her as Elise picked up her glass and walked outside. She wasn't angry at having to do the work, heck it was the best way to learn. No, she was angry at the underhanded way Colt had approached it. Taking a deep, calming breath, she eyed one of the rocking chairs on the porch.

Ever since her first day on the Lonestar, when she'd spied the rocking chairs moving in the wind on the front porch of the main ranch house, she'd wanted to sit and relax for a bit. Finally she did what she'd wanted to do. She pulled over a rocking chair close to the railing, propped her boots up on it and leaned back to sip her glass of lemonade.

Her anger diminished as she let her gaze scan the ranch. It was such a welcoming sight. The office was painted white and set off to the right of the main house. The stables were their natural brown color and the barn, painted a deep burgundy with a hunter green roof, stood off next to the stables. But the main ranch house was the most inviting. Painted white with hunter green shutters, the main house had a long front porch with several rocking chairs, a hammock on one far corner and a porch swing on the other. She'd really come to like the Lonestar, well, minus her lowdown, underhanded, slave-driver partner, she mused as her thoughts returned to Colt.

Relaxing low in the chair, she made sure to pull her hat down over her face so it looked like she was sleeping. Just let Colt say "boo" to her! Grrrr! After a half an hour of sitting and brooding, boredom took over. She started to get up and go back to the office when she heard someone walking with purposeful steps across the porch toward her.

Before she could prepare herself, her feet were swept off the porch railing to land with a loud thump on the wooden floor. She pulled her hat off her head and glared up at Colt.

"What're you doing lazin', Elise?" Colt demanded. "There are plenty of things to do around here. If you don't have enough to do, I'll be glad to find you something."

She looked up at him, letting the rebellion she felt reflect in her gaze. "I'm taking a much-needed break."

Colt gave her a hard look. "A break?"

She sat back in her chair and put her hat back on her head, staring pointedly at him. "Yes, seeing as how I was doing the work of several of the ranch hands while they leisured over breakfast, I felt I deserved an hour to myself."

Silence greeted her. Colt's jaw started ticcing again. Good. Let him be mad. The rat!

"You need to know what ranch life is like." His stubborn expression told her he wasn't about to apologize for his subterfuge. He picked up her hand and turned it over. The blisters on the palms of her hands had started to heal. He ran his thumb across the small scar that had formed on her wrist from the barbed wire. His brief touch sent shock waves radiating through her arm. Her stomach fluttered when he pressed his thumb against her pulse and met her gaze. "Ranching is a way of life, Elise. It's not a nine-to-five job."

Elise jerked her hand away from his heated touch. She was annoyed with him. She didn't want to feel anything else at the moment but anger, certainly not desire.

"I know that. And as mad as I am at you right now, I appreciate the lesson."

Realization at his motives dawned. "And that is what it was, right? A way to try to get me to leave?" Colt didn't bother to answer. His silence spoke volumes.

Elise looked out over the plains. She knew her eyes held a stubborn glint. "Well, I'm not going anywhere, Colt. What I have learned will come in handy." She turned and locked eyes with his. "When I'm needed to pitch in, I'll be right there with the best of them."

* * * * *

Noting the obstinate tilt of her chin, the determination in her eyes, Colt walked away from Elise. The woman was serious

She had no intention of going anywhere. *Now* what was he going to do with her? He knew what he wanted to do with her, but it involved getting up close and personal and that's the last thing he needed. He rubbed the back of his neck in pent-up frustration at the fireball sitting on his porch.

Chapter Three

Elise arrived at work early the next morning. She awoke at the same time she had the prior two weeks and couldn't go back to sleep. So she got up, showered and headed for the ranch. As she pulled into the parking lot, Colt was leaning against his truck with a horse trailer hooked to the back of it.

She hopped out of her car, said a merry, "Good morning" to him and walked past him toward the office.

Colt put a hand on her arm. "Where are you going?"

Elise raised her eyebrow at the hand on her arm. "I'm going to work on the website."

"No, you're coming with me."

She sighed. She didn't mind learning with the best of them, but not when it seemed to be more about a battle of wills than learning for learning's sake. "No more lessons, Colt. I'm all tapped out right now."

Colt dropped his hand from her arm and as she turned to go, he continued, "Suit yourself. I thought you might like to go to a horse auction with me."

Elise stopped dead in her tracks. A horse auction? She turned back to face him. "Now *that* I wouldn't mind doing." She noted his satisfied grin and chose to ignore it as she rounded to the passenger side of his truck.

Climbing in, she snapped the seatbelt around her. He was in the process of getting in the truck when she said in an impatient tone, "Let's go, Colt."

Colt laughed at her exuberance.

He started the truck and headed down the long drive. Once he turned out of the drive, he leaned over and picked up his cup of coffee from the coffee holder, taking a sip.

The smell of the fresh roasted coffee beans permeated her senses. Elise inhaled, enjoying the aroma. "Man, that smells good. I planned to have a cup at the office."

A grin rode up his face and he handed her his cup. "Here, knock yourself out."

Elise gave him a grateful smile as she took the cup from him, her fingers brushing his. Her heart sped up to a rapid pace as he held fast until she had a firm hold of it. Elise put the cup to her nose and inhaled before she took a long sip. She looked over at Colt. His eyes held an intense look as he glanced over while she drank from his cup. She knew he thought the same thing she did. How could drinking after someone seem so innocent yet so intimate?

She handed the cup back to him with a small smile on her lips. He took a sip and handed it back to her, giving her a heated look before he fixed his gaze back on the road. Just like the coffee warming her mouth and throat, her insides started to melt at the look he just gave her. Her breasts tingled and her stomach tensed when his gaze had briefly dropped to her lips, then her chest before returning to the road once more. The silence in the vehicle became way too intimate. As Elise lifted the cup to her lips, she asked, "So, how often do you go to the horse auction?"

He kept his gaze on the road and answered, "Four times a year."

"I thought you bred your broncs."

"Sometimes we do. Most of the time, it's easier to buy to fill in the gaps where our stock is weakest."

Elise nodded in understanding.

"What did you do before you came to Texas?" Colt asked her out of the blue.

Surprise he asked, she answered, "I worked for a start-up dot com company." She gave a wry smile. "One that's still doing very well."

"Why'd you leave? Why come all the way to Texas?"

Elise shrugged. "I have no ties to Virginia, other than my parents. When this opportunity came along, I jumped on it."

Colt flicked his gaze her way, curiosity reflected in his steel blue gaze. "Why?"

"I don't know. I guess I wanted a chance to be a part of something. To be involved with something that doesn't have anything to do with my dad's money or his influence." She smiled. "Plus, I get to spend as much time outdoors and with horses as I want."

Colt laughed at her thumb-her-nose attitude. "I take it your parents didn't approve of your love of horses?"

Elise looked at the road ahead of them. "They were fine with it when I was young." She didn't elaborate any further and was thankful Colt didn't ask because they had arrived at their destination.

Once he turned the truck into the driveway of the horse auction, she hopped out and followed him over to the makeshift pens that held horses up for auction.

"Are pleasure horses auctioned here as well?" she asked. She had to walk at a brisk pace to keep up with his long strides.

"Yes," Colt replied absently.

When they arrived at the pens, Elise listened as Colt asked to see some of the latest stock and their bucking action. After he picked out a couple of horses, the man saddled one of them. As Colt moved toward the chute and pulled on a glove he had in his back pocket, Elise grabbed his arm, her heart racing. "You aren't going to ride him, are you?"

He flashed her a devilish smile. "How else am I going to find out if he's rank enough to be in my rodeo?"

Elise sighed and let go of his arm, though apprehension still gripped her. Colt knew what he was doing. This was his way of life, she reminded herself, trying to breathe through the tightness in her chest. She watched him move around to the chute to settle himself on the horse. Once he was seated and had the rope securely gripped, he nodded to the men and the gate opened.

Elise's heart stopped in her chest as the horse shot out of the chute and did its best to buck Colt off. Watching him on the back of that horse was like a symphony in motion. His body was so in tune as if he knew just which way the horse planned to buck. It was over in a matter of seconds when Colt loosened the rope and jumped off the bucking horse to land on his feet.

Elise gave a sigh of relief that he survived, but her heart sped back up when he pointed to the other horse he had picked out, entered the chute once more and climbed on the new horse.

This time as the gate opened, she noted an immediate difference in the bucking action of this bronc. He snorted, moved in a more haphazard, unpredictable manner, and was basically as mean and ornery as he could be. Colt stayed on, but it was a battle. He didn't jump off easily this time. He landed on his side and rolled away from the bucking horse's hooves. When he jumped up grinning, Elise wanted to shake him at how very close he came to getting hurt.

When Colt moved out of the fence to stand beside her, he said with a grin, "That's the one I want."

She couldn't help but ask, "Let me guess, the more 'rank' the better?"

He tapped her upturned nose with the tip of his finger. "You're catching on, Princess. As the owner, it's my job to provide the most challenging stock for the rodeo."

"Just don't expect me to ever do that," she mumbled. Colt laughed outright at her expression. While he attended the auction, Elise walked around for a while until she saw a beautiful horse that drew her gaze—an all black mare.

She approached slowly and reached up to rub the horse's nose. The animal had a jagged white streak between her eyes. It was the only patch of color on her otherwise all black flesh. As she spoke to the horse, she looked up to see a tall man approach, his blond hair peeking out from underneath his black cowboy hat.

"You make a perfect match." His sexy smile showed perfect white teeth.

Elise laughed. "I wasn't planning on bidding today."

The man cocked his head to the side and put his hand out. "Name's Josh Kelly. You're not from around here, are you?"

She shook his hand and smiled. "Let me guess, my accent gave me away."

He winked at her and grinned, tipping his hat with his fingers. "Yep."

"I'm new in town, yes," Elise answered his question. "My name's Elise Hamilton. I'm part owner of the Lonestar."

"Ah, so that's the way the wind is blowing." He released her hand, his teal green gaze amused. "We're neighbors. My family's ranch, The Double K, borders the Lonestar land."

"Uncle Josh, Uncle Josh. Did you see Colt riding that bronc?" A blond-headed boy, about ten years old, came running up.

Josh looked down at his nephew with a smile on his face. "No, Ben, but I'm sure it was a sight to see."

"Ready to go, Elise?" Colt walked up. When he stood a little closer to her than usual, she gave him a curious look.

"Colt! " Ben said, his voice all excited, "That was sooome great ridin'."

"Thanks, Ben," Colt grinned down at the boy as he ruffled his hair. "We should have some stock coming back from the rodeo later this week. Stop by for a visit."

Ben turned hopeful eyes to Josh. Josh chuckled. "You have to ask your momma and daddy, Ben."

The boy turned and ran off calling his parents' names. Josh turned to Colt. "You shouldn't encourage him, Colt. His parents don't want him to rodeo."

Colt shrugged. "He's a kid. Kids like to be entertained."

Even though they spoke in a friendly manner, Elise could sense some undercurrents of tension between the two men.

Josh addressed Colt once more, "I heard you gave Earl one of your bulls. We could've used another bull."

Colt raised his eyebrow. "I traded a bull for an exceptional bronc with the option to buy first offspring of that bull at a cheap price, Josh. It was a business transaction."

Josh eyed Colt, his look assessing before he turned his attention back to Elise. "Since you're new in town, Elise, I'd like to invite you to the Fireman's Local Charity Dance tomorrow night."

"Really? That sounds like fun," Elise said.

"What time can I pick you up?" Josh asked.

"I'll bring Elise," Colt answered for her.

Elise noticed the sharp look Josh gave Colt. She didn't want to cause trouble. Turning to Colt she said, "How about I follow you there?"

Colt fixed his penetrating gaze on her, an annoyed look on his face. When she glanced up at Josh, the man was grinning from ear to ear.

"Great! I'll see you there," Josh said. Then he patted the black horse's neck and winked at her. "I'll hold onto her for you in case you change your mind."

Once they loaded up Colt's newest bronc in the trailer, Elise and Colt climbed into the truck and headed back to the ranch.

After they'd been on the road for a few quiet minutes, Colt glanced at her. "What was that all about?"

"What was 'what' all about?"

"I brought you to the auction to learn about buying horses, not to make dates." He sounded angry, disgruntled.

She looked at him, surprised by his comment. "Not that it matters, but I'm driving myself, Colt. I didn't make a date with Josh."

Colt shifted his gaze back to the road, his expression shuttered. "I think Josh might think otherwise."

* * * * *

The next day flew by for Elise. With Colt no longer handing out morning chores, she got a lot accomplished on the website. It still needed a lot more work to be completed, but she felt good about her progress. Elise looked at her watch. It was almost 6:00 p.m. She shut off her computer, picked up her duffel bag and headed toward the bathroom. She had invited Mace to go to the dance too, but he'd waggled his eyebrows up and down suggestively and said he had *other* plans. Elise just shook her head and laughed. Mace was such a hoot. The man was the ultimate ladies' man, she'd quickly discovered.

She emerged from the bathroom dressed in a spaghetti-strapped, black tea-length dress with a modest slit up the side and matching high-heeled strappy sandals. The dress was made of a jersey type material, so she felt it was dressy without being too pretentious. Elise had pulled her hair up in a French twist but no matter how hard she tried to make the style look slick and chic, little wisps of hair kept falling around her face. Finally she gave up and let the pieces fall.

She walked over to Colt's office and lightly knocked at his open door. "Ready to go, Colt?"

Colt glanced up from his paperwork and did a double-take. Elise couldn't help the grin that rode up her face. She turned in a small circle for him.

"I clean up okay, wouldn't you say?"

Colt looked back down at his paperwork and crushed some paper in his hand. She was surprised when he didn't throw it in the trash. He stood up and looked anywhere but at her as he put his hat on his head and said in a gruff voice, "Come on. Let's go."

Elise climbed into her car and followed Colt's truck to town. When they arrived in the Fireman's Hall parking lot, Colt immediately walked over to her car and opened her door for her.

Elise looked up at him as he helped her out of her car.

"Thanks, Colt."

With his impassive expression, she had no clue as to what he was thinking. He gave her a curt nod, placed his hand on her elbow and propelled her toward the building. As they neared the door, Josh pushed off the sidewall where he'd apparently been waiting and walked up with a huge grin on his face. He reached out and snagged Elise's hand saying to Colt, "Thanks for escorting Elise, Colt."

Before Elise could utter a word, Josh pulled her into the crowded room, full of music and laughter, food and lots of people dancing.

Elise laughingly berated Josh as he ushered her onto the dance floor and immediately swung her into his arms to the rhythm of the upbeat music. "Josh, that was really very rude. I'm not your date for the evening, you know."

Josh gave her an unrepentant smile. "Not yet, but the night is young."

Elise couldn't help but laugh at his optimistic attitude.

"By the way," he looked her up and down, "you look gorgeous."

Elise murmured a thank you and let him twirl her around the dance floor while they discussed the horse she'd considered purchasing the day before.

The music ended and a slow song started up. Elise looked up to see Colt tapping Josh on the shoulder. "I believe the lady said the next dance was mine, Kelly."

Josh glanced at Colt and his hold tightened when he turned his gaze back to her. Elise gave him an apologetic look as she allowed Colt to pull her away.

Colt shrugged. "It's not my fault the next song was a slow one." His words may have been lighthearted, but the look he gave Josh wasn't anything of the sort.

As Josh grudgingly walked off, Colt pulled Elise into his arms. "What was that all about?" She threw his words from the day before back at him.

Colt spoke close to her ear. "What was 'what' all about?"

Touché, she thought as his warm body pressed against hers. She noted his firm shoulder muscles under her fingers and the hard planes of his chest, brushing against hers every so often with the beat of the music. Her breathing changed at his nearness, turning shallow. "You and Josh." She fought to regain a hold of her rioting senses.

"Josh and I have been friends and neighbors for a long time."

"More like friendly rivals, it seems," she laughed.

Colt chuckled. "That too, at times, I suppose."

As they moved to the music's slow beat, his hands trailed down her back, massaging the base of her spine. His touch sent tiny shockwaves skating up her skin, causing goose bumps to gather on her arms. And if that wasn't enough, every so often, his thigh would brush in between hers. Elise's nipples hardened at the erotic rhythm of his seductive movements.

He released her waist and slid his hands to her upper back. The heat of his hands permeated her dress, igniting her entire body as he pulled her closer so he could whisper in her ear, "What do you want, Elise?"

He could be asking her a million different things with that one question, but only one thing came to mind. Elise wanted to know what it felt like to have his lips on hers. And not in a kiss meant to put her in her place, but in a kiss where he put his emotions behind it. Would he be a fast or a slow kisser? Would he use his hands or words to arouse her or heaven forbid, she bit her lip, both? She wanted to know what he'd feel like pressed against her, naked, hard…she knew without a doubt he'd be an aggressive lover.

She felt his breath on her neck and thought for an instant he'd actually brushed his lips lightly against her skin. She drew in her breath, her stomach tensing.

"Tell me," he demanded.

He'd stopped moving and pulled her flush against him, his

heated gaze locked with hers. At that moment the music ended and the spell was broken. Colt seemed to shake himself out of the sensual scenario he had created around them and he set her away from him. It took Elise a little longer to let go of the feelings rocking through her. She was saved from answering one way or the other when Josh walked up and escorted her away to introduce her to some of his fireman buddies and their girlfriends and wives.

Colt didn't ask her to dance the rest of the evening, but he didn't leave either. When the dance started winding down, Elise told Josh she had to head home. She had work to do tomorrow.

Josh pulled her in his arms for one last dance and this time it was a slow one. As she danced in his strong embrace, Elise's gaze met Colt's across the room. He leaned against the wall, his arms crossed over his chest. His gaze met hers, willing her to keep her eyes locked with his bold stare, so heated, yet so emotionally distant. Elise couldn't stand the sweet agony, wanting one man while she danced with another. She finally just closed her eyes to stop the dual torment.

When the dance ended, Josh walked her out to her car while Colt followed them out. Josh gave Colt a pointed, "shove off" look, but Colt ignored him and walked up, pulling Elise's car keys from her hand as she retrieved them from her purse.

"Thanks for escorting Elise out, Josh." He turned to unlock her car door for her and held it open, waiting.

Josh's eyes narrowed on Colt, his expression angry, before he turned to Elise. "I would like to see you again," he paused, glancing over to Colt, "without the additional company next time."

With the strong emotions for Colt churning inside her, Elise felt she should be honest with Josh. "Josh, I don't—"

As if he knew she planned to turn him down, Josh quickly leaned over and kissed her, cutting off her words. "Think about it. I'll call you soon." He turned, flashed Colt a triumphant smile and headed toward his truck.

Colt's jaw ticced as he handed her the keys. "If you play games, you'll get burned," was all he said before he turned on his heel and headed for his truck.

Chapter Four

Elise thrilled at the wind in her hair as she raced her horse across the open plains. She missed this. She'd grown up riding horses. Had even won a few ribbons. Her parents let her compete for the prestige. She did it because she loved being around horses. She loved grooming them, caring for them and most of all, the exhilarating freedom she felt when riding full throttle.

After the interesting evening the night before with Colt and Josh, she'd spent the whole next day working on the website, nonstop. When her workday ended and others had gone home for dinner, she'd stayed a little longer and then decided to go for a ride on Bess. She knew the ride would help ease her sore shoulders.

As she neared the main stable, she slowed Bess to a trot so the horse could cool down before she brought her into the stables. Letting her gaze take in the whole ranch from this angle, she smiled at the welcoming sight. Everything about the ranch made her feel at home. Bess had slowed to a walk when Elise spotted Colt. He stood outside the stables, his thick arms crossed over his chest. Even with his hat pulled low on his head, she could see he was scowling at her. What now?

Elise pulled up beside him and met his gaze. "What is it, Colt?"

When he turned to Sam and asked him to take the horse, she said, "I planned to groom Bess myself."

"Not today. We need to talk."

Elise slid off the horse and handed Sam the reins with an apologetic smile.

Colt took her elbow and propelled her around the stables

until they were alone by the main barn.

He turned to face her, his mouth set in a firm line. "Don't go off like that again by yourself. Do you understand?"

Elise leaned back against the barn's wall, closed her eyes, and counted to ten. She didn't want to get into a fight. Opening her eyes, she said, "I'm an accomplished horsewoman, Colt. There's really no need to worry."

"What if you'd taken a fall? Who would've known? And another thing. You're a beautiful woman, Elise, and while I believe the cowboys working on the ranch are good men, I wouldn't want to test that theory too much."

His words made her heart trip in her chest. Elise smiled at him. "You think I'm beautiful?"

Colt clenched his jaw and curled his hands into fists by his sides. His eyes bored into hers. "Yes, I find you beautiful," he admitted as if she had to drag it out of him.

"That's nice to hear, because I like what I see in you, too." She eyed him up and down with a slow smile. "So, what are we going to do about this mutual liking we've got going on?" she asked, letting her voice drop to a husky and suggestive tone. When conflicting emotions lit his deep blue eyes, her stomach tensed and she wondered if maybe she'd misread him.

"Then again, maybe it's not such a good…"

She didn't get to finish her sentence before he took the two steps between them in one long stride. With a hungry look that singed her all the way to her toes, he pulled her against his hard chest, his mouth descending on hers.

Elise welcomed his kiss, the feel of his body pressed against hers. She slid her hands up his shoulders to his head and knocked his hat off so she could run her fingers through his hair. Colt slowed his pace as his lips moved over hers, his tongue enticing her, drawing her in. If she could put a movement to the way the Texan drawl sounded, it would be his hot, wet tongue sliding seductively into her mouth, taking his time, making her want to find out what else he could do with his talented tongue.

Elise's heart beat hard against her chest, her breasts swelled and her nipples ached as she ran her hands down his thick, muscular back to pull his shirt out of his jeans. She wanted to touch his skin. Feel it against hers. Colt groaned and slid his hands down her back, clasping her rear and pulling her against his hard arousal. She moaned as he backed her against the barn wall and ground his erection against her sex. The pressure did little to assuage her throbbing ache. If anything, it intensified it.

"Damn, I'm so hot for you, I can't get close enough," he groaned as he trailed his lips down her neck while he rocked his hips against hers, applying delicious pressure.

"That's ditto, Cowboy," she said breathlessly. She gasped as he dipped his head and his hot mouth closed around her nipple through her shirt and skimpy bra. Her gasp turned to a low moan when his hand moved lower, stroking her mound through her jeans.

She pushed against his hand, wanting all of him, everything he could give.

Suddenly, Colt stepped back, his nostrils flaring, his heated gaze full of desire and want. He ran a hand through his hair, clearly frustrated. "What *am* I doing?" he ground out as if he weren't allowed to indulge in his sexual desires.

By the detached look in his eyes, Elise could tell he had pulled away and not just physically. She dropped her hands and pursed her lips, saying in a light tone, lighter than she felt, "It looks like you're going to leave me high and dry."

Colt leaned over and picked his hat up from the ground. He hit it against his leg, as if out of habit, before putting it on his head.

He met her gaze, his face a hard and unreadable mask. "I'm sorry, Elise. It won't happen again," he said before he turned and walked off toward his truck.

* * * * *

The next few days slid by in a blur for Colt. Refusing to

accept Elise working for the Lonestar for free, he'd set her up on an equal monthly partner's salary. He still hoped she'd decide to sell to him, but until then, paying her was only right in his mind. Other than that one interaction with her, he'd spent as much time outdoors as possible, avoiding her as best as he could considering they worked down the hall from each other.

His actions the other day by the barn made him feel like a real bastard leaving her there, leaning against the wall, wanting—her jaw red from his five o'clock shadow, her lips swollen from his kisses. But self-preservation had finally called his brain back to order since the damn thing had taken a flying leap at her sexy, emerald eyes and saucy invitation. Sure he could've gone for the sex, but there was something about the way he reacted to her that scared him. His physical response to her went deeper than any other woman he'd ever been around.

He didn't want to fall into the same trap his father had. No matter what anyone said, he believed his father died of a broken heart at the young age of forty-nine. When Colt was a teen and his mother walked out on them, saying she missed the parties and high society, he'd never forgiven her. She had come from old money when she'd married his father, and he knew his dad never felt like he really deserved his mother.

Walking away from Elise was the hardest thing he'd ever done. And he *had* suffered for it. The past few days he walked around constantly half-aroused; his body jumping to full arousal at the smell of her seductive, floral perfume, the sound of her slightest laugh, especially the throaty one he would hear when she spoke to Mace—the same voice that was torturing him down the hall, even now, as she and Mace talked about the online advertising and promotion aspects of the Lonestar. It grated on his nerves that his happy-go-lucky brother got all of her attention. It didn't matter to him that the website she worked on fell under Mace's PR purview.

There went that sexy laugh again. His chest contracted in anger and something else he didn't care to examine too closely. That did it. Colt stood up and walked over to the spare office down the hall. He began moving boxes full of rodeo overflow stuff from the office to his truck. After his third trip past Mace's door, he looked up to see Mace leaning nonchalantly against the doorframe, watching him approach with a box in his hands.

"Whatcha doin', bro?" He grinned at Colt.

"What does it look like I'm doing? I'm cleaning out this office so Elise can have her own office and you can get some work done," Colt replied, his tone clipped.

"Oh, I don't know, Colt. I think I'm just fine." He turned his head quickly back to Elise. "How about you, darlin'? You feel like you aren't getting any work done over there?"

Elise didn't even look up from the keyboard; her brow was furrowed in concentration as her fingers flew across the keys. She flipped her hand saying, "Sure, no problem, I'm fine," before she returned her fingers back to the keyboard.

Mace turned triumphant eyes back to Colt. "See, we're fine. You're going to throw your back out for nothing."

"That's why you're going to get your lazy butt out here and help me." Colt said with a meaningful look in his eyes.

Mace raised his hands. "Fine, I get the picture," he said grudgingly as he moved to retrieve a box from the back office.

"You can take Cade's computer and Elise can take yours since she needs a more powerful PC to do the website stuff," Colt commented as Mace loaded the last box onto Colt's truck.

His little brother turned to him, a knowing grin on his face. "Hey, if you want her, go after her."

Colt met Mace's curious gaze. He knew Mace saw the emptying of the other office for what it really was. A sinking feeling made his stomach fist into a knot. "It's not that simple, Mace."

Mace slammed the door on the back of the truck closed and met his gaze, "Yes, it is."

"She's upper class. Enough said."

Understanding dawned on Mace's face. "Colt, Elise is *not*

Mom." Then, he shrugged his shoulders. "And hell, even if she is, who said you have to marry her. There's nothing that says you shouldn't have a little fun in life, big brother."

When Colt didn't answer, Mace continued, as he rounded to get in the passenger side of the truck, "Hey, she's a desirable woman and if you don't take a shot at what's right before your eyes, there'll be plenty of men lining up at her door who will." He flashed Colt his best playboy smile before he hopped into the truck. "Including me."

Colt felt as if someone had just kicked him in the gut. The very thought of another man, even his own brother, touching Elise, drove him fuckin' nuts. He got into the truck and slammed his door harder than necessary. He didn't say a word to Mace as he drove toward the storage shed.

* * * * *

Colt looked up as he heard Mace walk down the hall. Earlier, he had seen Elise pass by his door to go outside, but she had come back in and was now in the bathroom. Colt stood up and stretched. It was the end of the day. Time to go home. He was glad it was the end of the week. He walked over and leaned in the doorway as he watched Mace standing patiently near the front door of the office.

Colt turned at the sound of Elise exiting the bathroom, a duffel bag slung over her shoulder. She had changed from her everyday jeans, boots and cotton T-shirt to a thigh high spaghetti-strapped dress that showed off her gorgeous shoulders and flared around her firm thighs. The dress was fire engine red and the contrast with her dark hair fueled his desire like none other. He looked down to see matching strappy high-heeled sandals on her feet and hardened instantly.

"Hi, Colt." She smiled and walked over to stand next to Mace. "Ready to go?"

Mace let out a low, appreciative whistle, took her hand and twirled her around in circle. "Gee wiz, Elise. I don't know about taking you to Rockin' Joe's tonight. Maybe I'll just keep you all to myself."

Elise elbowed him in the stomach. "Hey, you've been promising me all week you would show me how to do the two-step. No backing out."

Elise glanced at him. "Wanna come, Colt?"

Hell yeah! Colt pushed himself off of the doorjamb of his office. "Sure. Why not? I haven't been out in a while. Let me get my hat." He may not plan on touching Elise, but there was no way he'd to let Mace take her out alone. No fuckin' way!

When he came back out of his office, they were gone. Colt walked outside to see Elise getting into Mace's red convertible Mustang.

Mace pulled up beside him. "We'll meet you there, bro."

Before he could insist on riding with them, Mace took off in his car.

Colt grumbled to himself about sibling rivalry as he made his way to his truck.

* * * * *

Rockin' Joe's was just as he remembered it, a good-time bar with lots of drinking and dancing. As he walked through the dim, smoke-filled room, country music playing in the background, he spotted Mace and Elise sitting in a secluded corner booth. He'd bet his last dollar Mace had brought many dates to that very booth. Colt set his teeth and headed for the table, his boot heels making a dull thud on the wood floor as he walked.

When he slid into the bench seat beside Elise, she was now sandwiched between both Tanner brothers. Just as he'd settled in his seat, Mace grabbed Elise's hand as "All My Ex's Live in Texas" started up in the background.

"Come on, Elise, they're playin' our song," he drawled as he pulled her out of the other side of the booth.

"See you in a few, Colt." Elise turned and smiled back at him before she let Mace lead her to the dance floor.

Colt watched his brother swing Elise in his arms. His chest tightened as she laughed up into Mace's face when she missed a step and tripped. Mace caught her and pulled her closer. Colt fisted his hands beneath the table and set his jaw. He wanted to punch Mace square into the middle of next week.

Thankfully the song ended and Mace escorted a breathless, rosy-cheeked Elise back to the table.

She fanned herself and smiled. "Can you get me something to drink, Mace? It's hot in here."

Mace slid back out of the booth. "Anything in particular?"

"How about Sex on the Beach?" She grinned at him and gave Colt a sideways look. "I haven't had that in a while."

Colt groaned inwardly. The woman was way too sassy for her own good.

Mace gave him a suggestive smirk before he swaggered away. Colt turned his gaze to Elise and chose a neutral subject. "Looks like you had a good time out there."

Her sparkling green eyes met his. "Yes, I did. I've never danced the two-step before. It was fun to learn."

"How's the website going?"

"Great." Her face became more animated as she talked. "It's been a while for me, so I had to pull out my textbooks. The code was a little trickier than I had initially thought." She noticed his raised eyebrow and rushed to assure him, "But I think I have it all figured out."

Colt looked at her sincere face. "Something about you tells me you wouldn't let it go until you got it right, Elise."

As she gave him an appreciative smile, Mace returned with a whisky for himself, Sex on the Beach, complete with a cherry on top, for Elise, and a beer for Colt.

"Thought you could use one, bro," Mace said as he handed Colt a longneck.

"Thanks."

"Don't mention it."

As soon as Mace sat down, a redhead slid into the booth beside him, her arm going around his shoulders.

Her arrival made Mace scoot over and Elise in turn was forced to move closer, pressing her thigh against Colt's. A jolt of electricity shot through him as the heat of her leg touched his. With blood rushing straight to his erection, he had to focus to concentrate on what the redhead was saying to Mace.

"Where have you been, darlin'?" she drawled as she cut her eyes over to Elise, sizing her up.

Mace laughed and said, "It's good to see you, too, Lana," before he turned and introduced her to Elise and Colt.

Lana turned pouty lips to Mace as a slow song started to play. "Come dance with me, Mace honey."

Mace glanced at Elise as if asking for permission.

She laughed and shooed him on. "How could you possibly turn her down?"

As Mace slid back out of the booth, this time to be led away by the lady, Colt and Elise watched the well-endowed redhead wrap her arms around Mace and pull him flush against her body.

After a few minutes, Elise must have realized she was still pressed against him because she breathed out an embarrassed, "Oh," and moved over a few inches in the booth.

Colt wanted to tell her to stay but knew better. He didn't say anything even though he missed her soft heat already.

They drank their drinks in silence. He felt her inquisitive gaze on him as if she were probing him and wondering about his thoughts.

He refused to look at her. He didn't want to look down into those gorgeous emerald eyes, the kind of eyes a man could lose himself in if he wasn't careful.

Mace and Lana came back to the table laughing, arms

Colt's Choice

wrapped around each other. They sat back down, on the other side of Elise, forcing her to move back over against him once more.

Colt swallowed hard. He didn't know how much more he could take. He and Elise listened as Mace and Lana exchanged all kinds of sex innuendos. His own libido had kicked into overdrive with the first brush against Elise, he didn't need any more stimulation. He felt like yelling, "Will you two get a room, already?"

He chanced a glance at Elise. Big mistake. She had finished her drink and proceeded to suck the last of the drink out of the cherry. She met his gaze and popped the whole cherry, stem and all, past her luscious lips into her mouth.

He went rock-hard instantly but resisted the urge to growl out his sexual frustration.

Lana slid out of the booth and said to Mace, "Come on, sexy."

"Sorry, Lana, but I brought Elise tonight."

Lana frowned and Elise cut in, "It's okay, Mace, Colt can take me home."

And straight to bed, Colt thought without really thinking. He was thinking with one part of his body, that's for damn sure. He wanted her so bad his balls throbbed. Why was wanting her such a bad idea again? he argued with himself as the seductive pull Elise seemed to have over him reached out, grabbed hold of his gut and squeezed. Tight.

When Lana licked her ruby red lips in a suggestive manner, Mace turned to Elise and Colt, saying as Lana pulled him away, "I love it when a woman knows how to use her tongue for more than just talkin'." He saluted them both as he walked in the direction of the exit with Lana.

Colt looked back at Elise, his body literally aching. Aw hell, he could keep his emotions out of the mix. The truth was, physically he'd never wanted a woman as much as he wanted this one. One way or the other, he'd convince her to make their unplanned date tonight a real one.

"Don't worry, Colt. I'll get a cab. I just didn't want Mace to worry about having to take me home."

When she finished speaking, she smiled at him. With a secret look in her eyes, she touched her lips, then put something in front of him on the table. "Night, Cowboy," she said in a sexy Virginian accent as she started to slide out of the booth.

Colt looked down at the table in front of him. Sitting on the table was the cherry stem tied in a nice, tight knot. And damn, she had done it all with that delectable tongue of hers.

"Not so fast, Princess." He put a staying hand on her thigh.

Elise turned questioning eyes his way.

He continued in his best Texan drawl, "You're going to have to learn you can't tease a cowboy like that and leave him hangin', darlin'."

She raised an eyebrow. "Oh? I don't know… I think turnabout is fair play."

Colt stared intensely into her eyes and let his tone turn serious. "I've thought about nothing else for days. How much I regretted walking away from you instead of doing what I really wanted to do," he paused, and swept his heated gaze down her gorgeous body then met her gaze once more. "I want to make it up to you," he finished as he trailed his hand higher up her leg, then firmly gripped her inner thigh.

When her pupils dilated, he smiled, letting his touch grow bolder as he continued his hand's ascent until his fingers teased the edge of her panties.

Elise's eyes widened in surprise and she inhaled deeply before she slowly exhaled and said, "Where? Here?"

Colt raised a challenging eyebrow. "Where better?"

"But we're in a public place." She looked around, her gaze wary.

"Then you'll have to keep your screaming down," he said as his grin turned lascivious.

Elise laughed outright at his arrogance. "You're pretty damn sure you'll succeed, aren't you?"

"There's only one way to find out," he countered as he removed his hand and placed his arm on the back of the booth's seat behind her. Aligning his body with hers, he reached for her thigh once again with his other hand.

Elise looked up into his eyes. The rapid pulse beating at her throat told him how much the idea aroused her. It made him hot knowing the thought excited her. He wanted to damn well make sure the reality was equally as fulfilling.

Chapter Five

Elise couldn't believe she was actually considering his offer. Her heart racing, she looked around one more time. Well, their booth *was* secluded and there was a tablecloth on the table. Her stomach tightened and her nipples hardened as she looked up into Colt's deep blue eyes, now full of blatant desire.

"More power to you, Cowboy," she said in a nonchalant tone.

Colt gave her another sexy grin as he slid his hand along the smooth flesh of her inner thigh, slowly massaging the muscles.

She held her breath in anticipation and almost let out a whimper of pleasure when his knuckles brushed against her mound through her panties.

"You're wet for me already," he chuckled, sounding pleased. "Or was it all that talk about getting-it-on in a public place that got you all hot and bothered?"

Embarrassed, Elise looked away and lied, "It was the second part."

"We'll just see if we can't remedy that then," he said as he rubbed his fingers against her clitoris through the material.

Elise's blood pressure roared in her ears and she drew in her breath at his touch. Colt applied more pressure, this time in a circular motion, making her want to rock her hips with his movements. She closed her eyes at the sensations his knowing touched elicited.

"Keep your eyes open, or people may wonder what we're doing over here," he said. Her eyes snapped open as he slid a finger past the edge of her underwear and rubbed her own moisture against her throbbing nub. "It might help if you look at me, else people will wonder why I'm so close to you, darlin'."

His deep, baritone voice, coupled with that sexy, seductive, Texan drawl, sent chills up and down her spine. Elise looked up into his eyes. As she did so, he pushed his finger deep inside her, causing her to gasp and involuntarily rock her hips forward. The sensations she experienced felt so good and so naughty at the same time. She knew she wouldn't take long.

"Like that, do you?" he teased, his blue eyes smoldering as he watched her.

Elise looked away, her cheeks flaming with heat.

"Don't look away, Lise. I want to see the passion in your eyes."

His voice was so sincere, so compelling. She turned her gaze back to his.

"I'm so close," she whispered, then bit her lip, arching her back as she pressed against his hand.

"Not yet," he said while he slowly slid another finger inside her channel, his touch intimate and thorough.

She groaned at the added thickness rubbing against her. "But I can't wait," she panted and grasped the table for support.

"Yes, you can, Lise," he whispered into her ear before he trailed his lips down her neck to place a hot kiss on the bare skin along the sensitive curve of her shoulder. Goose bumps formed on her arms at the brief brush of his lips against her.

Colt removed his fingers from her body, causing her to glance up at him sharply. His look was intense as he started to pull her thin wisp of panties down her hips. "I don't want anything in my way," he rasped, his expression determined, aroused. She lifted her hips to help him as he slid her underwear down her legs and over her heels.

Colt shoved her underwear in his back pocket and slowly trailed his fingers back up her leg, driving her insane with his unhurried movements. Just when she decided to grab his hand and put it where she wanted it, he surprised her by grasping the inside of her thigh in a firm grip and lifting her leg up and across his muscular one. With her leg draped over his jean-clad thigh, she felt open and wanton, exposed to his every whim. Elise held her breathing in check, because it had suddenly gone very shallow as she awaited his next move.

He looked down into her eyes; his own had turned a deeper shade of sapphire blue. His sexy five o'clock shadow made her want to rub her hand against the rough surface. Tiny tremors skittered through her body as he gently brushed his fingers across her, teasing her, running the pads of his fingers up and down her most intimate places in a slow, tantalizing rhythm.

"You're hot and wet, responsive to my touch. I want to know what it's like to be inside you. I'm jealous of my own damn hand right now."

Elise gave a nervous laugh at the fierceness of his tone combined with his humor. But her laugh hitched in her throat when he immediately thrust two fingers deep inside her core. She couldn't help the gasp that escaped her lips as he added his thumb to the mixture, finding her hot spot and applying just the right amount of pressure.

Elise tried not to cry out as her body spiraled and finally spasmed around his fingers, but she just couldn't do it. Colt must have sensed she couldn't hold back for he covered her mouth with his, thrusting his tongue against hers at the same pace his fingers moved within her, slow and sure, drawing out every tremor.

When the overwhelming spasms stopped, he withdrew his hand saying in a gruff voice, "Look at me, Elise." Elise's body still shook from the orgasm he'd just elicited from her, but she managed to meet his gaze. He gave her a sexy smile that was all too cocky. "I like the fact you couldn't keep quiet. It's a helluva turn-on to know I can make you lose control like that. Want to go for round two?"

Elise placed her hand on his jeans where his hard flesh pushed against the fly of his pants. She raised an eyebrow and gave him a saucy grin. "I don't know how much more you can take, Colt."

Colt's laugh sounded forced even to himself. "Maybe you're right. Care to go for a ride?"

She gave him an innocent look, blinking her eyelashes for effect. "Does that mean I get to be on top?"

He meant his truck and she damn well knew it. Colt chuckled and helped her slide out of the booth.

When he pulled the door open for her to exit the bar, a draft of warm Texan heat blew in, causing her dress to lift up in the air. Elise let out a startled gasp and pushed the front of her dress back down. Colt immediately moved flush against her back as they walked through the door to keep the back of her dress from flying up and exposing her naked backside.

Once they were outside, Elise laughed. "I was feeling a little too footloose and fancy free in there." She turned and put out her hand. "Can I have my underwear back now?"

They were alone in the dark parking lot, standing beside his truck, the muffled country music floating back to them from the bar. Colt pulled her underwear out of his pocket and gave her a devilish look. "These?"

Elise reached for her black lacy underwear, but he held them aloft with one long finger. "Nah, honey, I don't think so. Why bother when I'm just going to take them right off you again anyway?" He crushed the soft material in his hand and put the underwear to his nose, closing his eyes and inhaled. When he opened his eyes he felt a rush of satisfaction to see Elise's lips part in surprise at his thoroughly intimate gesture.

Colt shoved the underwear back in his pocket and pulled her soft body against his harder one. "Faint smells may prime me, but I'm a very visual and sensory man. I want to experience *you* firsthand."

Elise ran her hands up his arms and across his shoulders. Pulling his head to hers, she whispered in his ear, "Well then, you'd better get a move on, darlin' because I'm one ahead of you."

She pushed away from him, her seductive laughter floating

behind her as she moved to the passenger side of the truck. Colt immediately followed her and opened the truck door for her to climb in.

Her voice reflected surprise as he grasped her hand, "Oh, a cowboy and a gentleman. What a treat!"

"I didn't realize they were mutually exclusive," he replied in an amused tone as he smoothed her skirt across her backside while she slid into the seat.

She gasped as his hand cupped her rear end and turned laughing eyes his way. "Okay, a cowboy who plays at being a gentleman so he can cop a feel."

Colt gave her his sexiest grin. "I take my opportunities as they arise, Elise. Doesn't mean I'm not a gentleman." He pulled the seatbelt and snapped it closed around her before he shut the door and moved around to his side of the truck.

As he turned his truck onto the highway, he glanced her way. Elise had turned very quiet. He hoped he hadn't somehow offended her.

When his gaze met hers, she gave him the best come-hither-look he'd seen in a long time. Holy hell, he wanted her. She moved restlessly against the leather seat, her green eyes beckoning him. Her movements reminded him of a sexy cat, calling to her lover with her sensuous, lithe movements.

"I'm way too far away over here, Colt," she complained as she moved to unbuckle her seatbelt.

"Uh-uh, Elise. Keep the seatbelt on. We're almost to the ranch."

She licked her lips, then pouted. "I was hoping to even the score."

Colt groaned at her suggestion. "We'll have plenty of time—"

His cell phone started ringing on the floor of his truck. Colt leaned over and picked it up. "Tanner, here."

"Colt, it's Rick. One of your prize bulls is actin' funny.

Thought you might like to check him out."

"Call Evan. Tell her to meet me there. I'll be there in a few." Colt swore as he hung up the phone. His gut clenched in disappointment at the shitty news.

"I take it our date is off," Elise quipped. "Is everything okay at the ranch?"

Colt shifted his gaze to her. He wanted to throttle someone. Of all the rotten luck.

"Sorry, Elise, but Rick needs my help. Duty calls."

Once he'd driven up the long drive leading up to the ranch, he stopped the truck and cut off the engine. Propping his arm on the steering wheel, he faced Elise, regret in his voice. "You don't know how sorry I am."

"Oh, I think I do," she laughed softly in the dim light of the truck. Suddenly, her eyes brightened and she squared her sexy shoulders. "Tell me what's wrong. I could help you."

Colt shook his head and smiled as he ran a finger down her cheek. "Elise, if you come along, I'd spend all my time looking at you instead of helping out like I should." In his mind, there was no need to drag Elise into this. It could be a bad run of luck, but it smelled more like Riley's doing.

Leaning over to brush his lips against hers, he said in a low, dark tone, "I know you'll be worth the wait."

* * * * *

Feeling more than a little tired as she drove up to the Lonestar the following Monday, Elise thought about her long weekend, or at least that's what it felt like — long!

After she left Colt on Friday, she'd arrived home to find no less than five messages on her cell phone from her parents. She'd shut off her answering machine a week ago because her father kept leaving her messages asking when she'd be coming home. Then he'd started calling her cell phone instead. Hence the reason she left it at her apartment. Every message on her cell phone related to her parents wanting to make sure she would be back from her vacation before the late summer party. According to them, they'd planned it as a special occasion.

Elise knew she had to tell her parents in person that she had made a new life for herself away from Virginia. She also had a few more of her things in storage she wanted to have shipped down to Texas. Her parents' persistence just stepped up the timeframe sooner than she'd expected.

The next morning she'd taken the first plane flight out to D.C. She'd considered giving Colt a call to let him know she'd be gone for a few days, but they weren't in a relationship. Plus, a phone call from her might have given him the impression she perceived them as a couple and as such felt the need to check in with him. Not!

Ugh, going home hadn't been a pretty scene.

"You're going to what?" her father had railed.

"Now Fred, don't go getting your blood pressure up," her mother said in a calm voice as she smoothed her blonde bobbed hair against her neck. "What Elise meant was that she wanted to spend the rest of her summer tending to her investment."

"That's not what I said," Elise interrupted as frustration knotted her stomach at her parents' complete disregard for her hopes and desires, once again. "I said that I plan to move to Boone permanently. It's my home now."

"Look here, young lady," her father began, drawing his bushy, dark brown brows together in a frown. "You so much as even think of moving to Texas for good and you can kiss your inheritance goodbye."

Elise had stiffened at her father's ultimatum. Once again he'd tried to use the lure of money to keep her in Virginia and working for Hamilton's. The problem with his plan was that she didn't care about the money.

She'd narrowed her gaze on her father, then tilted her chin in a defiant manner. "I'll be back here at the end of the summer for the party. I haven't forgotten my obligation to the Save a

Heart Charity. If I have to give them the donation from my own funds, so be it."

Her father had snorted in anger at her response, then he nodded as if pleased with himself. "Twenty thousand dollars is a lot of cash, Elise. You might have done well when you sold your share of that dot com company you helped start, but somehow I doubt you have that kind of cash lying around."

She'd refused to answer him and had to listen the entire rest of the weekend as her father hounded her about her duty and responsibility to Hamilton Industries. In her heart, she understood he wanted her to help maintain and manage the fortune he'd amassed over the years. Unfortunately, she couldn't force herself to live that life just to please her father, especially not now that she'd found the perfect life for herself at the Lonestar. She'd decided that no matter what happened between herself and Colt, she knew her heart belonged in Texas.

Leaving D.C. on the red-eye last night, she'd gotten very little sleep on the plane. Needless to say, this morning she was beat.

When she walked into the ranch office and shut the door against the early morning heat, she turned to greet Mabel and saw the secretary jerk her head toward Colt's office, a warning expression on her face.

"Mabel, is that...?" Colt called out as he stepped into the doorway of his office.

"Where the hell have you been!" he barked at Elise. He crossed his arms over his chest as a frown creased his brow.

"Well, happy Monday morning to you, too, Colt," Elise quipped.

As Colt's frown turned into a scowl, she asked, "Is something wrong with the website?" She cut her gaze over to Mabel to remind him they had an audience.

Colt must have realized her intention because he immediately straightened and lowered his arms. "Uh, yeah."

"Okay, I'll go take a look at it." She turned and walked

down the hall feeling the weight of her long weekend dragging her body down.

Sighing, she sat down in her chair and booted up her computer. Colt had been right on her heels and was now demanding her attention. Closing the door behind him, he stood there, his stance tense, anger emanating from his body.

"Where have you been?" he repeated.

"Is there a problem, Colt?" She looked up from her computer.

He waved his hands in the air. "Problem? You've got me wound tighter than a stallion downwind of a mare in heat with no way to get at her and you ask if I have a problem?"

"You *did* say I would be worth the wait," she said with a smirk, even though her heart raced at his words. Damn, his metaphor was effective.

"For the whole weekend!" he said, his voice growing louder. When she arched her eyebrow, he immediately lowered his voice. "I tried calling you several times and when I didn't get an answer, I got worried and drove over to your apartment. I wanted to make sure you were okay. Imagine my surprise when your neighbor told me she thought you left town. You could have at least called."

"And said what?" she countered. "'Sorry, I can't make it for a *jollies* session, but I have something I have to take care of.' It's not like we're in a relationship, are we?"

She had him stumped there. Colt seemed to be at a loss for words. She could tell this man was used to getting what he wanted when he wanted it. Good. She liked to keep him guessing.

Looking back down at her keyboard, she began typing once more. "If you want to keep tabs on me, buy me a pager." She gave him a meaningful look. "Preferably one that vibrates."

Colt turned on his heel, opened the door and stalked off down the hall.

Three minutes later, Elise looked up from her keyboard.

The sensation of someone watching was just too great to ignore. Mace leaned casually in the doorway.

"I've seen the looks between you two. If you don't do something soon, the man is going to rip someone's head off. He's been meaner than a rattlesnake all morning and not at all likable to be around."

Elise laughed at Mace's doomed version of Colt's situation. "Mace, worry about your own love life."

Mace pushed off the doorjamb. "Hey, no problem there, darlin'."

"So I gather," she teased.

"What can I say? I'm just the kind of guy the girls fall all over." He gave her a wide grin, not at all apologetic.

Elise scanned his six-foot-one, muscular body from the top of his light brown, sun-streaked hair to the tip of his scuffed boots. He was leaner than Colt, his muscles less bulky, but there was something in his green eyes that called to a woman's heart. He had dreamy eyes. "I guess I can see where some women might find you attractive, Mace."

Mace raised his eyebrows. "Just some women?"

Elise laughed at his cockiness. "Yes, *some* women. You can't possibly have them all to yourself."

Mace turned to go. "Yeah, but it sure is fun tryin'." He walked off toward his office chuckling.

Elise turned back to her computer. Mace was right. She should try to make it up to Colt. She waited until eleven-thirty and then told Mabel she had to run an errand. Knowing Colt typically worked through lunch, she went out and bought sandwiches for them.

The office was quiet when she got back. Mabel and Mace must have gone out to grab something to eat. She reached up and lightly rapped on Colt's closed door.

"What!" he barked.

Oh boy. This was going to be fun.

Elise opened the door with a flourish and said, "Lunch is served," as she walked in carrying a white paper bag.

Colt looked up from his desk, his eyebrows pulled together, frustration written all over his face. "Unless it involves you, naked and laid out like a sampler platter, I'm not interested."

Her insides turned to butter at his vivid description. He might be blunt, but the man certainly did have a way with words. "You have to eat, Colt."

Colt grunted as he looked at the bag in her hand. "What's that?"

She held up the bag. "I brought you a sandwich."

Chapter Six

After Elise handed him a sandwich, Colt watched with growing anticipation as she sashayed behind his desk and settled her lovely butt on the surface. As she proceeded to eat her own sandwich, he looked up into her face. She had her dark hair pulled back in a clip, giving him a full view of her face. It was such an expressive face with high cheekbones and a stubborn chin. But right now, her lips were driving him wild. As she chewed and stared down at him, it was all he could do to swallow the food in his mouth.

He didn't want her to know how much it bothered him that she left without so much as a word to him. He'd spent a long Friday night with Evan trying to figure out what was wrong with his bull. The animal was so agitated he'd acted stoned. Evan—the best vet around to be so young—decided to test his urine. Sure enough, faint traces of Jimson weed laced the sample. Even though the animal's urine only had enough of the toxic plant to whack him out, he was so messed up, he was throwing himself against the barn and the barbed wire fence.

Anger boiled through Colt at the discovery. The hallucinogenic wild plant only grew in the spring and it was summer. This stunt had Riley written all over it, but there was no way to prove the bastard did it.

Coming home in the early morning hours, he knew it was too late to call Elise. He fell into bed with the knowledge he'd see her the next day and they'd have all weekend together. When he'd discovered she'd left town, he didn't like the sense of panic that gripped him. He knew his raging emotions stemmed from the fact he hadn't been able to touch her, to slide against her sweet flesh the way he wanted.

Over the course of the weekend, Colt had moved from irritated mode to "maybe it was for the best" mode. By the time Sunday rolled around, he'd started to wonder if she'd changed her mind about Texas and gone back home to stay. If she really had left for good, maybe it was best he didn't get to know her better. While he was doing his laundry that weekend, her panties fell out of his jeans back pocket. He picked them up and frustration filled him all over again until it slowly burned into simmering anger. He admitted to himself he'd never wanted a woman as much as he wanted Elise.

By Sunday night he still hadn't heard from her, nor did she answer her phone, he began to worry. But he didn't know who to call since Marie was on vacation. He'd decided to give her until Monday and then he'd dig out his documents with her home address in Virginia to call her family and check on her.

When he'd seen Elise waltzing into the office this morning as if she hadn't just taken off without a word and left him hanging, his temper flared. Now that he knew she was fine, his libido kicked in once more. She'd offered, then not shown to deliver. And he sure as hell wanted to take her up on that seductive offer, damnit.

Colt munched his sandwich in silence for a few minutes and then he casually asked, "So, where did you go this weekend?"

Elise raised her hand in the air at his question to indicate she wanted to finish chewing before she spoke.

"I went home."

"To Virginia?"

"Yeah, I wanted to get some more of my stuff from storage."

That sounded promising. He wondered if she was serious about staying.

"What does your family think about you moving so far from home?" he asked in a conversational tone.

Elise looked away as she answered, "Let's just say, they

aren't thrilled." She shrugged. "But they'll just have to get used to it. It's my life. Plus, Aunt Marie is here. Well, she'll be here in a few weeks once she gets back from vacation."

Colt continued to eat, wondering about the conflict with her family. When he finished his sandwich, Elise was chewing her last bite. She picked up her napkin and dabbed at her lips.

He had to touch her. Her alluring floral scent had already reached out and wrapped around him, drawing him in. Colt ran a finger along the edge of her lips, rubbing off a bit of mustard that had collected in the corner of her mouth.

"Missed a spot," he said. He knew his voice sounded gruff. He didn't care as he put his finger in his mouth and sucked the mustard off. When her pupils began to dilate, he knew she was turned on. Good. That's just the way he wanted her. He gave her a devilish grin and started to put his hands around her waist.

Before he could reach for her, Elise jumped off his desk and quickly began collecting the bag and leftover wrappers.

"What are you doing?" he said, frustration evident in his voice.

Elise looked up from her task. "I'm cleaning up, silly. What does it look like I am doing?" She walked around the desk toward the door of his office.

"Elise!" He was losing patience fast.

She turned her head and gave him a saucy grin. "Hold your horses, Colt. I'll be right back."

Colt waited. Impatiently. A couple of minutes passed and he deemed she'd been gone longer than necessary to dispose of the trash in the kitchen. He was about to go get her when she appeared in the doorway again and shut the door behind her.

He studied the natural sway of her hips as she walked back to his desk. He felt the blood pumping in his body and his heart rate kicked up several notches. She settled herself on his desk, this time right in front of him. Her pink tongue darted out, wetting her lips as she cast him a saucy, come-hither look.

He didn't have to be asked twice. Rolling his chair closer,

he reached for her slim hips. His heart jerked in alarm when she planted her booted foot a little too close for comfort on the chair in between his legs, stopping the chair from moving forward.

"Not so fast, Cowboy."

Colt jerked his gaze to her face. What kind of game was she playing? Before he could form the words, with a swift push of her foot, she shoved his chair until the back of it slammed against the credenza behind him.

"We haven't finished lunch yet," she said as a small smile formed on her lips.

"Elise, I'm done eating." His patience with this woman's teasing ways hung by a thin thread.

She hopped off the desk and put out her hand. "No. I'm ready for dessert. How about you?"

She held one of those small paper containers that usually held ketchup at fast-food restaurants. As she waved it under his nose, his sense of smell kicked in. Mmmm, chocolate syrup. She must have warmed it in the microwave because its rich scent clung to his nostrils as she moved it back and forth in a teasing manner.

He smiled as he put his hands around her waist and started to pull her shirt out of her jeans.

"Uh-uh." She stepped back and set the container on his desk. Turning, she began to unbutton his jeans with nimble fingers. "This is about you, not me. I've been told you've been quite ornery lately and we can't have that, now can we?"

Colt's heart jerked into hyperdrive. He held his breath while she finished unbuttoning his pants and let out a deep groan when she put her hand on him through his boxers.

"I love a man in boxers," she murmured.

And just how many men had she done this to? he wondered. No, he didn't want to know. Colt just gave into feeling. She stroked him through his underwear, her hand moving down the full length of him. She shifted gleaming eyes to his half-closed ones, a smile on her face.

"My, my, I think your name should've been Stallion instead of Colt," she said, her voice full of amused appreciation.

He chuckled at her "hung like a horse" reference. But his amusement quickly turned into a groan of anticipation when she found the opening to his boxers and slipped his hard cock through it.

The feel of her hand on his exposed flesh lit him on fire. He reached over and pulled the clip out of her hair, sending the weight of her glossy black hair rolling down her back. Sliding his hand into the thick mass, he rubbed the dark tresses before gripping a handful. He didn't have to wonder anymore. It did feel as soft as it looked.

"You sure know how to seduce a man," he groaned as she slid her hand up and down his arousal.

She looked up at him and gave him a wink and a knowing grin. "You ain't seen nothing yet, darlin'." Retrieving the container from the desk, she tipped it over him and warm chocolate drizzled down his sensitized flesh. Colt rocked his hips forward at the sensation of warmth rolling down his cock.

She gave a throaty chuckle. "Now close your eyes and just experience," she said before her mouth descended on him.

The feel of her wet, hot mouth sliding around him just about sent Colt over the edge. He had to measure his breathing to keep from losing it as soon as her mouth touched his skin. She must have sensed it too, for she said in a husky voice, "See how long you can hold out. I promise it'll be worth the wait."

Colt ground his teeth at the feeling of her delicious tongue sliding up and down and around him. He could feel the pressure building, his lower belly tensing. "Elise," he said in a tight voice. He crushed her hair in his fist, his heart ramming in his chest.

Pulling her mouth off of him, she teased, "Not yet."

Colt opened his eyes and look down at her, not sure if he wanted her to tease him more or not.

"Let me know when you're almost there, okay?"

He nodded and gave her a brief smile before closing his eyes again. She moved her mouth back to surround him and the sensation of warmth washed over him once again. Sensing the welcome tightening deep in his groin, Colt knew he couldn't hold back much longer. "Elise," he warned, expecting her to pull away.

And she did for a brief second, then he felt a sudden rush of coolness bathing him along with her warm mouth. The drastic change in temperature was all he could take. His body shuddered with a mind-blowing climax as he thrust his hips against her again and again. Elise kept her mouth moving over him until he was completely spent.

When she pulled away, he opened his eyes and started to say, "How did you...?" when he saw her sitting back on her heels. A Cheshire grin lit up her face as she stuck her soda straw in her mouth and sucked seductively on it.

"Gotta love a cold drink," she said with a wink.

Colt grinned at her and just shook his head. What a woman.

With a pleased look on her face, she stood up, set down her cup and moved in between his legs. "Feeling better, Cowboy?"

Colt put his hands on her waist and pulled her onto his lap. "I won't feel better until I am buried in you. I want to hear your screams as I rock your world." He watched the desire flicker in her eyes and knew they would be good together. Colt cupped her head and pulled her to him, giving her a thorough kiss.

Elise lifted her head and arched an eyebrow. "Such promising words, Cowboy. The question is...can you deliver?"

He was about to answer her when he heard Mace's voice, as he entered the main office door. Elise stood and he gave her a heated look while he fixed his pants.

Once he was dressed, Elise walked over to the door. Before she opened it, she turned and blew him a kiss. "Here's to open-ended promises, darlin'." She opened the door and left the room.

Elise walked back to her office feeling very happy. She

liked Colt. Liked the way he made her feel. And she wanted him. So much so she did things with him she had never done with another man. It just felt so right with him...so natural to be less inhibited and more...wild. She smiled as she sat in her chair and moved her mouse to get rid of the screen saver. And she *had* made his day. Boy, had she made his day!

She chuckled to herself at the look of surprise on his face at her aggressive behavior. She really didn't know where it was coming from. Normally, she didn't act like this. Colt must just draw the bad girl out of her. She liked it, liked the power of it. Lost in thought, she looked up to see Mace standing in her doorway for the second time that day.

"I don't know what kind of magic you worked on my brother, but keep it up." He grinned. "I just might get a raise, yet."

Elise feigned a puzzled expression. "I don't know what you're talking about." Even though she was secretly pleased she could bring about such a swift change in Colt's mood, she didn't need or want to broadcast their relation...er, whatever it was, just yet.

Mace laughed. "Yeah, right." He continued to stand there as if waiting for her to respond.

Elise stared him down, waiting for him to get bored and leave. With a shrug and a wide grin, Mace turned to walk away. He swiftly glanced back and said, "I like your hair down." An innocent expression crossed his face as he continued, "Is that the way you wore it this morning?"

Elise involuntarily put her hand to her hair. She had forgotten about her clip Colt had removed in his office. Her cheeks grew hot as Mace walked away, a deep, knowing chuckle following in his wake.

* * * * *

Colt stared at the clock on his desk. Man, it felt like an eternity until six. He lost count of the number of times he stopped working and glanced at his watch, willing it to move faster. He hadn't seen Elise since lunch. Earlier, he heard her talking on the phone, heard her sexy laugh and he instantly hardened. This was the longest damn day in his life. His body reacted as if Elise hadn't satisfied him just a few hours ago. If anything, her knowing touch only managed to make him want her more.

Another long hour passed.

Colt said goodbye to Mabel as she waved goodnight. On his way out, Mace leaned in his doorway. "Have a good evening, bro, ya hear?" His brother winked at him and laughed heartily as he turned and walked out the main door.

His heart already pounding faster, Colt forced himself to wait until Mace turned toward the main house and Mabel's car disappeared down the long driveway.

He pushed his chair back, picked up his hat and set it on his head as he made his way back to Elise's office.

A grin rode up on his face as he pushed open her partially closed door. He was surprised to find Elise, her head cradled in her arms on her desk, fast asleep. Colt felt the disappointment course through his body, but it was quickly replaced with concern as he stared down at her, watching her sleep.

He walked over and scooped her up from the chair into his arms. "Come on, sweetheart, time to go home."

"Wha...?" She looked up at him, dazed and confused. Wrapping her arms around his neck, she mumbled into his neck, "I'm sorry...must've fallen asleep...that'll teach me to take the red-eye back." When Colt moved to walk out of her office, she quickly lifted her head. "My keys." Colt turned back and she swiped her purse and keys off the desk.

After he set her down next to his truck, Elise looked around. "My car's over there."

Colt put a finger on her jaw and turned her face toward his. "You're too tired to drive yourself home. I'll drive you."

She stared into his eyes for a long moment and then sighed.

"I guess you're right."

He opened the door for her and she slid into the seat. Once she'd buckled her seatbelt, he walked around to his side of the truck. Climbing in, he put his hat on the seat and started the engine. As his truck rumbled down the gravel drive, he saw Elise's eyes begin to close once more.

Colt pulled into the parking lot in front of Elise's apartment and she lifted her head when the car stopped. "Are we here already?"

He chuckled and got out of the truck. Opening her door for her, he leaned over and grabbed her keys from the seat. When she stumbled as she stepped down from the truck, Colt lifted her in his arms once again.

"Colt! I'm fine to walk myself," Elise complained.

"I like holding you close, Lise," Colt said as he nuzzled his face into her neck, inhaling her scent and wishing for more.

Elise sighed and wrapped her arms around his neck as he walked up the stairs to her apartment. Without setting her down, he unlocked her door and walked inside. Kicking the door closed behind him, he asked, "Which way to your bedroom?"

Elise pointed and he followed her direction. As Colt walked toward her bedroom, he vaguely noticed an overstuffed cream-colored sofa and chair with a rattan frame and a matching round side chair. Several boxes were still sitting around, waiting to be unpacked.

He laid Elise on her bed and started to move away.

"Where are you going, Cowboy?" she said in a sultry voice, her green eyes gazing up at him with sexy promises.

His jaw tightened. He fought the wave of desire coursing through his body at her suggestive question, the thought of her warm body pressed against his for hours.

Colt planted a brief kiss on her forehead. "You need to sleep, Elise." He moved to untangle her arms she'd wrapped around his neck.

"You can't leave me now." She tightened her hold and pressed closer to him.

How did she manage to sound incredulous and alluring all at once?

Colt tamped down the hunger raging throughout his body. He looked directly into her eyes. "Elise, darlin', the last thing I want to do is leave your delectable body alone right now. There's nothing more I would like to do than bury myself so deep in you that neither of us would be able to tell where one left off and the other began." He heard her intake of breath at his lascivious words, saw her pulse racing at her throat and his body throbbed.

Running his hand down her side and across her breast, he never relinquished her gaze. "I want to see every inch of your beautiful body, to know that my touch makes it hum." He skimmed his fingers over her stomach and lower where he cupped her sex possessively through her jeans. Her heat radiated through the fabric and he felt his own body grow instantly hard at its fiery promise. She arched her back at his touch, moaning softly.

God, she was so responsive.

He removed his hand before all his good intentions slipped away in a haze of lust-filled passion. "I want you. But I want you rested and ready, not tired and half asleep."

Elise sat up on her elbows and he instinctively dipped his head toward hers. She closed the small distance between them and drew his bottom lip in her mouth. After she'd sucked on it, she let his lip slide through her lips as she laid her head back on her pillow.

"You'll pay for this," she said with a disappointed sigh.

Colt chuckled at her petulant behavior. "Is that a fact?"

Elise bit her full lower lip and then ran her tongue slowly along it. She nodded. "Yes, it is."

He arched an eyebrow. "Well, then, I'd better make the payback worth my while." Lowering his head, he ran his tongue along her lower lip where she had just moistened her mouth.

Elise opened her mouth to speak and he took advantage, sliding his tongue into her mouth, intending to plunder her senseless. Elise kissed him back and began to suck on his tongue the same way she had sucked on his cock earlier. Her seductive act sent a jolt of raging lust slamming into his groin.

Colt jerked away, breathing hard. He stood, straightening beside the bed. "Good night, Elise. Sleep well." Turning on his heel, he walked out of her apartment as fast as his boots would take him. As he closed her apartment door and used her keys to lock it, he heard her throaty laughter floating from her bedroom. His body reacted, winding even tighter.

Damn the woman and her talented mouth. Now, he'd be the one dragging tomorrow. Fuckin' hell, he knew he wouldn't get a lick of sleep tonight.

* * * * *

The next morning, Elise awoke to the aroma of fresh roasted coffee. It smelled strong, as if it were right under her nose. She inhaled again, drinking in the inviting scent and actually felt the heat against her skin. Her eyes flew open to see Colt sitting on her bed with a hot cup of coffee from the local coffee shop down the street in his hand. He pulled it away from her nose and took a sip.

"Morning, Princess. Sleep well?" His eyes crinkled in the corners as he smiled at some hidden humor.

Elise harrumphed and rolled away from him, pulling the covers over her head. "What time is it?" she mumbled. She vaguely noticed the sun had barely begun to rise outside.

"Time to rise and shine, sunshine," he said in a voice way too awake for her. "I brought you coffee."

"Go away and come back in two hours," she said ungraciously. The truth was she didn't feel very gracious toward Colt. He'd left her wanting.

Again.

All she did last night was dream about his handsome face. His hands touching her. Everywhere. She tossed and turned and slept fitfully for the first hour until the lack of sleep from the night before finally caught up with her. She slept like a rock the rest of the night. But she still felt like she could use a couple more hours.

She drew in her breath when Colt's large hand landed hard on her backside.

"Get up, Elise. If you want to get to the office before Mace and Mabel do, get a move on. Else, they'll wonder why your car is there and you aren't yet."

Man, she hadn't thought of that. Elise threw back the covers and gave him a fuming look. "Oh, all right." She rolled out of bed and stomped off toward the bathroom, not even sparing him a backward glance. Stopping off at her dresser, she quickly grabbed some clean clothes and closed the bathroom door behind her. As she slipped out of her silk pajama set, she heard his deep chuckle.

"So, how'd you sleep last night?" he inquired through the door.

"Like a baby," she replied. There was no way she'd let this man know he kept her awake last night. No way!

"Uh-huh," he replied, disbelief evident in his tone.

Elise turned on the shower and waited for the water to warm up.

"Don't take a long one. We need to be at the office no later than seven," he called out over the patter of the water hitting the shower floor.

It would serve him right if she took a long one. But, then they would get to the office late and she didn't need to give Mace anything else to tease her about. As she stepped under the warm water, it occurred to her how she could get Colt back. Elise said in her most suggestive voice, "It's too bad we don't have much time, Colt. You could have taken a shower with me." When she heard no comment, she continued, feeling braver since she had locked the bathroom door behind her, "Well, there's no use wasting a good shower." She picked up the soap and ran it all over her body. "I guess I'll have to imagine your hands all over my wet skin."

Moving her hands over her breasts, she moaned loudly just for Colt's benefit. The latest shampoo commercial sprung to mind, making her smile. Oh, she had the urge, all right. *Maybe I should kick it up a bit.* She threw back her head and closed her eyes as she ran her hands down her stomach. "Yes, yes, oh, yes, that's it, YES."

A cold draft of air, chilling her skin, caused her to jerk her eyes open. The soap slipped from her hand as Colt pulled the shower curtain completely back. His eyes burned with open desire as he raked his gaze over her wet, naked body. His look darkened as he watched the rivulets of soapy water disappear into the dark hair between her legs.

"I may as well see what I am missing out on," he said in a light voice that didn't quite mesh with his predatory gaze as it stayed locked on her body.

After a brief initial embarrassed heat infused her body, Elise regained her composure. "Colt!" She reached over to pull the shower curtain closed.

He grabbed her hand, staying her attempt to pull the curtain. His eyes locked with hers and held. "I told you I'm a very visual man, Elise. Did you not take me at my word?" His gaze challenged her to finish her shower while he watched.

Sexual power surged through her at his suggestive eyes. This man better learn she never backed down from a challenge. She gave him a seductive smile as she pulled her hand away and bent to pick up the soap. Straightening, she met his gaze once more and said, "Are you sure you can handle it?" as she began to rub the soap over her breasts and down her stomach once more. Through half closed eyes, she watched and relished Colt's reaction. His jaw hardened and his grip on the coffee cup in his hand was so tight the cup bowed inward.

Elise chuckled inwardly at him and at herself. She was actually getting all hot and bothered at the idea of him watching her. Lifting her leg, she set her foot on the edge of the tub so she would have better access when she ran her hand lower. As she inched her hand toward herself, she looked up in time to see Colt turn to leave the bathroom.

"Hurry up. You have five minutes," he called out over his shoulder in a gruff voice.

When he shut the door sharply behind him, she chuckled out loud, knowing she'd won that round. She spent the next ten minutes getting dressed and drying her hair. As she walked out of the bathroom, Colt grabbed her by the shoulders and pushed her against the open door, thrusting his thigh between hers.

His mouth came down on hers, hard and invading, the thrust of his tongue in her mouth, taking…everything. Elise kissed him back, returning his fervent kiss. She loved the way he kissed, fast and hard or slow and heated. She didn't care. She loved the way he tasted. This morning he tasted of coffee and cinnamon.

Colt slid a hand from her shoulder down her body to cover her aching center. His thumb pushed against her sensitive nub through her jeans. Elise arched into his touch. He applied more pressure but didn't move his hand an inch beyond that. Elise tried to move her hips, but his thigh had her locked in place.

Colt lifted his head from hers and stared into her eyes, his eyes blazing with undisguised lust mixed with anger. "Don't ever do that to me again when you know I don't have time to do anything about it."

Elise opened her mouth to defy him. Colt moved his thumb ever so slightly, giving her the sensation she sought. She gasped and tried to rock her hips. But then he immediately stopped and applied straight, frustrating pressure once more.

"I mean it, Elise. Am I clear?" he ground out.

Elise bit her lip and narrowed her eyes on him before she spoke, "Yes, I get the picture."

Colt slid his hand up her stomach and laid it on her shoulder. Pulling her close once more, he planted a firm kiss on her lips before he turned and walked away. "Let's go, Princess. The office awaits."

She wanted to scream in frustration at the man's retreating back. Instead, she grabbed her purse and backpack and followed him out the door, all the while mumbling about irascible cowboys.

Chapter Seven

Colt held the truck door open for Elise, but didn't say a word to her. His face was an impassive mask as he shut her door behind her and walked around to his side of the truck. He started the engine and pulled onto the road. Elise couldn't stand the tense silence anymore. She turned to look at Colt's profile as he stared at the road.

"Colt…" she began. But that was all she got out before Colt reached over and laid his hand on her thigh. The gesture was heart-stopping.

Elise dropped her gaze to his hand. The warmth of it penetrated her jeans, soaking into her skin, radiating throughout her body. She let her eyes shift from Colt's hand back up to his face. He didn't say anything, just let his gaze drift slowly over her. It wasn't so much an apology he held in his eyes but something…deeper. His intimate, visual caress coupled with his heated touch conveyed his feelings more than any words ever could have. Elise locked eyes with him as she laid her smaller hand on top of his.

Colt finally broke their gaze to return his to the road, but his hand stayed where it was, branded on her thigh. They rode the rest of the way to the ranch in silence.

When they reached the ranch, he removed his hand from her leg to turn off the engine. Turning to her, his eyes reflected his pent up desire. A tight smile formed on his lips before he spoke, "It's a good thing I have a lot of errands to do on the ranch today. I don't think I would be able to spend today in the office with you without yanking you into my office and having my way with you."

Desire shot through her body at his words, spreading from

her hard nipples and below. Elise gave him a pouty smile. "Well then, Cowboy, what kind of thoughts are you leaving me with today?"

Colt's tight smile changed and broadened a full-fledged grin. "Hopefully, the same kind of torturous thoughts I've been having ever since you turned those sultry green eyes my way and said, 'Nice to meet you, Colt.'"

Elise laughed as she opened the door and slid out of the truck. She turned and looked at him with his arm slung over the steering wheel. "You have a good day bouncing around out there on Scout, ya hear?" Shutting the door, she swayed her hips a little more than normal just for his benefit before she disappeared inside the office.

Once inside, she settled in her chair, booted up her computer and opened the file to the website. The ticket sales seemed to be working just fine. Colt made sure to keep in touch with his manager of The Lonestar Rodeo, Tom Hoffman, to let him know about the significant changes in the ticket selling process. Yes, tickets could still be bought at the rodeo, but the website should help smooth the process.

Clicking around the website some more, she thrummed her fingers on the desk. Lately something had been bothering her about the website. She clicked on the pictures she'd loaded on it the other day for Mace. These were the pictures Jim Peterson supplied of various rodeo shots. While they were action shots, showing what happens at their rodeo, Elise thought it would also be nice for people to know what goes on behind the scenes of a rodeo. To kind of give the website more depth for folks visiting it—make it more personalized. People could always relate to the behind the scenes people doing their jobs to bring them entertainment.

She reached over and pulled her camera bag from her backpack. Unzipping the case, she slid her Pentax 35MM camera out. The camera was one of the items she'd left behind in Virginia. As she searched through the camera bag, she realized she was out of film. Before she ran out to the store, she decided to give her friend Alex a call.

"G'day." Alex's breathless voice, her Australian accent in full swing, came across the phone line.

"Hi, Alex. Got a minute?" Elise asked. She hadn't spoken to Alex since a couple weeks before she inherited her half of the Lonestar.

Alex laughed. "Elise, you rat! You haven't called me in a month. Now, right when I'm on my way out of town to another photo shoot, you decide to call me? You're not playing fair. I want to talk, but my plane leaves in an hour."

Elise's grin rode up her face upon hearing her girlfriend's good-natured ribbing. "Sorry, Alex. I've been a little busy. Call me once you get a free minute or two and I'll fill you in on the details. You can either call my cell phone or my work number." She gave Alex her number at the office.

"That's no Virginia area code," Alex said, suspicion in her voice.

Elise laughed. "I'm glad to see all that world traveling hasn't dulled your mind."

"Ooh, Elise, I want you to spill, but I don't have time right now. I'll call you as soon as I get a free minute. I want all the juicy details." Alex's excited voice floated through the phone.

Elise chuckled at her longtime friend's exuberance. "I know you have to go, so I'll ask my question. I want to take some outdoor action shots. Which film is best for me to use under those circumstances?"

Alex drilled off the best types of film saying it depended a lot on lighting. "I'll call you as soon as I can," she promised before she hung up.

Elise looked up to see Mace leaning in her doorway, one boot crossed over the other, his eyebrow raised as a curious expression filtered across his face. "Mornin' Elise. Who's Alex?"

Elise realized by Mace's tone, he thought Alex was a guy. She let a devilish smile spread across her face. Why dispel the theory?

"Alex is a friend of mine. I needed some advice and Alex has always been there with the answer."

"Be careful of the guys with all the answers," he warned.

Elise laughed outright at his ironic words. "Like you have room to talk, Mr. King-of-the-Smooth-Talkers."

He gave her a cheeky grin. "It takes one to know one, darlin'."

Elise decided she might as well ask Mace about her idea while she had his attention. "While you're here, I wanted to run something past you." She outlined her idea to add personalized shots of the people who work the ranch, the people behind the scenes of The Lonestar Rodeo. "I could write up what each person does to contribute to The Lonestar." She winked at Mace. "Even your good-for-nothing mug will be on the website."

Mace nodded his head as she talked. "I like it, Elise. Great idea!" He rubbed his jaw as he thought through it. "Tell you what, I'll write the introduction to the new section and you can do the individual write-ups, okay?"

Elise gave him a broad smile. "Sounds like a plan."

He grinned back at her. "Guess I'd better get started on that intro." He headed off to his office.

* * * * *

As lunchtime neared, Elise decided to run out and get the film Alex recommended. On the way to her car, Colt caught up with her. "Now where are you going?" He had that frustrated look on his face again.

Elise raised her eyebrow at his demanding manner. "Remember the pager, Colt," she reminded him in a cool tone.

Before he could respond, a red truck pulled down the drive. A man who looked to be in his early fifties got out and shut the door.

"Howdy, neighbor," the man with salt and pepper hair said as he plunked his gray Stetson on his head.

"What are you doing here?" Colt said in a rough tone.

Elise turned and looked at him in surprise at his abrupt manner.

"I came to meet your new partner," the man said in a jovial tone as he stuck out his hand to her.

Elise laughed and shook his hand saying, "I'm Elise Hamilton and I must say, news travels fast around here."

"Jackson Riley," the older man said.

"Oh, you're—" she started to say when Colt cut her off. "Elise was just on her way out to run an errand."

"Colt!" she said, shocked by his rudeness.

"Par for the course," the man said, seeming unruffled by Colt's attitude toward him. "How's that bull of yours, Colt. Heard he wasn't doing too good this weekend. Seems a shame since I heard you'd given your other top bull to Earl."

Colt crossed his arms, rocked back on his heels and replied, "He's doing just fine." His gaze narrowed on Jackson. "How do you know about my bull?"

The old man shrugged. "I saw Evan's truck leave your ranch, and well, it is a small town."

Colt started to speak when Mabel poked her head out of the office door, "Colt, Tom's on the line for you."

"Tell him I'll call him back."

"He said he needed to speak with you now."

"Uh-oh. Don't have trouble with the rodeo now too, do ya?" Jackson said.

The lack of sympathy in his voice made Elise look at him. Good Lord, what was going on with these men?

Colt's jaw muscle jumped before he turned and headed to the office.

"I would think you'd want to unload this troublesome place," Jackson said to her as soon as Colt walked inside.

Elise met his gaze. "On the contrary. That's what makes it

so wonderful. There's so many ways we can improve it."

"I'll raise the offer another eight grand," he said, his voice hopeful.

She sighed. "I told you when I received your offer a few weeks ago that I wasn't interested in selling, and I haven't changed my mind," she responded in a firm tone.

The man stiffened and all friendliness fled his expression. As he turned to get back in his truck, he looked back at her and said, "You'll want to sell one day. My offer still stands."

Shaking her head and wondering at the animosity between the two men, Elise got in her car and followed his truck off the property on her way to the store for the film.

* * * * *

When she arrived back on the ranch, Colt met her at her car. As she got out, he pushed his hat back on his head and forced a smile. "I'm sorry for coming across abrupt when I spoke to you earlier. I was just hoping we could have lunch together."

Elise gave him an apologetic smile. "Sorry, I grabbed something to eat while I was running my errand."

He ran a finger down her cheek as he gazed into her eyes. "Maybe it was for the best anyway. I don't think an hour would be nearly long enough."

Elise felt her pulse quicken at his words and a bolt of desire shot from the place he touched on her cheek all the way down to pool in a pulsing ache between her legs. She involuntarily clamped her legs together at the frustrating sensation.

She stepped away at the knowing look in Colt's eyes. He knew she was affected by his touch.

Seeking a distraction, she asked, "By the way, what's up with you and Jackson Riley?"

Colt stiffened and his expression turned cold. "He's just a troublemaker I could do without having around."

She tilted her head to the side. "I wish you had told me

about the sick bull. I would've delayed my trip to help you out."

He stepped close to her and slid his fingers down her neck. His expression softened. "All is well, darlin'. No worries."

"Colt, I want to be informed—" she started to say when he interrupted.

"I didn't think you'd be interested. I promise next time I'll tell you."

Elise nodded her head in agreement then said in a brisk tone, "Go back to your ranching, Cowboy. I have work to do," before she headed toward the office.

Colt's low chuckle followed in her wake. The sound made her square her shoulders and walk with her head held high as she opened the door and walked into the office.

As she walked down the hall, Elise was in the process of pulling the film out of the bag when she ran right into Mace.

"Whoa, there," he said as he steadied her with his hands on her arms.

"Oh, sorry, Mace, I wasn't looking where I was going."

His green eyes twinkled. "Apparently not." He looked down at the film in her hand. "Ready to take pictures?"

Elise nodded. "Have you written the intro yet?"

"Yep. I emailed it to you so you can look over it. That way, you'll already have a copy of it when you are ready to add that page to the website."

"Thanks, Mace."

"Don't mention it." He gently chucked her on the jaw, winked, and gave her a broad grin before he walked off toward the main office door.

Elise shook her head as she watched him swagger out of the office. That man could charm the scales off a rattlesnake. One of these days Mace was going to meet his match. And watch out! A broad smile formed on her lips. She could only imagine the type of woman it would take to tame Mace Tanner. She chuckled to herself as she made her way to her desk.

Once she read the email Mace had sent her, she sat back in her chair for a minute, thoroughly impressed. Now she knew why Mace was in charge of public relations. Not only did the man have a way with women, he also had a way with words. It wasn't just the smooth cadence of his writing that struck her, but the way in which he pulled the reader in, making one *want* to click the button to find out about the people behind The Lonestar Rodeo. More than satisfied, she saved the document on her hard drive and closed out the email.

Elise finished loading her film in her camera and was leaning over to put the camera bag back in her backpack, when she heard something land on her desk. She looked up and saw a black cowboy hat sitting next to her computer. Allowing her gaze to travel upward, her attention landed on faded blue jeans stretched across lean hips, a nice belt buckle and a chambray shirt. She sat up and looked at Colt.

"Come on, Elise. You may as well tour the ranch again while I'm out and about."

Elise flashed him a brilliant smile. "Now, how can I resist an offer like that?"

She picked up the hat Colt brought her and put it on her head. As she stood, she swiped her camera bag back out of her backpack.

"What's that?" Colt asked as she pulled the strap over her shoulder and walked around the desk to stand beside him.

"A camera."

He raised an eyebrow. "Thought to do some sightseeing?"

"No, it's a project I'm working on." She winked at him. "You'll see."

"Hmmm," was all Colt said as he put his hand on her elbow and propelled her down the hall.

* * * * *

Elise let Bess follow Colt and Rick's horses out of the stable.

She lifted the camera strap over her head so it was on one shoulder while the camera bag lay against the opposite hip. As they made their way across the range, she took pictures of the scenic view. Colt and Rick moved their horses across the plains, shifting cattle from one grazing area to another. Elise lifted her camera and snapped a couple of pictures of Rick and Colt working as a team to keep the cattle in line.

She even got a picture of Vaquero, the Border collie that worked the ranch with the men. He paced back and forth, his head held low, barking occasionally if any cattle strayed. And just to be fair, she clicked a picture of Caboose, the dog that, well…was always trailing in the rear as if he would rather be doing anything else other than working the cattle, but she could tell he didn't want to be left out either. She had to chuckle as she realized how these dogs got their names. She guessed their mannerisms more than anything else was what earned them their names.

They were almost done for the day when one of the calves moved away from the herd and trotted off. Vaquero started to go after him. Rick whistled the dog back, causing the calf to bolt. Rick looked at his watch and said to Colt, "You're on, boss."

Colt gave him a huge Texan grin. He put a short rope between his teeth and took off after the calf, already swinging his other rope. Elise slowed Bess to a stop and readied her camera, thankful she had a long-range lens. Through her viewfinder, she watched in fascination as Colt managed to rope, jump down, flank—a term she had read about on the website, which basically meant put it on its side—and tie the calf in mere seconds. The fluidity in which he and his horse worked together was amazing to watch. She had never seen a person move so fast. Clicking shots, she lowered her camera. She knew her expression was full of awe.

Rick pulled up beside her. His brown eyes twinkled as he showed her his watch. "Yep, he's still got it in 'em. Just under eight seconds."

Elise turned surprised eyes to Rick. "In reviewing the old

website, I read that Colt did a bit of rodeoing but…wow, that was impressive."

Rick nodded. "He was the reigning world champion for three years running in the calf roping and saddle bronc riding events, until…" Rick cleared his throat as if realizing he was saying too much. "Um, until his dad passed away and he was needed to run the ranch."

Elise nodding her understanding to Rick, then laid her camera against her hip as she walked Bess over to where Colt had untied the calf. The animal jumped up and Colt swatted his hindquarters, sending him in the general direction of the herd. The calf happily trotted back to its momma.

"Now that was a sight to see," she said looking down at him, her eyes full of appreciation.

Colt looked up at her as he began to wind the rope back up in his hands. With his hat on the ground, he squinted into the afternoon sun. "Didn't I mention I was pretty handy with a rope?"

"No, you forgot to mention that little tidbit," Elise said with a smile as she watched Rick move on with the cattle. She turned her gaze back to his face.

She saw a knowing grin tilt the corners of his lips before Colt looked down at his hands to finish winding the rope. "Must've slipped my mind."

Elise chuckled. "What other surprises do you have in store for me?"

Colt raised his face to hers, his blue eyes full of fire. "Oh, I can think of a thing or two I can show you that you might never have seen before."

Elise felt the heat of his laser gaze penetrate her body, causing a singeing sensation to spiral through her. She had to fight to clear the lustful fog from her mind.

"Do you miss it? The rodeo?"

Colt raised his eyebrow at her question then let his gaze roam the land around him.

"No. I don't miss it. I have all I ever wanted right here." His eyes landed on her as he said the last words, "Well, almost."

If she thought her body couldn't get any hotter, all she had to do was look into Colt's eyes. The man had a way of making her body feel constantly on fire. The promises in his eyes made her a mass of quivering, sensitized nerves. She needed to get away from him before she launched off the horse and right into his arms, no matter what ranch hand happened to be riding by. With a smile she turned her horse away and called over her shoulder, "See you back at the ranch house, Colt."

Colt watched her ride away on her horse. He smiled at her straight back, the curve of her hips as her body swayed in motion with her horse. She looked so right riding Bess, the Texas plains and cattle in the background a beautiful backdrop behind her. He thought he could spend the day away from her, but that afternoon his resolve had broken and he decided to track her down for lunch. When he hadn't been able to have lunch with her, it had eaten at him more than he cared to admit.

Finally, he gave up and went and got her. He wanted Elise by his side. He wanted her to experience the range, the fresh beauty of it, the peacefulness it could bring. The hot Texas sun had him reaching for his hat, dusting it off and plunking it on his head. He gave a wry smile. Then, there was the sweltering Texas heat, the dust and loneliness that can sometimes accompany one on the range as well. Who was he kidding? Elise, and what was between them, was only temporary. But he was tired of waiting. He wanted to know exactly what *was* between the two of them.

Chapter Eight

It was late in the day. Most everyone had gone home and the ranch hands were currently at the ranch house eating dinner. Elise had spent the rest of the day taking pictures and talking to the ranch hands, finding out what they do. She even took a picture of Nan in the process of making the evening meal.

Elise took advantage of the quiet around the place as she leaned on the fence near the stables just as she had done her first day on the ranch. The sun was sinking low in the sky, making the beautiful scenery before her too irresistible. She snapped the last few pictures left on the film and was in the process of lowering the camera from her face when something landed on her shoulder.

Elise drew in her breath as Colt's warm, hard body pressed fully against her back. His frame touched her from the top of her shoulder blades to the back of her thighs as he leaned over and whispered in her ear, "Just wanted to show you how handy I can be, Princess."

She glanced down and saw a rope lying on her shoulder. She chuckled that he was throwing the same words she'd said to him on her first day on the ranch back at her. But the amusement died on her lips as she watched the end of the rope drop to the ground in front of her. She used the camera strap to slowly lower her camera to the ground as Colt slid a hand between her legs from behind her, causing her body to tense in anticipation.

Instead of touching her, he reached for the rope dangling in front of her and pulled it through her legs and upward between their bodies, effectively looping the rope around her body from her shoulder to her crotch. As the rough ridges of the rope slid against the denim of her jeans, creating a humming rub right against her most sensitive area, Elise sucked in her breath. She was so turned on from the feel of his body against hers and his suggestive words, she almost climaxed from the mere friction it caused.

Colt chuckled as he pulled the rope tighter. "I think you like my skill with a rope." Elise moaned at the pressure the tightening of the rope caused. While he held the rope with one hand, he skimmed his other hand down her side. Placing his palm on her thigh, he held it there as he had done that morning. When Elise turned her face to the side, wanting to be closer to him, he kissed her temple with a tender brush of his lips. She realized what he had meant by his touch. It was his promise of what was to come. After a few seconds, he slid his hand upward across her hip and back down across her taut stomach. She throbbed painfully, wanting the contact, needing his touch.

Colt let the rope go and Elise watched it drop to the ground at the same time he cupped her fully through her jeans, his touch possessive and sure. She gasped at his touch, bucking at the contact, wanting to press herself closer. Colt skimmed his lips down her neck as his fingers applied pressure in just the right place. When he used the heel of his hand for good measure, she bit her lip as her body thrummed in response to his touch.

Colt wrapped his other arm around her waist and pulled her full against him, whispering in a husky tone, "Let go, Lise. You want this as much as I want to give it to you." He put a booted foot between her legs and nudged her boot's heel across the dry dirt, opening her legs at the same time he slid his hand down and back up, applying oh-so-perfect pressure. Elise's breath hitched in her throat and she was lost in a maelstrom of spiraling desire until her body finally succumbed to the sexual tension that had been building since she last felt his intimate touch.

When she tried to turn her head into his neck to muffle her cry of pleasure from her orgasm, Colt captured her lips with his. Once the tremors stopped, she turned in his arms, wrapped her arms around his waist and laid her head on his chest. Closing her eyes, she absorbed the sensations assailing her, the warmth of the setting sun, the smell of outdoors and Colt's own natural scent permeating her senses, the feel of his hard body pressed against hers, the sound of her own heartbeat as it slowed from her climax and Colt's steady heartbeat under her ear. It was a special moment in time she would never forget.

After a few minutes she looked up into his deep blue eyes. They were filled with longing and hunger.

"I want to know, Lise," Colt said.

She knew what he meant. He wanted to know if they were as good together as he thought they'd be. Elise gave him a saucy grin. "What are you waiting for, Cowboy?"

His expression turned serious as he grabbed her hand. Elise barely had time to scoop up her camera before he dragged her behind him with a determined gait. As they passed her car and headed toward his truck, she laughed and said, "Leaving my poor car behind again, are we?"

"Damn straight," he mumbled in response, not once breaking his stride.

Once they settled into his truck and he started the engine, Elise reached over and tried to slide her hand up his leg.

He cut his gaze over to her and said in a gruff voice, "Keep your hands to yourself, darlin', if you want to make it back to your apartment. I'm too on-the-edge right now."

Her body tingled all over at his intense comment. She leaned back against her seat, her stomach tensing in anticipation. While he drove, she noted that he never looked her way the entire trip. When they arrived at her apartment, she hopped out before Colt had a chance to come around her side. Walking ahead of him, she'd almost made it to her apartment door when she stopped dead in her tracks. Crap! She didn't have her keys. Lovely, now they'd have to drive back to the ranch to get them. She wanted to scream in frustration.

Elise had stopped so abruptly, Colt almost ran right into her. He chuckled as he took a step back. "What's the matter?

Wondering where these are?"

She turned as he dangled her keys between his fingers. Giving him a winning smile, she took the keys and moved to her apartment's burgundy door to unlock it. As she tried to insert the key in the lock in the dim evening light, Colt slid his arms around her waist and down the front of her thighs while he pressed his hard length against her backside.

His movements caused her hands to shake, making it all the more difficult to unlock the door. Standing on her hunter green welcome mat in front of her door, her heart racing, Elise smacked at his hands as he moved them upward toward her breasts. "Colt, you're distracting me. I can't unlock the door."

Without a word, he pulled the keys from her hand and turned her around until her back was against the door. Her breath caught in her throat as he leaned over and kissed her full on the mouth. Elise thrilled in his persuasive mouth and warm tongue darting past her lips, seeking a response. When he pulled away, he turned the key in the lock and opened the door.

Once they'd entered her apartment, Colt pushed the door shut behind him. Elise set her camera down, flipped on the entryway light and turned to face him, her nerves making her insides jangle in tense excitement. They both stood there, staring at each other. Now that they were alone, it was as if neither one wanted to make the first move. She licked her lips and said, "Well, do you want something to drink?"

She turned to walk toward the kitchen when Colt's hand snaked out and grabbed her arm, propelling her back against his hard body.

His eyes held that hungry look in them again. "Uh-uh. I've got all the sustenance I need right here, darlin'."

He put his hands on her upper arms and pushed her against the wall as he lowered his mouth to hers, giving her the hottest kiss she'd ever experienced. There was just something about his warm lips moving over hers, the evening stubble chafing her face while his tongue thrust seductively against hers in a sensual dance that mimicked the sexual act—the heated kiss singed her nerve endings all the way to her toes.

Elise kissed him back with all the pent-up passion she'd been holding back since he left her wanting the other night. While their tongues tangled for dominance, she mumbled between kisses, "This time you'd better not leave me hanging or I'm liable to do you some real damage."

Colt lifted his head and stared deep into her eyes. He moved his hands to the wall on either side of her body and pressed his erection between her thighs. Rocking his hips upward against her mound, he lifted her slightly off the floor. She gasped at his aggressive, sexual movement.

"Don't worry, you and I aren't going anywhere until this fire between us has been thoroughly doused."

Thrilling at his promise, she gripped the tight muscles in his upper arms to steady herself, since her feet were barely touching the floor. Colt moved back from the wall, lowering her to the floor once more. He put his hands around her waist and pulled her closer.

As he leaned over to kiss her, he slid his hands down her back and tugged her lavender cotton shirt out of her jeans. Splaying a large hand against her lower back underneath the material, he ran his palm across her skin.

"Your skin is so soft, just as I knew it would be," he said in appreciation as he moved his lips over her jaw and down the column of her neck.

Elise shivered at his touch and his words. She let her head fall back as he kissed the hollow in her throat. Before she could offer to help, he lifted her shirt over her head and dropped it on the floor beside them. Reaching out, he traced the swell of her breast that peeked out over the curve of her silky bra.

Elise bit her lip at the sensations his slightest touch evoked. She gave a soft whimper when he dipped a finger inside her bra and brushed the rough pad against her nipple. She'd moved to unhook her bra but stopped when he said, his voice hoarse with desire, "No, I want to do it."

She lowered her hands and waited as he leaned his tall frame close and skimmed his lips across her bare shoulder. Goose bumps gathered on her skin at his touch, the heat of his nearness, so close but not touching her except for his mouth. He slowly slid one strap down as his lips followed its path across the curve of her shoulder.

Elise grasped his blue chambray shirt tight in her hands. She wanted him to hurry but the man seemed to want to take his sweet time. What was wrong with him?

When she was about to voice her opinion, she felt her bra give way around her as Colt unhooked it and slid if off her arms. He devoured her breasts with his heated gaze then moved to touch her. Before he made contact, Elise batted his hands away and gave him a sultry look. "Uh-uh, Cowboy. My turn."

Sliding her hands up his muscular chest, she enjoyed the firm hardness underneath her fingers. When she reached the opening of his shirt, she gave him a sultry grin saying, "I love western shirts." The snaps gave way as she quickly pulled his shirt apart, revealing his thick, sinewy chest.

Colt chuckled at her aggressive act, but his chuckle turned into a groan of pleasure as she ran her hands over his chest and up his shoulders to push his shirt down his arms until it fell in a heap behind him. Elise skimmed her fingers back up his arms and across his chest before she dropped her hands to his taut, flat abdomen. His body was perfection. Not an ounce of fat, nothing but pure muscle jumped under her touch. She moved closer and slid her hands around his waist to press her breasts against his chest.

"I've wanted to know what it feels like to have my skin touching yours, Colt," she whispered as she laid her head on his chest.

Colt wrapped his arms around her body and drew in a jagged breath when she planted a kiss on his upper chest. He didn't bother asking, but leaned over and quickly scooped her up in his arms, making his way back to her bedroom.

Once he set her down, Elise didn't bother turning on the lamp in her room. Enough light filtered from the hallway. She worked at the buttons of his jeans as he kicked out of his boots and pulled off his socks. Colt snapped the button of her jeans and slid them down over her hips while she stepped out of her boots and peeled off her socks.

Colt stripped off his boxers and watched as Elise slid out of her panties. They stood there, naked, inches apart, staring at each other. Colt lifted his hand and ran a finger down her chest, over her breast to stop at the tip of a puckered nipple. He circled the taut nub. The rough skin on his finger was a tactile, erotic sensation against her soft flesh. Elise reached out, grasped his rigid flesh in her hand and used her hold on him to pull him flush against her heated body. "Let's find out just how good we are together," she boldly said, before she kissed him full on the mouth.

Colt kissed her back, hard and demanding, before he abruptly broke the kiss. Stepping away from her, he picked up his discarded blue jeans to retrieve a condom. He pulled out a nearby straight-backed, wooden chair from the desk and sat down to roll the condom on. Even in the dim light, his dark, burning gaze stayed locked with hers. All she could think of while he stared at her with that hungry and possessive expression was... *God, the man makes me melt.*

Elise expected Colt to walk over to her once he put the condom on. Instead, he beckoned her with his hand and a promising look in his eyes. "Come here."

She walked over to stand beside him and let out a squeal of surprise when he quickly grasped her around the waist and effortlessly lifted her in the air until she straddled him across the chair. He held her there, the tip of his erection touching her heated center and said, "I got damn tired of seeing these firm thighs wrapped around my horses, Lise. I want to know what it feels like to have your beautiful legs wrapped around me." As he spoke, he slowly lowered her over him. Inch by inch, Elise thrilled as her body stretched to accept his gradual entry.

She moaned at the stimulation zinging through her while Colt slid into her body. Placing her hands on his shoulders, she held herself steady as he pushed into her. It seemed like an eternity before he finally filled her to the hilt, but she drew in her breath as her body came to a sliding halt. She'd never felt so completely filled. When he rocked his hips for the first time, his muscles bunched and contracted under her fingers. She thrilled at her body's reaction to him inside and out as she reflexively gripped his shoulders.

Colt moved his hands from her waist to her breasts where he cupped them fully in his hands. Her pulse thrummed at the flash of undisguised desire in his eyes while he skimmed his thumbs across her hardened nipples. Elise arched her back at his touch, moving against him, causing Colt to groan in pleasure. He leaned over and circled his tongue around one nipple while he rolled the other between his fingers. When Colt sucked her nipple into his mouth, Elise closed her eyes and moaned at the erotic duet. She clenched her thighs and rolled her hips against him.

"Look at me." His voice sounded raw, unchecked when he spoke.

Elise opened her eyes and stared into Colt's stormy blue ones. His eyes were lustful and intense as he lowered his hands to her waist and commanded, "Ride me, Lise."

Elise put her arms around his neck and tentatively touched her lips to his before she opened her mouth and deepened the kiss. She began to move her hips in a seductive, rocking motion until she heard Colt's breathing pattern change and felt his heart pound against her chest.

"E-lise." his voice broke as he said her name in a reverent tone, before he kissed her jaw and then her neck.

Encouraged by his reaction, Elise sat back and looked him in the eye. "You forget, half the horses are mine." She gave him a siren's smile. "And there's only one way I like to ride and that's full throttle." Grabbing his shoulders in her hands, she lifted her toes off of the floor and hooked her feet on the lower rungs of the chair, changing the pace of her movements. She pulled almost completely off of Colt before pushing against him once more, sheathing him fully inside her. Upon hearing his hiss of satisfaction, she threw her head back and enjoyed the sensation of her long hair dangling down her back as she arched against him.

Elise welcomed his powerful counterthrusts, the feel of his hands on her waist, helping her move, making sure she came down on him as completely and as hard as possible.

Colt whispered, "You feel so good, Lise, a tight glove made just for me."

Her own breathing turned rampant at his further words of encouragement, and she felt the tightening of her stomach muscles as her climax built within her. Unable to stop herself, she breathed Colt's name out in a throaty sigh as the pulsating rhythm took over.

Colt coaxed, "Scream for me, Lise." He thrust into her, hard and fast.

She answered his request as she experienced the most mind-numbing climax she'd ever had in her life. Right behind her orgasm, Colt tensed underneath her, calling out her name when he reached his own passionate plateau. Elise collapsed against his chest, her heart racing, her body throbbing and a sheen of sweat on her skin. She realized she would never ride a horse again without thinking of her first time with Colt.

While she lay across his chest, panting, Colt skimmed his fingers up her spine, flattened his hands on her back and slid them back down her body.

"Good lord, Lise. I had no idea." He sounded awed, surprised.

Elise chuckled against his shoulder. "Me either."

Sitting up, she moved to get off of him. He grabbed her waist and stilled her departure. "Where are you going?"

"I thought you might want to get up off the hard chair you're sitting on." She moved to get up once more.

"No," Colt said, restricting her movement once again. He shifted and effortlessly lifted them both off the chair. Elise sighed and wrapped her legs around his waist as he walked toward the bed. She welcomed the feel of his warm skin, the weight of his body on hers when they sank into her soft bedcovers.

Colt looked into her eyes, his cobalt ones searching her face. He smoothed back her hair with his hand. "You are so beautiful."

She felt him growing hard within her once more and gave a surprised gasp.

He chuckled. "See what you do to me, Lise? Instead of being doused, this fire between us is only growing. I wonder if it will ever be put out."

Smoothing her hands over his shoulders and down the hollows of his chest, Elise smiled up at him. "I guess the best we can do is try to contain it then."

Colt dropped his head to bury his nose in her neck and hair and mumbled, "I could stay buried in you for a week."

Elise started to chuckle at his words when Colt rocked his hips, pushing further into her, his hard length filling her, causing delicious friction. At her sigh of pleasure, he put his hands underneath her thighs and pushed them up so her knees were bent on either side of his chest. Lifting himself up, he placed his hands beside her on the bed as he pulled out and slowly sank back in once more. His intemperate expression made her heart skip a beat.

"Come for me, Elise. I want to feel your body humming around me again."

Elise closed her eyes and arched her back as he slid into her once more. She tossed her head and moaned at the drag of his body against hers, the feel of his muscular arms touching her legs. His hold on her gave her very little chance to move her legs, so she made up for it with her hips. She met his thrusts with accepting ones of her own, her breath hitching at the strength behind his thrusts into her. It was as if he planned to imprint himself on her, branding her as his very own.

Colt's movements created a ripple of sensations that began to rock throughout her body. "You're close, Elise. I can tell," he rasped as he pushed as far into her as he could, grinding his hips against hers.

Elise opened her eyes and met his gaze. "Yes, Colt, YES!" Her fingers flexed on his shoulders as she tightened her muscles around him, trying to still his movements, keep him deep within her forever. She cried out as she surrendered to her climax and shuddered around him.

Colt knew his eyes glittered with satisfaction and fierce possessiveness when he felt the featherlight vibrations of her body as she spasmed around him. It was the hottest turn-on he had ever experienced. He closed his eyes and rocked in and out of her, once, twice, until he finally gave into his own satisfying release.

Rolling over, he pulled Elise against his chest and ran his hand through her hair as they both lay there, catching their breath. With a sigh, she laid her head on his chest and placed her hand over his beating heart as she snuggled close to his body.

Colt listened until Elise's breathing turned even in her sleep. He rolled her onto her side and leaned up on an elbow to watch her sleep. As he ran a finger across her shoulder, she moaned in her sleep and his body began to tighten once more. Would he ever get enough of her? He gently pushed her onto her back so the moon's light streaming through the window would land on her beautiful face.

Colt balled his hand into a fist and held it to his side to keep himself from touching her again. He wanted to touch her, to run his hand lower, wake Elise and coax her into another mind-blowing experience all over again. He couldn't believe their explosive lovemaking. He'd known they would be good together, but he had no idea just how good! His sexual encounters with other women didn't begin to compare with what he and Elise shared. They had a...connection. And the thought knocked him in the gut as effectively as a sucker punch.

Elise was supposed to be a diversion. Instead, he could see his need for her easily turning into an addiction. Colt didn't want to get caught in that trap. If he forced himself to leave, he wouldn't give himself an opportunity to get used to waking up with her in his arms.

Pulling the covers over Elise, he slid out of bed. She turned over in her sleep and made little sexy sounds. Colt ground his teeth and forced himself to look away from her as he gathered his clothes, dropped the used condom in the bathroom trash and dressed in the dark.

Chapter Nine

Elise woke with a start. She lifted her head and reached out for Colt to find an empty bed beside her. Sitting up, she looked at the clock. It was three in the morning. Her gaze roamed the room, but there was no sign of Colt's discarded clothes. Pulling the covers back up over her cold shoulders, she laid back on the bed. Why did Colt leave? Damn, she regretted falling asleep. It just felt so right not to have to say anything with him—as if no words needed to be spoken. Now that he was gone, she'd lost the opportunity to say anything.

Rolling on her back, she stared at the ceiling as her regret turned to anger. It angered her that he'd left without a word. Elise reached over and set her alarm clock before pounding her pillow with more force than was needed. Laying her head down, she waited for sleep to come.

※ ※ ※ ※ ※

Even though it was a while before she'd succumbed to sleep, Elise jumped out of bed when her alarm clock blared three hours later. Since Colt drove her home, she knew he would have to come get her for work. She didn't want to have a dulled, sleepy mind when she faced him this morning. She quickly headed for the shower.

It was almost 7:00 a.m. Elise finished the last bite of her bagel and wondered where in the world Colt was when she heard a knock at her door. She smiled and felt immediately better at the sound of that determined knock. She moved toward the door and opened it with a ready smile. Her smile faded somewhat when she saw Mace standing at her door.

"Mornin' Elise." Mace touched the brim of his hat as he

gave her one of his sexy smiles.

Before she could stop herself, she asked, "What are you doing here?"

A wounded expression crossed his face. "You don't have to look so disappointed." Sobering quickly, he explained his presence, "Colt and Rick are working to ready the stables for the rodeo stock coming back today, so Colt asked me to come pick you up." He gave her a knowing look, then continued, "He said you had car trouble, so he had to bring you home last night." Mace stood there as if waiting for her to say something to confirm or deny the story.

She chose to do neither. What she *did* want to do was hit something. Instead, she turned on her heel, gathered her camera and followed him to his car. While Mace drove to the ranch, Elise became lost in her own thoughts. Why did Colt feel he had to make up some excuse as to why he'd brought her home? Why did he care what other people thought about them being together? Did he just want to get her out of his system and nothing more? She squared her shoulders. Well, if that was the case, she could pretend indifference with the best of them.

Elise perked up when she saw the various trailers that took up space in the Lonestar ranch's parking lot. Horses and bulls were being unloaded. Men worked to clean out the trailers as the animals exited.

"They're preparing for the second string," Mace said, referring to the rodeo stock that would eventually be loaded into the trailers.

"Second string?" Elise cut her eyes over to him as he parked his car along the side of the long drive.

"Yeah, think of it like football, except in reverse. We let the least rank rodeo stock tour the high school and college rodeos, but we put our most rank stock in the professional circuit rodeos."

She nodded her head. "And rank means, toughest to ride, right?"

He smiled. "See, you're getting the lingo down, city girl."

Elise returned his smile as she pulled out her camera. "I don't want to miss this opportunity for behind-the-scenes shots."

Mace led her over to introduce her to the members of The Lonestar Rodeo team. She locked gazes with Colt over his truck bed, now full of hay. He put his hand up and brushed his hat rim to acknowledge her but nothing else flickered in his eyes. His face remained an unreadable mask.

Elise gave him a tight smile and turned to meet Tom Hoffman, a gray-haired man in his fifties who managed and traveled with the rodeo. After she took Tom's picture, she asked if she could interview him later for the website. His agreeable response was overshadowed by a boisterous, feminine voice calling out, "Yee-haw, Colt Tanner, I'm back and yours for the takin'." A busty woman with long blonde hair threw herself into Colt's arms, wrapped her legs around his hips and planted a wet kiss on his lips.

Colt put his hands on her waist and grinned, "Welcome back, May."

Elise turned to Mace and raised her eyebrow. He leaned over and whispered, "Elise, meet May Winston."

As jealously shot through her, Elise said in a dry tone, "Let me guess. She works for the Lonestar rodeo."

Mace's gaze searched her face, then he answered, "Yep, she's responsible for selling the rodeo paraphernalia at our shows."

Elise looked down at her camera and adjusted the lens, mumbling, "Great, can't wait to interview her."

When Colt set May down, the woman continued talking animatedly to him. More than a little annoyed, Elise walked over to the main ranch house. As she entered the kitchen through the side door, Nan looked up from kneading dough on the counter.

"Mornin' Elise," she called out in her booming voice.

"Good morning, Nan."

Nan turned her deep brown gaze to the window. She tilted her chin toward the activity beyond. "I see folks are back."

Elise walked over and pulled a cup out of the cabinet. She turned to Nan with a grin. "I hope you're prepared for a much larger crew than normal for lunch and probably dinner."

Nan's full bosom shook with her laughter. "No problem there, child. I'm always ready for a big crowd."

Elise poured herself some fresh squeezed orange juice from the fridge and walked over to stand beside Nan. "That's good," she said absently as she took a sip of her drink and stared out the window. May was still talking to Colt.

Nan flipped the dough and pounded it hard.

"Not any more, Elise," she said, her words coming from nowhere.

Elise turned and gave her a confused look. "Pardon?"

Nan jerked her head toward the window. "Colt and May. They dated for a while, but they aren't anymore." She pounded the dough again and grumbled in a low tone, "Despite her best efforts."

Elise cut her eyes from the window to Nan and back. "Really? Interesting."

She could tell Nan didn't like May much. Well, May *was* the type women loved to hate. With her beautiful face, voluptuous figure and flirtatious ways, no wonder. But Elise knew Nan's feelings were more maternal in nature. After all, Nan had helped to raise the Tanner boys, or so Mace told her.

"She's only after one thing," Nan continued.

"Oh? What's that?" Elise couldn't resist asking as she took another sip of her drink.

Nan looked up and gave her a how-could-you-not-know expression. "She wants the ranch, of course."

Elise chuckled. "Considering I own half of it, she'll have to marry both of us for her dreams to come true."

Nan chuckled too. "Yeah, there *is* some justice in this world after all." She sobered as she looked back out the window and saw May place a hand on Colt's chest. "But as my Daddy always said, 'Nan, honey, when there's a will, there's a way, especially if there's a very strong will.'" Nan turned to Elise. "Watch that one."

She met Nan's gaze and tried to sound disinterested, "It doesn't really matter to me what Colt does, Nan, as long as it doesn't interfere with business."

Nan gave her a doubtful look and turned back to her dough. "Mmm-hmmm."

Elise walked outside and looked over at Colt and May. They were still talking. Her spirits plummeted as she made her way over to stand beside Mace. Elise turned to say something to him when she saw a couple of people riding up on horseback. It was Josh with Ben. Excitement stirred in her heart to see the black horse Ben was riding—the one from the auction. Ben slid off Lightning and ran over to Colt. Elise had already come to think of the mare with that name since the jagged white patch on her nose looked just like a slash of lightning against the night sky.

"Colt, I've come to visit." Ben was so excited he jumped up and down, a nervous ball of energy.

"I've come to visit too, Elise," Josh said as he looked down at her. He touched the brim of his hat and leaned his forearm on his saddle's horn. "Thought you might like to go for a ride."

Elise beamed up at Josh. "Has anyone ever told you that you have perfect timing?"

Josh gave her a roguish grin, then winked at her. "Why, yes ma'am. On more than one occasion and in many varied ways."

Elise didn't miss the sexual undertones of his words. She just chose to ignore them. She turned and handed her camera to Mace. "Here, take a few pictures for me. I'm going for a ride."

Mace gave her a long, assessing look then flicked his gaze to Colt before he took the camera from her hand.

Elise put her foot up in the stirrup and lifted herself up on

Lightning's back. Her gaze met Colt's across the parking lot. He'd looked up from talking with Ben. May was still hovering by his side. Elise turned away and pulled slightly on the reins, tightening her thighs on the horse as she kicked and said, "Hee-yah" to nudge the mare into a full gallop back in the direction Josh came.

She must've taken Josh by surprise, because he was a little behind her as she took the horse at breakneck speed across the plains toward Double K property. She felt the clip fly out of her hair, but she didn't stop. The sensation of the hot wind whipping around her felt too good. Lightning was a very smooth ride. More and more, she considered purchasing her.

Elise slowed her horse to a trot so Josh could catch up. After stopping and dismounting briefly, Josh got back on his horse and rode up beside her, his green eyes twinkling. "You ride well." He looked down at Lightning and grinned. "You two really do go well together."

Noting a ranch up ahead, Elise slowed the horse to a walk and then stopped to pat her horse's neck. She looked at Josh. "You're right. We do seem to do well together. Maybe I'll consider buying her."

"That's my girl," Josh said with a grin. He handed her the clip that had fallen out of her hair. "Thought you might want this." Lifting his hand to her hair, he touched a strand. "But personally, I like it down much better."

Elise smiled and hooked her clip on her jeans' belt loop. "Show me around The Double K, Josh."

Josh straightened his shoulders. "It would be my pleasure." He steered his horse toward the main ranch house.

Once they arrived at the ranch, Josh immediately jumped down and put his hands on her waist to help her down off of Lightning. "Thanks, Josh," Elise said with a smile at his chivalry as she lifted her leg over the horse to face him, then leaned forward and put her hands on his muscular shoulders to accept his help. What she didn't expect was Josh to pull her flush against his hard frame as he let her body slide down his own until her boots touched the ground.

When he didn't immediately release her, she glanced up into his face with a questioning look and was surprised at the desire she saw reflected in his gaze. "Um, I'm on the ground now," she reminded him with a chuckle.

"It's just that you feel so perfect right where you are," he shot back with a devilish grin, his grip tightening around her waist.

"Who've you brought for a visit?" An older man called over to Josh as he walked out of the stables with a horse in tow.

With a reluctant expression, Josh released her and stepped away, introducing her to his dad, Kenneth. Then he took her around the rest of the ranch where she met his brother, Ben Senior, and his wife, Lacey. Unfortunately, she didn't get to meet his mother since she was running errands. She loved the feeling of acceptance that settled within her while Josh introduced her to his family as "a new neighbor from the Lonestar ranch".

They walked around the main stables and were alone in the side yard when Josh stopped and grabbed her hand. Pulling her close, he sat her down on a bench against the barn, then settled beside her.

Elise smiled up at him. "Thanks for bringing Lightning over for me to ride."

"Lightning?" Amusement shown in his eyes. "I see you've already named her."

Elise laughed. "Yes, I suppose I have."

Josh's eyes turned serious. "Elise, you know the horse wasn't the only reason I came to visit. I wanted to ask you out. So what do you say?"

Elise was about to answer him when a shadow fell over them. Colt stood there holding Ben's hand.

Ben ran over and started talking animatedly to his Uncle. "Uncle Josh, man, they have some mean-looking bulls over there!"

"Ben wanted to tell his Dad about all he had seen. I told him I would bring him back." He looked pointedly at Josh. "Since I didn't know when you would be returning."

Josh flashed him an I-got-the-prize smile.

Elise stood up. "Well, I'd better get back. I have a website to work on." She put out her hand to Josh. "Thanks again for bringing Lightning."

Josh shook her hand but held fast when she started to let go of his. "And my other question?"

She didn't want to hurt Josh, so she deliberately misunderstood him. Withdrawing her hand from his, she smiled. "I'll think about buying Lightning from you."

She turned to follow Colt as he walked toward the horses. Colt mounted Scout and Elise mounted Bess. She waved to Josh and Ben as well as the rest of the Kelly family, as she and Colt walked their horses back in the direction of the Lonestar.

As soon as they were out of sight of The Double K, Elise kicked her horse into a full gallop. She heard Colt call her name, but she didn't stop. She didn't want to be alone with him. She wanted to ask him about leaving in the middle of the night, but she didn't dare. Maybe he really meant for it to be a one-night stand. Plus, May put a whole new twist on things she hadn't anticipated.

Elise slowed Bess to a trot once she reached the ranch. Colt was not too far behind her. She made it to the stables and dismounted. Where was everyone? The stables were empty. She listened, then she heard laughter and realized it was coming from the kitchen in the ranch house. It sounded like Nan was busy.

She hurriedly unbuckled Bess's saddle and slid it off her back. She turned to put it on a sidewall hook when she looked up and saw Colt standing outside Bess' stall holding Scout's reins. Her heart skipped several beats until he led Scout to his stall without a word to her. She gave a sigh of relief that she wouldn't have to talk to him right now.

Turning, she picked up a brush and began grooming Bess.

"Did you enjoy your ride?"

She jumped when Colt's warm body pressed against her back. She chose not to turn around, but continued grooming the horse. "Yes, it was exhilarating, as always."

Colt wrapped his arms around her waist and pulled her flush against his body. Elise stiffened while he ran his hands down her thighs and back up the vee they made at the top of her legs. She gritted her teeth at the tantalizing sensations he created, but she refused to let him seduce her. Colt must've realized her resistance in the stance she took, because he immediately turned her around and walked her backwards until her back touched the stable's wall.

His eyes glittered in anger. "When you're with me, you're with *me* and no one else." As he finished the last word, his mouth came down on hers, hard and punishing. Elise kissed him back. She was so turned on by his anger and possessive tone she couldn't do anything else. At least she hoped his actions meant he cared.

He pressed his erection against her, causing her to moan at the hard contact. She dropped the brush and wrapped her arms around his neck, eliciting a growl of satisfaction from him. His hands skimmed down her body, across her breasts, then around her waist to land on her hips. Lifting her, he pulled her thighs around him and arched into her. Trailing hot kisses down her throat, he gave her a nip or two along the way.

Elise turned her head to give him better access to her neck, gasping at the rhythmic thrust of his body against hers. The idea of the unfulfilled throbbing she knew she'd have to endure for the rest of the day, if they didn't finish what they started, made her press herself harder against him.

"Do you want me, Elise?" His whisper in her ear was sexy and seductive.

He stopped moving and just held her there, suspended in air with his hips, his erection pressed intimately against her. She tightened her arms around his neck. "Yes, I want you."

Colt set her legs back down on the ground and took a step back, a guarded look on his face. "Then show me you want me."

Elise was glad he'd thought to shut the door to the stall. She gave him a saucy grin as she moved to pull off her shirt. When she saw Colt's nostrils flare, she stopped.

"Do you want *me*?" she asked, throwing his question back at him.

Colt's stare was so hot she thought she just might melt right there at his feet. She had her answer. She stared boldly into his eyes as she lifted her shirt, pulled it over her head and tossed it on the floor. Colt's gaze gravitated toward the twin curves of flesh peeking above her bra. She moved to take off her bra, but stopped, then smiled knowingly. "Do you want me to take it off?"

Colt clenched his fists by his side. This was his game after all. He flicked his gaze away from her breasts to meet her eyes for the briefest of seconds. "Yes, I want you to take it off. Now."

Elise unhooked the bra but didn't remove it from her breasts yet. "Colt," she demanded his attention, "when you're with me, you're with *me* only. Am I clear?"

He locked his gaze with hers. "As a bell."

Elise gave him a siren's smile before she removed her bra and tossed it on top of her shirt.

When Colt moved to touch her, she held up a hand. "Not yet."

Balling his hands into fists once again, he let them fall to his sides, his expression intense, his control barely held in check.

Elise walked over and pulled his shirt open to reveal his bare chest. She put her hands down by her side and moved closer to him until the tips of her breasts touched his body. Leaning over, she went up on her toes to kiss the pulse beating against his throat, letting her breasts brush his chest in the process. She smiled when she heard Colt's breath hiss out.

Elise moved lower and ran her tongue over his nipple. Straightening, she met his burning gaze. "You can't use your hands, but you can use your mouth…"

Before the words were barely out of her mouth, Colt captured her lips with his. The thrust of his tongue was nearly her undoing until he moved his mouth down her neck to her shoulder where he bit her gently.

"That's for leaving with Josh, Princess."

Elise gasped at his aggressive behavior. She leaned over and licked his nipple once more. When she put her teeth on the tiny nub and bit down, Colt sucked in his breath.

"That's for kissing your ex in front of me, Cowboy," she said, meeting his gaze.

Colt raised his eyebrow, then leaned down and grasped her nipple in his mouth. He sucked long and hard until she was a mass of highly sensitized nerves, arching against him. Just when she thought she couldn't take it anymore, he nipped at her nipple, stood straight up and looked her right in the eyes, his expression intense. "That's for letting Josh think he has a snowball's chance in hell of ever getting in your pants."

With a determined look, he started advancing on her. She had to back up so she wouldn't fall. Before she knew it, Colt had her backed against the stable wall. He planted his hands against the wood on either side of her body. Elise gasped when he leaned down and ran his tongue in a slow, seductive circle around her nipple.

"Do you want me to touch you, Elise?" he asked, his voice a sexy purr.

Elise knew he wanted her to ask. She refused to be the one. She shook her head.

"Are you sure?" Colt licked her nipple again and this time blew on it for good measure. It tightened into an even harder bud, if that were at all possible.

Elise squeezed her eyes shut, but jerked them open again as Colt traced a lazy trail with one finger from her collarbone down across her chest to the top of her breast until he reached the tip of her wet nipple.

When he raised his eyes to hers and she saw the longing and unchecked desire reflected in them, Elise whispered, "Touch me."

With a low growl, he placed both palms on her breasts and cupped them fully in each hand. Grazing his work-roughened thumbs over each nipple, he lifted one of her breasts to his descending lips. After he'd sucked the firm peak into his warm mouth and drew on it tenderly, he moved to the other breast and treated it with the same tenderness.

Elise moaned at the vibrations flying throughout her body at his gentle touch. Her heart raced as Colt moved his hands lower and unbuttoned her jeans, his movements changing to a faster pace as his eyes blazed with need.

"I've got to have you...now!" he ground out.

Before he started to lower her jeans, Elise toed off her boots. She then kicked her jeans and underwear the rest of the way off. As Colt pulled a condom out of his pocket and opened the packet, she unbuttoned the top button of his jeans. She didn't bother with the rest of the buttons, she jerked and they all gave way. While she pushed his jeans down as far as his boots would allow, Colt rolled on the condom.

Elise barely had a chance to straighten up before he'd lifted her and settled his erection against her sex. Pressing her back against the stable wall once more, his eyes burned with unadulterated lust as he let gravity slide her body down on top of him. Elise moaned and felt her climax begin before he was even fully seated inside her.

Colt leaned over and kissed her to muffle her cries of ecstasy. "God, Lise, you take my breath away," he admitted when her body finally stopped contracting around him.

Holding her gaze, he withdrew and pushed back in as far as her body would let him go. Elise gasped at the pleasure of being so thoroughly taken. Her breathing turned more erratic as

Colt increased the tempo, pressing into her, taking their lovemaking to a higher pitch, a harder, faster ride. She locked her legs around his waist and laid her head back on the stable wall. "I'm yours for the taking."

"Mine," he gave a satisfied growl as he pumped into her once more. He held himself still as she called out his name while she vibrated around him once again, before he continued thrusting until his body was completely spent.

He let his head fall on her shoulder as their panting turned to even breathing. While Elise stroked his shoulders lightly with the palms of her hands, he lifted his head and stared directly into her eyes. "I'm a one-woman man, Elise. I don't want to see you go off alone with Josh again."

She pursed her lips. "Same goes for you. But, you and May have a history. It's a little different."

Colt arched his eyebrow. "You said the operative words. We 'had a history,' as in past tense." Setting her down, he kept his gaze locked on hers. "The only person I can't seem to get enough of is you."

A satisfied smile rode up her face. "Just so you remember that."

Colt pressed his lips to hers before he moved to get dressed. He looked around for a place to dispose of the condom before he pulled it off, then gave her a wry smile as he pulled up his pants, saying, "Guess I'll be a bit uncomfortable until I get to the bathroom."

She couldn't help but laugh. Once he was dressed, he turned to her. "I'll go out first."

Elise nodded and picked up her clothes. She was pulling on her boots when she heard May say, "There you are, Colt. I've been looking for you. I heard the most disturbing news. Something about that brunette being part owner of the Lonestar?"

Elise smiled to herself. *That should throw a wrench in May's plans.*

Her smile faded when she heard May continue, "So, what are you going to do to get rid of her?"

Elise didn't hear Colt's answer for Bess chose that moment to neigh loudly.

"Colt, I miss you, honey. We were soooo good together," May purred.

Okay, *that* comment had her quickly moving to the stall's door. Elise opened the door to the stall and walked toward the entrance of the stables where Colt and May stood talking. Colt's back was to her and May faced her direction with her hand on Colt's chest. Elise knew May noticed her because she stopped talking as she approached.

Winding her hair up as she walked toward them, she reached for her clip from her belt loop and slipped it in her hair. She only stopped her brisk pace for the briefest of seconds to tuck in a corner of Colt's shirt that hadn't made it into his pants. Elise gave Colt a brazen smile and tucked it in for him, "Here, let me help you out, Colt. You're not quite tucked." She noted the suppressed mirth in his eyes and the indignant gasp from May when she dropped her hand to pat his firm buttock before she continued her walk toward the office.

Elise chuckled to herself as she opened the office door. Never had she so blatantly and thoroughly branded a man as hers and it felt good. Damn good!

Unfortunately, she ran right into Mace as she walked in the door. "Mace!" she called out his name in surprise. How much had he seen? she wondered.

Mace crossed his arms over his chest and chuckled, then gave her a wide smile. "Now that has to be the fanciest piece of maneuvering I have ever witnessed, Elise, and I consider myself an expert on the subject."

Well, she didn't have to wonder anymore. She smirked then asked with a frown, "Tell me you've already taken her picture."

Mace's grin deepened. "Yes, fortunately for you, I did. I

thought it would be best, seeing as how you might just put a picture of a heifer up on the website with her name and description below it if I didn't."

Elise raised her eyebrow. "Now there's a thought."

Chapter Ten

Elise sat down at her desk and worked steadily until lunchtime, writing up interview questions for the rodeo personnel to answer. She even spent ten minutes having a bit of fun with May's questions. *When did you first realize Colt was your ticket to owning a ranch? What? You mean rodeo clown isn't your job?* With a grin, she deleted the questions, intending to ask May the same questions she asked the other rodeo employees.

When lunchtime arrived, she started to pull out her camera bag to take the film to be developed when she suddenly remembered she never finished grooming Bess properly. Guilt washed over her as she put her camera bag back in her drawer. Shutting down her computer, Elise left the office and headed straight for the barn.

"Hiya, 'ol girl," she cooed to Bess as she entered her stall. Picking up the brush from the shelf, she spoke in a low, conspiratorial voice, "I'm sorry I left you hanging, but I got a bit distracted. I'm here to make it up to you."

As she started to brush her neck, Elise ran her hand across Bess's coat, then paused at its sleek feel, not a bit of dust clung to the horse's hair. "You've already been brushed," she said with surprise in her voice.

"Imagine that," May called out in her heavy Texan drawl from behind her.

Elise turned her head and raised her eyebrow, irritation rising at the woman's condescending tone. "Come again?"

May propped the door open, took a couple of steps into the stall, and folded her arms over her chest. "Colt took care of Bess, since you saw fit to leave her unattended after your roll in the hay," she said, unmistakable sarcasm dripping from her accusatory words.

Anger rumbled to the surface of Elise's emotions, laced with a twinge of guilt at leaving Bess's grooming half-done. Being distracted by Colt and then further distracted by May's fawning over the man, did show a lack of responsibility—even if she was here, foregoing her lunch in order to remedy her error. But hell would be fifty below before she'd ever let May know she felt any guilt at all.

Raising her chin a notch, she faced the woman head on. "What I do or do not do is none of your business." Narrowing her gaze, Elise continued, "It's my understanding your job is to run the promotional sales booth at the rodeos, not tell the *owners* what to do."

May's cheeks turned red and Elise could swear she literally saw steam rise from the woman's ears as she dropped her arms and curled her hands into tight fists by her side.

"I've taken care of more than my share of livestock for the Lonestar." May nodded to Bess and finished, "Including, Bess here. She's usually *my* mount when I'm home. So yeah, I think I have a bit of say-so in how she's treated."

Just who the hell did she think she was, talking down to her? Elise picked up on the woman's possessive tone and her own heart rate roared in her ears. It really shouldn't bother her that Bess was the chosen mount for females visiting the Lonestar, but knowing of May and Colt's past, she couldn't help the feeling of "taking May's seconds" that slammed through her at the discovery.

Carefully placing the brush on the wooden shelf, she stepped away from Bess and bent slightly at the waist, waving her arm toward the horse with a flourish. "Then, by all means, enjoy Bess along with the benefits of grooming her during your short stay."

May gave her a haughty look as she crossed her arms once more. "He might screw you, but that'll be all he'll want from you. I've asked around. You're too much like—"

"May." A man's deep voice cut May's words off.

She immediately stopped talking and sucked in her breath, turning toward the front of the stall.

Elise shifted her gaze to the man and felt her stomach drop to her knees. Standing a little over six feet tall and dressed in a black T-shirt and black jeans, the lean, fit man had his arms crossed over his chest. With broad shoulders, a wiry upper torso and defined biceps, the stranger was the ultimate cowboy from the tip of his black cowboy hat to the gold buckle at his trim hips, down to the spurs gracing his boots. He stood too far away for her to see the color of his eyes but one word came to mind...dark.

He leaned on the stall's entrance and narrowed his dark, penetrating gaze on May.

"Cade! It's so great to see you. I heard you placed first at the last three rodeos. I'm so proud..." she babbled like an incoherent school girl talking to *the* most popular boy in school.

Elise caught herself before she snorted out loud at the woman's complete change in demeanor. *So this was the rodeoing Tanner brother...*

Cade interrupted May, his tone curt, "Go make your mischief elsewhere, May."

"Cade!" she whined as if offended by his comment.

He didn't speak again, just stared at her with his intemperate gaze. The way he held himself, his very demeanor, told Elise he was not a man to be crossed.

"Oh, all right," May finally said in a disgruntled voice as she threw her hands up in the air.

As she passed by him on her way out of the stall, May said in an alluring voice, "Save a dance for me at Rockin' Joe's tomorrow night, okay?"

Cade didn't spare her a glance as she walked off. Instead he fixed his assessing gaze on Elise for a long, agonizing minute.

His impassive gaze skimmed down her body, then back to

her face. Elise knew, in a matter of seconds, he'd sized her up, measured her worth, and had her neatly catalogued in his mind.

She held her breath, waiting for an indication of his judgment.

Touching the brim of his hat, he tilted his head slightly, a devilish gleam in his eyes as he said in a respectful tone, "Afternoon, ma'am," before he turned and walked off.

A shiver passed through her at the memory of his penetrating look—how much he conveyed in so few words. God, the man was sex incarnate. But as much as she'd bet he'd be a relentless lover in bed, she wondered at the dark, distant look in his eyes...as if nothing or no one had ever been allowed to get close to him.

Picking up the brush once more, she slid the rough bristles across Bess's back, saying aloud to the horse, "So that's the Tanner boys. Other than loads of sex appeal, could they *be* any more different?" she finished with a chuckle, shaking her head.

That evening, for the first time since she'd joined the Lonestar, Elise ate dinner with the entire ranch and rodeo staff at the main house.

They all sat at the long kitchen table. Extra leaves had been added and chairs pulled up to accommodate the larger than normal crowd.

When a ranch hand near Nan started to pick up his fork, she slapped at his hand, "Not yet, Davy, we're waitin' on Cade to show."

Just then, Cade came in through the kitchen side door, the screen slamming behind him.

Standing up, Nan walked over to stand in front of him. "Well, it's about time you showed your face, young man—"

Cade stunned Nan in mid-sentence when he'd picked her up, twirled her buxom body in a big bear hug and kissed her on the cheek, saying, "But Nan, I just wanted to make sure I came to the table all clean and freshened up for ya."

Elise saw the deep love Nan felt for the boys as the older

woman's eyes misted. She shoved him away and ran her hands down her apron as if brushing out imaginary wrinkles. "Aw, go on with ya devilish self. Sit down so we can eat."

Cade winked and cast a devastating smile Elise's way as he sat down next to Mace and across from Colt. *Yep, dark*, she thought. His hair was as dark as Colt's—though worn longer. His eyes were a shade of blue so deep they appeared almost black.

Once Cade was seated, Colt surprised Elise when he introduced her as the Lonestar's half-owner and webmaster. Thank God he hadn't called her the webmistress or she was sure May would've had a field day with that one.

Cade gave her a respectful nod and said, "Nice to meet ya, ma'am." Not once did he acknowledge that he'd made her acquaintance in the stables earlier.

While Elise ate, she enjoyed listening to Colt and his brothers exchange amusing childhood stories. Their interaction included a good bit of teasing, but she could tell they held a genuine love and respect for each other. Colt even made sure to include her in a small way by winking at her when he started to relay one particular story of Cade dunking Mace in the horses' water trough in payment for some trickster deed Mace had done. She enjoyed seeing Cade laugh.

Elise realized the middle brother might be a man of few words, the kind who seemed to hold his emotions in constant check, a laugh or a smile a rare sight. But as evidenced with his deferential treatment of Nan earlier, he certainly had a helluva way with women when he turned on the charm.

As dinner came to an end, Tom walked outside and pulled in a cooler full of beer. Passing the longnecks to everyone, he held his up and said, "Here's to the rest of the rodeos, folks. May they be as busy and as profitable as the first half of the season."

"Yee-haw," everyone agreed at once, holding up their beers in salute. Elise did the same and smiled at Colt before she put the beer bottle to her lips.

Turning to Elise, mischief twinkling in his eyes, Tom said, "What time's my interview tomorrow, Elise?"

"Me too," another man said.

"Me too," a third man echoed.

Laughing, Elise turned to the men and started setting up an interview schedule for the next day. While she talked to the employees, she saw Colt, Mace and Cade slip out of the kitchen into the living room to talk.

Good for them. She figured with Cade's schedule it wasn't often that all three brothers got to spend quality time together.

As her interview schedule filled up, the kitchen emptied. When Elise got around to scheduling May's interview, the woman stood, then walked toward the screen door. "I see you saved the best for last," she commented, her tone irritated. She opened the door, her expression triumphant. "That's okay. Colt knows just how worth the wait I am."

When the door slammed behind her, Elise gritted her teeth and stood to help Nan gather the dishes.

Scraping food off a plate into the trash, Nan *harumped*. "I saw the way she was lookin' at Cade." She shook her head mumbling, "Goin' from one brother to another—that woman is trouble."

Elise gave a hollow laugh. "She told me Bess was *her* mount earlier today."

Nan looked up and her knowing brown eyes narrowed. "I think she needs to find another job. Anyone can run a concession stand."

"Don't say anything to Colt about this, Nan," Elise said. "If May is fired, I want it to be because she deserves it, not because she enjoys needling me."

Nan grinned. "Don't worry, Elise. Someday May's goin' to tie her own noose. I won't have to say a word."

* * * * *

Elise frowned at the swift knock at her door. She glanced at the clock. Ten o'clock. She'd washed her face, pulled on an oversized T-shirt that reached her mid-thigh and was just getting ready to climb into bed. It had to be Colt.

After she'd finished up with Nan, she heard Colt still talking with his brothers, so instead of intruding, she decided to head home. Now he shows up two hours later. Who knew he was such a talker? Then again, he could've been waylaid by May. Her heart sank at the thought. But he'd sounded so adamant when he'd said he was a one-woman man, she reminded herself. The memory of his steely tone calmed her nerves. She believed him.

Great, instead of a sophisticated Elise Hamilton, he would get to see a woman who looked more like a teenager with her hair down, no makeup on, sporting an old Hard Rock Café T-shirt and bare feet.

As she headed for the door, her chest tightening, she thought in defiance, *Maybe that's exactly what he needs to see. Me at my plain Jane-est. Second best to May, my ass!*

Feeling rebellious, yet very unsexy, Elise opened the door.

Colt stood outside, one hand on the doorjamb, waiting.

His cowboy hat hid his face in shadows from the bright parking lot lights. All she saw was his strong jaw with that muscle tic and her heart leapt. When he tilted his head and the light filtered across his face, the sight of his glittering gaze raking her body from the top of her head to the tips of her toes, then settling on the peaks of her nipples jutting against the soft cotton fabric, took her breath away.

Damn his smoldering gaze, as if he knew she wore no underwear beneath her shirt. And double damn her traitorous body for reacting instantaneously to his black cowboy shirt and faded jeans covering his tall muscular frame. The visual stimulation coupled with his intoxicating male scent and potent, seductive charisma, made her heartbeat roar in her ears.

"You left without sayin' goodbye, darlin'," was all he said, but his tense stance and the distinct muscle jumping in his jaw spoke volumes.

No way would she let him know how much the whole Bess thing had bothered her. Colt had never said anything about commitment, had even ignored her flippant statement about them not being a couple.

He walked inside and shut the door behind him, his look predatory as he advanced on her in long strides.

She answered, her heart racing, "You were busy talking to your brothers. I figured you had a lot of catching up to do."

Colt pulled his hat off and tossed it on the kitchen table. He continued to stalk her across her living room, his tone possessive, intense, "I had plans, Lise, things I wanted to do." His voice dropped to a seductive rumble. "To you."

Right when he finished speaking, the backs of her knees bumped into her Papasan chair and Elise lost her balance, flopping into its deep, circular cushion.

Oh God! The primal look in his eyes and the promise of his words, made her realize her T-shirt had hiked up her thighs, almost exposing her to his gaze. Her breasts tingled and her sex began to throb in tense anticipation.

Grasping the rattan outer edge of the chair, she started to pull herself up when Colt placed his big, warm hands on her naked thighs.

"No. Don't move," he ground out as he sunk to his knees in front of her.

Her breath caught in her throat and her heart rammed in her chest as he slowly slid his hands up her thighs.

Massaging her muscles, he pulled her legs apart and moved between them as his deep blue gaze locked with hers. Sliding his hands under the hem of her shirt, his thumbs teased her damp curls.

"I've wanted to taste you all day and when I discovered you'd left..." he trailed off, while his hardened expression told her how much her absence bothered at him.

"Colt, I—"

Elise's words trapped in her throat when Colt slid his hands around and grasped her naked rear, pulling her along the cushion, closer to the edge of the chair.

"Put your feet on my shoulders," he ground out.

"Colt—"

"Now!" The fierce expression on his face reflected his hunger, his pent-up desire to have her right then.

Elise had barely touched her heels to his shoulders when Colt swiped his tongue across her sex in a slow, deliberate lap, his action a territorial branding that spoke volumes to his intentions.

She grasped the edge of the chair and let out a mewing sigh of pleasure while he teased her entrance once more before delving his tongue deep inside her. Lapping her juices, he groaned his approval. The feral sound was such a turn-on!

His heated breath bathed her thighs as he spoke, his voice sounding tortured, "Everything about you intoxicates me. Your scent when you walk past, your throaty laughter, and now your taste…" He paused and let out a controlled breath. "It makes me want to have you again and again." He looked up, his clouded, dark gaze colliding with hers. "I've never claimed to be a gentle lover, Lise."

His intensity sent thrills up and down her spine. "I never asked you to be," she shot back, panting in expectation.

The look in his eyes shifted to satisfied determination. He lowered his head and found her clitoris. Sucking at the throbbing nub, he alternately nipped and pulled at the sensitive flesh, bringing her to the edge only to lave at her until her impending orgasm abated. Again and again he played her body to his own tune.

Rocking her hips to his torturous onslaught, Elise finally fisted a hand in his thick, dark hair and pressed him closer, hissing out, "You need to add sadist to your list of faults, damn you."

Colt's chuckle rumbled against her right before he thrust two fingers deep inside her and sucked hard on her sensitive flesh.

"Yes!" she screamed out at the welcoming sensation as her body began to clench around the fingers pumping in and out of her body. As Elise drew in her breath, her heart hammered and her stomach tensed right before a full-blown orgasm rolled through her in waves of intense pleasure.

Just as the tremors in her body started to dissipate, he lifted his head and grasped her hips. Backing out of the way of her legs, he swiftly pulled her out of the chair and rolled her over on her stomach.

Facing the chair, her knees now on the floor, Elise's heart raced at her quick change in position. All she could think about was having Colt inside her as quickly as possible.

As she pulled her shirt over her head and tossed it on the floor, the sound of Colt unbuckling his belt and ripping the buttons of his jeans apart only fueled her desire. Placing one hand on her hip, he pressed the flat of his other hand against her back, silently directing her. Panting in anticipation, Elise complied, bending at the waist as she laid her arms on the cushion of the chair.

When Colt grasped her hips, pressed his erection against her and slammed into her in one swift, deep thrust, she keened out her pleasure at the satisfying feeling of completeness. The sensation of his jeans rubbing the back of her lower thighs as he withdrew and sank back in made her feel wanton yet so very desired.

"Come on, Elise, show me what you've got," he encouraged in a rough rasp as his hips met her rear once more.

Feeling thoroughly challenged, Elise rose up on her hands and used the chair for leverage as she pushed back against him, clenching her inner muscles around his erection.

At the sound of his low groan of pleasure, she smiled and pressed harder.

In response, Colt laid his chest, his bare chest—aaah, he'd removed his shirt!—against her back and slid his hands over hers, clasping her hands and stretching her arms forward toward the back of the chair as he rammed into her. With each penetrating thrust, her nipples rubbed back and forth against the wooden edge of the chair, causing her to moan in delight.

"Damn, Lise, you match me well," he hissed out next to her ear, male satisfaction evident in his voice.

And she did match him, Colt thought as she sighed with contentment when her orgasm began. He enjoyed the sensation of her warm body convulsing around him and felt his own blood rushing in his ears as his cock throbbed harder with his impending climax.

When she pulled her thighs closer against his legs and clenched her walls around him, he lost all coherent thought as he exploded. He absorbed every single breath, every brush of hot skin against skin, the moisture of her body mixed with his as he slid in and out of her. God, she felt so damn good.

Pulling her against him, he stayed buried deep within her as they tumbled to the floor on their sides. As their breathing slowed and reason returned, he knew a moment's panic when he realized what he'd done.

"I'm sorry, Lise," he whispered as he started to withdraw from her, his stomach tensing. "I just realized I didn't put on a condom."

She reached behind her and clasped his bare buttock, pulling him back inside her with a throaty chuckle. "I believe after giving me oral sex oh-so-thoroughly you trust I'm clean, Colt. Don't worry. I'm on the pill."

His heart started beating again as relief flooded through him. So why did a small part of him wish she hadn't been on the pill? Colt ignored the nagging question and stroked her breast with his fingertips, replying with a chuckle, "I'm glad to know you'll match whatever I throw your way."

She shrugged her shoulder in an unapologetic manner, the

action unintentionally sexy, but arousing to him nonetheless.

"I believe in a healthy attitude about sex. How else will you learn what pleases you if you aren't willing to try new things?"

He grinned, liking her philosophy. Withdrawing from her, he rolled her over and slid his hand down to tangle in the curls between her thighs as he met her gaze. "I've decided you're sexiest with no makeup and just an old T-shirt. Screw lacey underwear. Hard-rock was *exactly* what I was thinkin' when you opened the door."

When he finished speaking, Colt shifted to his knees and pulled up his pants. Leaning over, he lifted her in his arms and walked back to her bedroom saying in a suggestive tone, "About those new things you said you'd be willing to try…"

Chapter Eleven

The next morning, Elise didn't have time to worry about the fact Colt hadn't spent the night once more. She had interviews back-to-back that kept her busy all day long. And when the day ended and she and Colt went back to her apartment, she didn't want to spoil their time together by asking him why he didn't stay the night before.

But when the next several days became a pattern for Colt, she found that her patience had run thin. The last couple of nights, she'd casually tried to ask him to stay, but his reply was always the same, "I've got early work tomorrow."

Feeling bereft all over again as she remembered his response, Elise stood there in front of the office's main window, staring blankly at the coffeepot and wondering if, after several consecutive nights together, he'd always planned to steal away once she'd fallen asleep in his arms. Waking up alone was somehow worse because she fell asleep with the hope he'd stay the night. The fact he left in the middle of the night bothered her a great deal, because it made her feel as if she were a one-night stand every night.

So what if Colt didn't want commitment, couldn't he at least feign that he felt comfortable enough with her to stay the night? Beyond her growing annoyance, she didn't examine the reason for her deep feelings on the subject.

After all, it's not like she planned to fall for the guy or anything. No, she hadn't fallen for him. Not at all, she denied as her heart rate kicked up when she spied Colt walking toward the stables, his chambray shirt stretched across his broad shoulders. Her gaze dropped to his rear end outlined by the chaps strapped to his trim hips and muscular thighs. What an ass the man had! She curled her fingers around her coffee cup. Man, she loved grabbing his hard, muscular butt as they made love.

Oh shit! She'd said it…well, mentally. Made love. But that was how she felt when she and Colt were together. He made love to her. It wasn't just sex. The way he touched her, rough, gentle—she didn't care because he was always considerate of her needs—he made her feel loved and cherished, even if he didn't say the words.

The sight of May trotting out of the stable on Bess's back drew her out of her musings. May had stopped and spoke to Colt while he grasped the horse's reins and responded to whatever she'd said. Elise's stomach churned and her chest felt as if someone had put a vise around it. The constricting sensation made it hard to catch her breath.

Her emotions running high, she turned away and ran right into Mace.

"Whoa," he called out, steadying her with his hands. "Man, I guess it's a good thing you hadn't poured your morning coffee yet or I'd be wearin' it," he laughed in a good-natured tone.

Feeling miserable, Elise looked down at her empty cup. "Guess it's best I skip coffee this morning."

"You okay?" he asked, his expression concerned.

She shrugged. "Yeah, just a headache." Brushing past Mace, she headed back to her office and shut the door.

After she'd flopped into her chair and stared at her computer, Elise let her anger at herself boil to the surface. *Screw second best. I'm going to do something about it, damnit.*

Picking up her phone, she called directory assistance and retrieved Josh Kelly's phone number. Once she punched in the number, she drummed her fingers impatiently on the desk, waiting for him to pick up.

"Hello?" an older man answered.

"Mr. Kelly? This is Elise Hamilton. Is Josh around?"

"No, he's not, Elise. Josh had a firemen's conference to attend. He should be back by Sunday. Want me to have him call you?"

Sunday? That was a few days away! Her heart sank at the news. "Yes, please have him return my call when he gets back."

"Will do."

Even though she couldn't reach Josh, Elise felt better. She had a plan. Lightning would be hers by the end of the weekend.

She worked steadily all morning, incorporating the info from the various employee interviews she'd conducted into the website. When lunchtime arrived, Elise took the film to the developer to have it put on a CD so she could upload the photos to the website. Thankfully, her errand kept her away from the office and out of Colt's sight. She was afraid if she spent any time with him, she'd ask why he hadn't stayed a single night with her. The last thing she wanted was to come across demanding or clingy.

She'd just finished her takeout lunch and was about to throw the bag away in the trash can underneath her desk when Colt walked in.

"I came by earlier but you weren't around," he said.

Crumpling the bag, she tossed it in the trash and turned back to her computer. "I took the film to be developed on my lunch hour."

Colt nodded his understanding, then grinned. "I noticed you haven't ridden all week. Come out on the range with me for an hour or so."

Her heart jerked at the invitation. Time alone with Colt. Outdoors. The fresh, open air blowing in her face. On Bess.

Which made her think of May and second best. Which made her think of him leaving her every night after she fell asleep.

Her heart stuttered and her euphoria died a quick death. Rubbing her forehead, she lied, "I've got a killer headache."

Colt's expression reflected his disappointment, then turned devilish as he raked his gaze down her white button-down blouse to the rise of her breasts, then back up to her face. "I guess I'll just have to settle for spending time with you tonight. Want to go out to dinner?"

She shook her head. "Not tonight. I'll have to pass. I'm tired." *'Cause waking up to an empty bed in the wee hours of the morning has a tendency to make me sleep fitfully until it's time to get up*, she thought with an inward grimace. Maybe if she spent an evening away from him it wouldn't bother her so much. Now why did she seriously doubt that?

"Just dinner then?"

She shook her head once more and noticed him visibly stiffen at her rejection. Why did she feel like such a shmuck? *Because you know you want to go out to eat with him, find out more about him, then spend the rest of the evening making love until you're both exhausted and spent, that's why…you shmuck!*

She couldn't even meet his gaze as her emotions swirled inside her, making her body tense and her stomach ache.

"I hope you feel better tomorrow, Lise," he replied before he turned on his heel and walked out of the room.

His use of her nickname, spoken in a low, deliberately husky voice reminded her when he usually called her Lise — while making love. Her nipples tightened and her sex throbbed in immediate response at the thought. Damn, she was like Pavlov's dog…just say the *pet* name and she's panting. Grrrrr!

Gritting her teeth, she willed herself to focus on work while she prayed she didn't see Colt for the rest of the day.

* * * * *

After she called "goodnight" to Mace and walked down the hall past Colt's office, Elise breathed a sigh of relief. Empty. Phew! She had a reprieve.

As she exited the building and made her way to her car, another disturbing thought wormed its way into her psyche

Colt would find someone else to fill his evening, namely May.

Her stomach churned at the thought and her hands shook so bad she dropped her keys as she tried to unlock her door. Bending down, she retrieved them and started to slide her key in the lock.

Someone reached over her shoulder and a big, warm hand came down on hers. Colt's distinct scent washed over her, leather, faint spicy deodorant and outdoors. God, he smelled so good. She wanted to lean back against him and keep inhaling.

Instead, she stiffened as he pressed his body against her back and whispered suggestively in her ear, his voice low and sexy, "Did I tell you I give great massages? I've been known to make a headache or two disappear."

Elise fought the desire swirling in her belly. She straightened and turned the key in the lock. "No, you hadn't mentioned that particular ability."

As she started to open the car door, Colt's hands landed on her hips and quickly turned her around to face him.

Before she could respond, he clasped her hips once more and stepped into her body, pressing his erection against the seam of her jeans running between her legs. With the car behind her, his action created arousing friction. Her heart rate jumped into overdrive. Elise fought the excitement flowing though her like an electrical wire overloaded to the max.

Colt's blue gaze searched her face as if he were looking deep into her soul, deciphering her mood. Without a word, he dipped his head and inhaled near her collarbone while a low growl escaped his throat.

"You're *sure* you don't want me to work my magic on you?" he purred into her ear.

Elise's self-serving, traitorous desires clamored for dominance. She so wanted to let him have his way with her — to work his *magic* as he put it. The very fact he was pressing himself against her, staking his claim in plain sight of any Lonestar employee within eyeshot made her feel special. She caught herself before she asked the question that had been nagging her brain. *Are you going to stay this time?*

Laying her hands on his chest, she worked hard to keep her breathing even as she pushed against his hard muscles. "Not tonight, Colt."

Colt's gaze met hers and narrowed. He leaned close once more and whispered in her ear. "Take your break for tonight, but don't think for one minute you'll put me off tomorrow." He finished his statement by pressing his erection against her once more.

She shivered at his fierce, possessive comment and couldn't suppress the thrill that zipped down her spine at the knowledge he wanted her that much.

When Colt let go of her and stepped back, she let out an unsteady breath and turned to open her car door. His next words made her freeze in her tracks and her heart stutter in her chest.

"Did you know that when you're very aroused you bite your lip?"

Elise glanced at him and slowly let go of the deathlock her teeth had on her lower lip.

Colt gave her a steely look. "Tomorrow night you'll tell me why you gave me the brush-off today, Elise."

✶ ✶ ✶ ✶ ✶

The following morning, Elise was on her third cup of coffee as she sat in front of her computer. Last night she spent a restless evening tossing and turning. The pillows and sheets on her bed smelled like Colt. Everywhere she turned in bed, she imagined his touch, his warmth. She'd missed him desperately.

Taking a sip of coffee, she set the cup down on her desk and realized the caffeine made her more jittery than wakeful. Or was it the fact she knew she'd have to face Colt and his determination to know why she'd ditched him the night before. She'd arrived very early this morning and every time the office front door opened she tensed.

She didn't want to tell Colt the truth because she'd be revealing too much of herself. Not that she wasn't a giving person, she'd tell him what bothered her in a heartbeat if he gave her the slightest indication his feelings ran deeper. So far he just seemed to be sexually attracted to her...well, okay, he was a bit possessive, too.

When Mace poked his head into her office to say, "Mornin' Elise," she jerked, gasping in surprise and bumped her coffee. As the brown liquid sloshed on her desk, she quickly mopped it up with tissues from a box in her drawer.

"Man, Elise, you're more jumpy than a long-tailed cat in a room full of rocking chairs. You okay?"

She nodded. "I'm fine. I think I made up for yesterday by consuming two days' worth of coffee this morning." With a grin, she continued, "I've already helped hay and feed the horses, made more coffee, took out the trash, cleaned the refrigerator and the kitchen, contemplated washing the kitchen floors, but decided I'd better get my rear in here and work on the website."

Mace gave a hearty laugh. "I think you just became Mabel's best friend." With a wink, he thumbed back toward the front of the office. "Hey, my car needs a good washin' if you're still in an energetic mood."

Elise picked up a wad of paper she'd crumpled earlier and tossed it at his retreating back. "Go to work, you slacker."

Once Mace had walked off, in her keyed-up mood, the sight of that lone, balled-up trash on the floor drove her nuts. Elise walked around her desk to her doorway and bent over to retrieve the paper missile.

The tip of a dusty, scuffed boot crushed the paper before she could pick it up. Her heart rammed in her chest as she lifted her gaze up Colt's jeans, past the bulge at his crotch, up his white button-down shirt to see his serious expression.

"Littering, Elise?"

She pushed at his boot and when he moved it, she picked up the paper ball. Standing, she met his penetrating gaze with a steady one, even as her heart beat in her chest in a staccato rhythm.

"Just working on my target practice," she shot back.

Colt took a step closer until his arousing aftershave tickled her nose. Without his hat on, she noted that his hair was curled and still slightly damp from his shower. She clamped her hand tighter on the wadded-up paper to keep from reaching up to touch those damp curls.

He raised a dark eyebrow. "Plan on trashin' someone?"

She laughed at his pun, then grinned. "Yeah, I'll spam 'em to death."

"Huh?" Colt looked confused for a second before understanding of her computer techie jargon dawned on his face. "Spammers should be shot."

Her smile faltered when his expression sobered. His deep blue gaze compelled her as he said, "Come ride with me."

"This early in the morning?" She shook her head. "Can't. Got work to do."

Colt stepped into her, his hard, muscular frame making her own body scream in slow, tortured agony. He pulled the clip from her hair at the same time he laced his fingers with hers.

"It wasn't a request, Lise."

Before she could form a reply, he took off down the hall with her in tow. Colt only stopped long enough to toss her clip in his office, let her throw the paper in the trash and retrieve his hat from the coat rack before he pulled her outside toward the stables.

When Elise saw Sam standing there holding Scout's and Bess's reins and an extra cowboy hat in his hand, she dug in her boot heels and tried to yank her hand loose.

"I told you. I have a lot of work to do." She'd be damned if she'd share Bess. She knew it was silly, but she couldn't help how she felt.

Colt had stopped briefly when she spoke. When she finished, he said in a low, controlled voice, "This isn't up for debate. You're riding out with me for a bit."

Turning, he made his way over to the horses, tugging her along.

Angered by his high-handed manner, Elise jerked her hand free. "I'm not riding out on Bess, Colt."

"Suit yourself," he replied as he approached his horse and swung his leg over Scout's saddle.

"I'm sorry you went to the effort on my account, Sam," Elise mumbled before she turned and walked back toward the office.

The sound of Colt's horse trotting behind her made her entire body tense, but she refused to move out of the way or be cowed by the man's obvious show of anger. Elise let out a surprised yelp when a strong arm reached out and pulled her up onto the saddle in front of him.

With her legs dangling down the horse's side and the saddle digging into her butt cheek, Elise grasped Colt's arm as fear of falling raced through her. She shot him a deadly look.

He just shrugged. "You're the one who said you weren't riding Bess."

"Put me down," she hissed.

Colt stopped the horse and wound the reins around the saddle horn. Thankful he seemed to be listening to her request, Elise tensed when he grasped her firmly around the waist, then swiftly shifted her until she sat facing forward in front of him on the saddle.

At his vise-like hold around her body, Elise let out a huff of irritation and threw her foot over the horse so she sat in the saddle in the appropriate manner.

Retrieving the reins, Colt turned his horse and trotted back to Sam, stopping long enough to grab the black cowboy hat from him and drop it on her head.

As they headed out to the eastern pastures, Colt kept one arm around her waist. His rock-hard chest pressed against her back and the heat where his body met her rear end felt so natural. Elise immediately stiffened, trying to keep from pressing against him. He was angry. And right now, so was she. He'd made her go out with him. Grrrr!

When Colt urged Scout into a gallop and she had to allow her body flexibility to move with the horse, Elise gave up trying to stay away from his hard frame. Instead, she removed her hat and held onto it as she leaned into him.

With the wind blowing in her face and the warm morning sun beating down on her head, she closed her eyes and thrilled in this unique experience of feeling so close to Colt. Even if he didn't feel the same way, she could imagine he wanted her company just…because.

After a few minutes of hard riding, Colt slowed Scout and Elise kept her eyes shut, not wanting to break the idyllic dream state she was in. But her heart jerked in her chest and her eyes flew open when Colt clasped her breast in his hand, then rubbed his thumb across her nipple. The bud immediately hardened, pressing against her thin bra.

Scout stopped and began to eat grass, while Colt ran his fingers under the curve of her breast before gently pinching her nipple. Elise looked around and saw they were in an unoccupied side of the ranch she'd never explored.

Her gaze traveled to the end of the property where the barbed wire fence stopped and beyond, past the rolling hills to a sprawling log style ranch house set far back on one of the highest hills.

"Who lives there?" she asked, her voice sounding more breathless than she intended.

Colt pinched her nipple again and pressed his lips to the spot behind her ear, then kissed her neck. Elise's heart skipped to a fast gallop and she almost forgot her question when he finally replied.

"That's my home."

Surprise rolled through her and she stared at the property, taking in as much detail as she could from such a great distance. "*Your home*? I'll bet you have a helluva view—" she started to say but gasped when he dropped his hand to her sex and cupped her body in a totally possessive manner.

"All I thought about last night was your soft body and the fact you might be out with Josh or some other man instead of me," he said in a calm, controlled voice as he slowly wound the reins around the saddle's horn.

Elise felt the tension in his body, then his hard erection against her backside as he gathered her closer and purposely rubbed against her.

"That's how I was all last night, Lise, hard, wanting and pissed. I swear if I'd have gone home with you yesterday, I'd have fucked you until there was never a question of what man you'd be spending your evenings with."

The roughness of his words and his intense tone made her heart skip a beat and her breathing turn choppy. Elise let her hat fall to the ground and put her hands on his hard thighs while she turned to look at him. Colt's mouth landed on hers, aggressive and dominating, his tongue thrusting into her mouth in a mimicry of his words—taking her hard, possessing her. God help her…she wanted to be taken just like that.

She tried to pull back, to tell him there wasn't anyone else, but Colt let out a low growl in his throat and said against her mouth, "No talking, Lise, not right now," before he stole her breath with another kiss while he clasped her thigh in a firm grip.

Elise let out a cry of surprise when Colt lifted her in his arms and turned her body sideways on Scout. The horse sidestepped for a second at the change in the weight distribution, but a calm command from Colt had him happily munching on grass once more as Colt settled her in his lap.

When his lips trailed down her throat, heated and tender, suddenly, she realized that with Colt, the passion he put into his lovemaking reflected his emotions. Colt *was* showing his feelings through his physical touch and through the depth of his need to be the only man in her life. She wrapped her arms around his neck and knocked his hat to the ground so she could slide her fingers through his hair. Pulling him closer, she kissed his jaw, encouraging him to return his mouth to hers. And when he did, she kissed him with just as much intensity.

Another low growl erupted from Colt as he slipped his hand between her thighs and cupped her body through her jeans. Elise broke the kiss and cried out in pure bliss as he used the seam on her jeans to his benefit, pressing it against her nub, while he whispered in her ear, "Imagine I'm sliding inside you, taking you against the wall, because honest to God, I'd be too damn horny to make it back to the bed if we were in your apartment right now."

The mental image he painted swirled in her mind, making her even wetter. Elise rocked her hips and gripped him close as her body tensed against his hand. Somehow, being up on the horse out in the middle of an open pasture, felt naughty, yet so very natural and right with this man. Colt's magnetism, his total male virility—he was not a perfect man, but he made her melt like no other man ever had.

Colt nipped at her neck and tweaked her nipple with his other hand. "Come for me, sweetheart."

His huskily whispered endearment made her emotions turn to sentimental mush. Elise pressed closer to his hand, rocking her hips to the rhythm beating inside her body. The creak of the leather saddle caused by her movements, Colt's clean scent and the smell of leather and outdoors surrounding her only fueled her arousal. She cried out as her body spasmed against the pressure of his fingers against her.

Chapter Twelve

When her body stopped trembling Elise sagged back against Colt. With a groan, he wrapped both arms around her, pulling her close as he said in gruff voice near her ear, "Lise, the thought of you with another man—"

"There's no one else," she assured him with a chuckle.

His grip tightened. "Then tell me why you ditched me last night."

Elise hesitated. She wanted to ask him why he wouldn't spend the night with her, but she just couldn't. Maybe she was afraid his answer would be that he never would. Hoping was better than an answer she might not like. Better to go with the other issue that had been plaguing her.

She sighed before speaking. "It's bad enough having your ex around but to learn Bess is usually her ride..." She let her words trail off and shrugged her shoulders, looking away from him.

"Ahhh." Colt chuckled as he lifted her leg over Scout's body to help her face forward in the saddle again before he dismounted and retrieved their hats. Putting his hat on, he handed the other one to Elise. When he climbed up behind her once more, his shoulders continued to shake in amusement.

Upset that he took her feelings so lightly, Elise jammed the hat down on her head and stiffened when Colt tried to pull her against his chest once more. "I don't find it amusing, Colt."

Colt ignored her rigid stance and pulled her against him anyway as he turned Scout toward the southern pastures. While they rode in silence, Elise stewed. He shouldn't ignore her feelings. He would be furious if the boot was on the other foot. She knew he would be.

As they approached the field holding the horses, Colt pushed her hat forward until it dropped down over her eyes.

"Hey," she called out as she tried to lift the brim.

"Leave it down," he ordered.

"What?" She ground her teeth and ignored his statement, trying to right the hat once more.

Colt's hand landed on the top of the hat, applying pressure. "Leave it."

She felt Scout slow underneath them and gave up trying to see until the horse came to a stop.

When Scout stopped and Colt lifted the hat off her head, Elise turned to him with narrowed eyes. "It's bad enough you just laughed at me… What was that for?"

He ignored her angry look and pulled her close. Lowering his chin on her shoulder he stared in front of them saying with a nod, "Look, Lise. What do you see?"

Confused by the pleased look on his face, Elise turned to stare at the horses in the gated area. Despite her frustration, she smiled as two horses frolicked and nipped at one another, obviously playing. Then her gaze landed on a black horse eating grass.

Colt straightened and whistled. The horse looked up and faced them, its ears twitching.

When Elise saw the white patch between the horse's eyes and nose, excitement made her stomach flutter. "What's Lightning doing here?"

"She's waiting for you to ride her."

She heard the grin in his words. Elise jerked her gaze back to Colt as tears gathered in her eyes. "Really?"

He nodded, his white teeth flashing in a broad smile. "Yep, she's yours."

When he jumped down and held up his hands to help her dismount, she grasped his shoulders. "You mean she's mine to ride while I'm here?"

When her feet touched the ground, Colt pulled her close and kissed her forehead. Pulling back he met her gaze. "No, sweetheart, I mean she's yours for keeps." He winked. "I put your name on the ownership papers."

"Are you sure, Colt? Not that I'm not appreciative, but that's an expensive gift. Please tell me you bartered some kind of deal to get Lightning?"

Colt grinned. "I'm a businessman, darlin'. What do you think?"

Heedless of who might see them, Elise whooped and jumped up into his arms, wrapping her legs around his waist. Cupping his face in her hands, she said, "Thank you," between each kiss she planted on his lips.

Colt's hands slid down to her buttocks and clasped her cheeks through her jeans. "Later you can thank me in other ways," he said in a suggestive tone before setting her on the ground. Giving her butt a firm swat, he continued, "But for now, go get Lightning saddled and let's ride."

Elise ran over to the fence and retrieved the bridle he'd left for her. She called to Lightning and the horse immediately trotted toward her. Pride surged through him that she was so impatient to see her gift, she didn't even wait to open the gate, but grabbed the post, bridle in hand, and climbed over the fence. Once the bridle was secure on the horse, she returned to the fence to retrieve the new saddle he'd also left for her.

As she mounted the horse, a fresh jolt of lust seared though his groin. Damn, he'd never be able to see her sitting astride a horse without thinking about their first time together in her apartment. She'd more than rocked his world!

Colt leaned on the saddle horn and watched her take Lightning for a trot around the enclosed area. He had to admit, she and that horse were a perfect match from their pitch-black hair to the spirit each female radiated. And the way they rode — perfect harmony.

Ever since May showed up, Elise had acted different,

skittish around him. After yesterday's rebuff, he walked around feeling totally frustrated. It bothered him a great deal that she'd turned him down and after an hour of denial, he decided he wanted to do something for her. Plus, he thought with a smug grin, trading a bull for Lightning meant he'd eliminated the one thing Josh Kelly could hold over him—having something Elise wanted. Good thing Josh was at that conference.

Colt didn't give a shit if his actions weren't totally altruistic. When it came to this woman, he'd fight like a junkyard dog to keep her attention…on his terms. So far he'd managed to avoid Elise's request that he spend the night at her apartment. His self-imposed rule was a different kind of torture, because each night he found it harder and harder to leave her warm body and her bed to go home.

Urging Scout forward, Colt opened the fence to allow Elise and Lightning to exit.

"What do you think?" he asked with a grin as she pulled her horse up beside his while he secured the gate.

"I think I've got a faster ride. Care for a race?" She flashed him a smile as she kicked her heels, ducked her head and urged Lightning into a full gallop.

As he nudged Scout with a squeeze of his knees, Colt laughed at her head start and the knowledge Elise wasn't beyond a little cheating herself to get what she wanted.

* * * * *

Elise let Lightning have free rein and the horse took off, full-throttle. The animal was a pure pleasure to ride, her gait so smooth. She'd never felt so free or happy in her life. The knowledge that Colt truly cared about her that he'd paid attention to her desire to have Lightning and had even put the horse ownership in her name…his gesture melted her heart and made her spirits soar. She'd worry about him never staying a full night another day. Today…ah, today she wanted to enjoy her gift and the man whom she'd begun to think she couldn't live without.

Gusts of wind blew around her, threatening to take her hat. She held onto her hat as she slowed her horse to an easy trot. Colt joined her, a grin on his face.

"How's she runnin'?"

"Like the fine-tuned engine she is," Elise replied, pulling on the reins until her horse stopped.

Colt pulled up beside her, his leg brushing against hers.

Elise leaned over and placed her hand on his thigh. She met his deep blue gaze, her heart beating hard at his closeness. "Thank you, Colt."

He lifted her hand and pulled it to his mouth, kissing her palm before moving his lips to her wrist. "You're welcome. Seeing your cheeks flushed from that run is reward enough for me."

As he leaned over to kiss her, another gust of wind blew around them so hard his hat went flying off.

Elise glanced up, following Colt's gaze to the darkening sky.

"Storm's blowing in." He jumped down to get his hat, then remounted. "We should get back."

Nodding her agreement, Elise turned her horse in the direction of the ranch and rode alongside Colt in silence.

When they were almost to the ranch he stopped to talk to a ranch hand. "Davy, go check the southwest fence's corner post. It's starting to show its age. Take Jim and Matt and have them help you temporarily secure that post until this storm blows over. Once the ground is dry again, we'll replace it."

As they made their way between the main ranch house and the stables, Rick rode out of the stables and stopped to talk to Colt.

"After the bull incident...I've got this feeling. Dunno why," he began leaning on his saddle horn and narrowing his gaze at the swirling dark clouds above them. "Guess it's the electricity in the air, but I wouldn't put it past Jackson to try something today, so I want to be out on the range for this one."

"Out in the open? In the middle of a storm?" Elise asked, surprised.

Colt cast a glance her way. "Don't you know just how tough Texan men are, darlin'?"

When Elise tossed him an are-you-nuts expression, his shoulders shook with laughter. "We have a few small houses, shacks really, but places to wait out the worst if you're caught out in a storm."

"Ah, I see." She grinned, nodding her head.

Rick touched his hat and dipped his head in her direction in a show of respect. As he walked his horse past hers, his gaze dropped to Lightning. "Nice addition to the ranch."

"The mare's Elise's," Colt commented.

She grinned, patting her horse's neck. "I'm sure Lightning will be just as much a fixture around the Lonestar as Scout and Bess are."

"Take care out there, Rick," she called after the foreman as he trotted off.

"He'll be fine," Nan called from the porch. She leaned on one of the columns and stared out at the range, a faraway look in her eyes. When the wind kicked up once more, she looked at Colt and rubbed her upper arms. "It's gonna be a doozy, Colt. I feel it in my bones."

"I know," he sighed, then reached out and threaded his fingers with Elise's. "I'm going back out with Rick. Why don't you go spend some time with Nan?" He looked at Nan and grinned as he continued, "She's never liked storms much."

"Harumph," Nan snorted. "Mind your manners, Colt. You're never too old for a good tannin'." Winking at Elise, she continued, "But I won't turn away some good company for a spell."

Elise returned the older woman's friendly smile. "Let me

put Lightning—"

Just as she spoke, a bolt of lightning streaked across the darkened sky, making the tiny hairs on her arms stand on end.

Rumbling thunder quickly followed. At the same time, Cade and Mace came trotting out of the main stable, wearing their Stetsons and orange rain slickers.

"Ready for some fun, bro?" Mace asked as he tossed a walkie-talkie and then a folded-up rain slicker to Colt, his eyes alight. Clicking his walkie-talkie, he spoke into it, saying, "Breaker, breaker, this is 'the Studmeister', you copy?"

Colt gave his middle brother a can-you-believe-this-wiseass look to which Cade lifted his own walkie-talkie to his lips, clicked the button, and said in a low, droll voice, "I think he's gettin' a little *too* into this, don't you," he finished with a deadpan expression, "*Little Mustang?*"

Colt's shoulders shook with laughter as he clipped his walkie-talkie to his hip. "Save me from smartass brothers."

Elise grinned and leaned over to kiss him on the cheek. She whispered in his ear, "Ah, you know you wish you could pitch a tent in the backyard and camp out in this storm like you did when you were kids."

Before she straightened in her saddle, Colt clasped his hand around her neck and whispered back, "Yeah, but don't ever tell these two wiseasses that or I'll lose all the respect I've gained over the years."

She winked at him and leaned back in her saddle to address his brothers. "He said you're both grounded when you get back."

All three brothers laughed and even Nan joined in until May rode up on Bess, wearing rain gear as well.

Thunder rumbled again and Bess tossed her head, prancing in the dirt.

"Sorry May, but you know how skittish Bess gets during storms," Colt said. His words sent a silent sigh of relief coursing through Elise. She didn't want to think about May out on the range with any of the Tanner brothers, but especially Colt.

Adjusting her bright yellow rain slicker, May pouted, "But Colt—"

"I mean it, May," Colt warned before turning his horse away. Mace and Cade followed, kicking their horses into a full gallop to keep up with him.

As they watched the men disappear over the hill, fat raindrops started to fall. Elise turned Lightning toward the barn, expecting May to follow. When May kicked her heels into Bess and took off toward the pastures, Elise started to call her back, but Nan interrupted her.

"Let her go, Elise. The woman will bring her own trouble. I imagine she's tougher than Bess any day."

Elise pressed her lips together then nodded. "Let me put Lightning away and I'll meet you in the kitchen."

Once she reached the barn and put Lightning in a stall, Elise started to unbuckle her saddle then thought better of it. Re-cinching her horse, she decided to leave Lightning saddled and ready to go just in case her help was needed.

She made sure her horse had water and food and before she left, she patted her on the nose saying, "We might be needed to help out. Hope you don't mind waiting just a bit longer, girl."

Lightning neighed and lifted her nose up and down as if she agreed with Elise's decision.

As she exited the stables, rain began to pour down. Elise picked up her pace across the yard to the front porch of the main house. Closing the screen door behind her, she entered the kitchen and accepted the warm mug Nan handed her with a smile.

Inhaling the rich smell of the dark coffee, she took a sip and yummed her approval as the warm liquid slid down her throat, chasing away the chills the rain had caused.

Elise sat down at the table and asked as Nan sat down across from her, "Tell me about Jackson Riley. I noticed tension between him and Colt when I met him. Why do Rick and Colt think he'd try something on the Lonestar property during a storm or at all for that matter?"

Nan took a sip of her own coffee, set it down and nodded, her deep brown eyes taking on a knowing look. "Jackson Riley's dad owned the Lonestar land a few decades ago but lost it in a high stakes poker game. The man who won the property sold it to Colt's daddy and uncle. After losing his property, Jackson's dad drank himself into an early grave. Jackson has always claimed the poker game was fixed."

Nan paused and shrugged. "Fixed or not, Colt's daddy and uncle bought the land fair and square and have raised their own cattle and horses on it ever since."

"Aaaaah, now it's all starting to make sense."

Nan's brow crinkled, her expression confused. "What's starting to make sense?"

"I never told Colt about this, but Jackson contacted me and tried to get me to sell him my half of the Lonestar. I told Jackson that if James Tanner had wanted him to have it, he would have put him in his will. Jackson wasn't too thrilled with my rejection of his offer."

"That Jackson's a wily one." She snorted.

Concern for Colt laced through Elise. "Do you think Jackson would sabotage the ranch?"

Nan nodded. "I know so, girl. We've had cattle rustled quite a few times, a prize bull inexplicably maimed to where he had to be put down, another bull recently go bonkers from a weed that only grows in the springtime, and a bout of bad water for some of the horses; there's no doubt in my mind."

That's what the whole bull thing had been about, Elise thought, angry for Colt's sake.

A couple of ranch hands opened the back door, their bodies drenched from the rain. "Hey, Nan, got any more slickers in the closet. There aren't any left in the usual place out in the stables."

Nan was already walking out of the kitchen. "I'll be right back."

Elise looked at the men. They seemed agitated, in a real hurry.

"What's wrong?" she asked out of intuition more than anything else.

The blond named Frank pulled on his hat to acknowledge her. "The southwest fence is down and the cattle are roaming, ma'am."

Elise's heart raced at the news. She jumped up from the chair right as Nan returned with jackets for the men.

"Got any more, Nan?"

"Nope, just a thin overcoat," she replied, then stopped. "You're not going out in that storm, young lady."

Elise gave her an oh-yes-I-am look as the men went outside. "The southwest fence is down. They need all the help they can get."

Nan nodded solemnly as she turned and walked out of the room.

Her adrenaline pumping, Elise gripped the back of the chair while she waited for Nan.

Elise breathed a sigh of relief when she returned with a short jacket. As she slipped into the expensive, albeit less serviceable coat, and pulled the cord tight around her waist, Nan said, "Sorry, it's the best I've got. It was Colt's mama's."

Elise jerked her gaze to meet Nan's serious brown eyes, but she didn't have time to fathom the reason why the woman's lips were compressed in anger. One thing she knew…Colt may have mentioned his dad, but he'd never talked about his mother.

Nodding her understanding, she pulled the hood over her head and left the kitchen. Dashing across the yard toward the barn, she ran as fast as her legs would carry her.

As she entered the stall, the smell of rain, wet hay and earth tickled her nose. Her sudden heightened sense of smell made the shiver of unease that rippled up her spine intensify. She shuddered despite the coat. When she leaned over and grasped

Lightning's reins, the horse neighed and pawed at the ground, nodding her head up and down.

"C'mon, girl. We might not have taken the round-up-the-freaked-out-cattle-class yet, but we know a thing or two about mending a fence."

Once she slid a pair of work gloves in her coat pocket, Elise put her foot in the stirrup, mounted Lightning and nudged the horse into a gallop as she exited the stables.

Chapter Thirteen

With the storm's strong winds blowing across the pastures, a chill in the air had replaced the Texas heat as the heavy rain fell around her. Ignoring the rain pelting her face, Elise raced across the open fields toward the southwest side of the ranch.

As she approached the downed fence, she slowed her horse and dismounted. Walking over to a secure area, she tied Lightning's reins to a post and sloshed through the puddles of water in the grass until she reached the area where a couple of the ranch hands and May worked to repair the fence.

Elise noted the barbed wire had broken in two sections of the fence right next to one another, making the repair even more difficult since they'd need leverage from a secured post in between to help stretch the barbed wire taut. Nor did the torrential rain help matters. She watched as they worked to pull the wire taut, but due to the saturated ground, the opposite post shifted whenever they tried to put their full weight behind it.

Dogs barking off in the distance drew her attention. Elise glanced up to see Colt, Mace, Cade, Rick and a couple other men rounding up groups of cattle that had apparently left through the broken area of the fence to huddle together under a couple of huge oak trees up on the hillside. The dogs worked the sides of the herd, keeping them in line as the group slowly moved back in the direction of the downed fence.

Seeing the cattle approach spurred her into action. She tapped Frank on the shoulder and pointed to the other broken area, yelling over the raging storm, "We've got maybe ten minutes before the herd is back inside the fence. Let's have the fence as ready to go as possible so that when they come, all we have to do is the final hook-up and stretch."

Frank nodded his agreement and called May to take over so he could help Elise start the next section.

Elise pulled on her gloves and she and Frank worked quickly. She felt every ache and strain in her muscles as she tried to use leverage to help tighten the barbed wire against the post, but her boots couldn't gain purchase in the wet grass and mud beneath her feet. The hood slipped off her head as she fell down in the muck. Now that her head was thoroughly soaked and the cold rain slipped down in the collar of her coat, drenching her clothes, she jumped back up and pulled even harder. Elise's heart raced as her adrenaline and anger at the situation coalesced to give her the additional strength she needed to complete her task.

She and Frank were almost done with their repairs, but they paused and moved out of the way as the herd walked through the opening in the fence. The animals' bodies were a slow-moving mass and they even seemed to moo their displeasure in unison. She couldn't decide if their incessant mooing was due to the fact they'd just lost their newfound freedom or from fear of the storm flashing and booming around them.

When the last cow entered the fence, immediately followed by the men and dogs, Elise and the ranch hand moved in to make the final repair to close off the fence.

Deciding to test the repaired wire one last time before they connected the broken pieces, Elise hooked the wrecking bar tool against a barb and pulled hard, putting all her weight behind it. To her surprise, the wire snapped. As she started to fall, the barbed wire came flying back toward her. She tensed and closed her eyes at the same time she turned her head, hoping to avoid the sharp barbs.

She heard a grunt of pain as a strong arm encircled her waist, catching her before she hit the ground. Opening her eyes, she saw Colt fling the other end of the barbed wire away.

Elise dropped the tool as he pulled her into his arms and held her close. "I meant to warn ya about the barbed wire. Old barb can still have a helluva recoil on it, sweetheart," he said in a hoarse tone.

She wrapped her arms around him and laid her head on his chest against his rain slicker. Even with the rain pouring around them, she could smell his masculine aroma. The comforting scent seeped into her bones, warming her despite the cold rain hammering down on her shoulders and jacket. While Colt held her, his hat provided cover for her head and face from the wet deluge.

Colt kissed her forehead and pulled her coat's hood back over her head. "Let's finish up so you can get inside and dry off."

Elise stared at him. Though he'd smiled at her for a brief moment, something was on his mind. His body felt tense, his tone had been matter-of-fact as he stepped away from her.

"What's wrong?" she asked.

He nodded toward the fence as Frank repaired the final barbed wire. "That was Jackson's handiwork."

"You think he sabotaged the fence? How do you know?"

Colt picked up some of the discarded old barbed wire that had snapped when Elise applied too much pull. He showed her one end. "See this, it's rusted and brittle." Flipping the wire around, careful to avoid the barbs, he continued, "Now look at this side. The edge is smooth and shiny. No oxidation has reached the inside." Pointing to the side of the wire, he indicated the two embedded ridges along the outside of the wire. "Whatever tool was used, it has a chip in it."

She jerked her gaze to his, her heart racing. "It's been cut."

Colt pressed his lips in a thin line. "Exactly."

He glanced at someone over her shoulder and called out, "Rick, you, Cade and Jim take first shift. Chase, Frank and I will take second."

Colt walked over and placed a hand on May's shoulder, "Thank you for your quick discovery. Who knows how many more cattle we would be rounding up if we hadn't acted so quickly once you alerted us to the downed fence?"

She flashed him a brilliant smile. "All in a day's work around the ranch, Colt. You know I always do my part." Her gaze shifted to Elise as she finished her last words.

Elise had stiffened when Colt's hand landed on May's shoulder, but she brushed aside her question of May's true motivations, considering the woman had literally saved the day. Apparently, Colt had forgiven May for disobeying him about bringing Bess out in the storm. Where *was* Bess? she wondered.

Colt approached her once more and wrapped his arm around her shoulder. Turning her toward Lightning, he said, "Frank's done. We've mended the fence until the rain stops and the ground hardens again. Go on back to the main house and get dried off. I've got to round up Bess. She's here in the pasture somewhere. I believe she took off when May dismounted to work on the fence."

He helped her climb up on Lightning and once she was settled, he laid his hand on her thigh. Elise could feel the heat of his palm through her pants.

"I'll see you in a bit." His steel blue gaze held hers as he gave her thigh a squeeze.

Her heart rate increased at his reassuring touch. Elise nodded and nudged her horse into a full gallop in the direction of the stables.

When she reached her destination, she dismounted and walked her horse into her stall. Tying her reins, she unbuckled and removed the saddle and wet blanket. After twenty minutes of wiping down and grooming Lightning, Elise heard May enter the stall next door with Bess.

As she used a towel to wring out most of the dampness in Lightning's mane, Elise paused and turned when May passed by her stall and said, "I see Colt bought you a gift." Pushing back her hood to display a mostly dry head of hair, May tossed her hair over her shoulder then continued, "Bet he still hasn't taken you to his house, has he?"

Elise's blood boiled at the woman's dig, but she held her silence.

May sniffed the air haughtily, saying with a laugh, "And don't expect him to either. Colt rarely takes a woman to his home." Twirling a strand of her long blonde hair, she said with a knowing smile before she walked away, "I wonder if it's changed much since I've been there."

Elise didn't give her the satisfaction of a reaction. She turned away, grabbed a brush and began briskly brushing the rest of the excess moisture out of Lightning's mane.

Bitch, she thought, her body shaking in anger. The woman just loved to provoke her. God, she'd be glad when the blonde bimbo left on the next round of rodeo tours. She'd be damned if she'd endure that woman's bullshit the next time around.

Flipping the section of mane hair she'd already brushed over Lightning's neck, Elise moved on to the next section, her mind whirling. She and Colt were going to have a talk about May. As half-owner of the ranch, which included the rodeo, she had as much say about its employees as he did. She'd looked at the sales figures for the rodeo paraphernalia stand May ran. Over the past couple of years, the stand's sales had been flat, yet the ticket sales had gone up each year. Elise had enough professional issues to discuss regarding May. The personal ones wouldn't even need to be discussed. There wasn't that much money in the paraphernalia stand. It was more of a courtesy to the fans than anything else. *Hey!* she thought as an idea struck her.

Elise perked up as the idea for increasing sales percolated in her mind. She finished the rest of Lightning's mane and stood on tiptoe to lean over the horse's neck to flip the hair back into place. As she started to move away to set down the brush, she realized her watch had snagged in the horse's mane.

She dropped the brush and used her other hand to try to untangle the watch. Unfortunately, nothing less than a good tug would free her. The watch she wore was her grandmother's and there was no way she was leaving it on Lightning's mane as an expensive barrette.

Grabbing hold of a portion of the entangled mane to keep from pulling Lightning's skin, Elise jerked with all her might. She pulled her arm free with a sigh of relief. Looking down to adjust her watch that had twisted around her wrist in her earlier movements, her heart jerked in her chest.

It was gone!

Glancing behind her, at the stall full of hay, she rolled her eyes. Great, the watch must've gone flying. Grumpy and uncomfortable from feeling like she took a cold shower—with her clothes on!—all she wanted to do was go home, dry off and have a cup of hot chocolate. Looking all around her stall, she couldn't find the watch anywhere. When she glanced at the slats of wood that made up her stall's wall, it dawned on her that her watch must flown over into Bess's stall.

Sighing, Elise trudged over into Bess's stall and scanned the hay. She had to move Bess a couple of times as she glanced over the stall. Nothing, damnit!

Sinking to her hands and knees, the smell of manure and hay invading her senses, Elise scanned the floor. She worked quickly, sliding the hay out of the way as she looked for her watch. Finally, along the far side of the stall, where the wall met the floor, her fingers brushed against the watch face. Grinning in triumph, she stood and examined the timepiece, relief flooding through her. The pin holding the band to the watch was missing, but that could easily be replaced.

As she turned to walk out of Bess's stall, her foot hit something hard under the hay near the far stall wall. Elise frowned and kicked the hay aside. When her gaze landed on a pair of wire cutters, she picked them up and opened them. Noting a nicked edge along one side of the metal cutters, she clenched the tool in her hand. Her heart pounded in her chest as anger caused heat to rise in her cheeks.

* * * * *

With the exception of Elise, the rest of the crew, who'd helped during the storm, had cleaned up and dried off and were now convened in the kitchen drinking hot coffee.

Colt's blood boiled as he thought about his ruthless neighbor. This, on top of the stunt with the bull…he'd wanted to go after Jackson right away, but he knew putting in a showing in the kitchen and thanking everyone personally for their help was a "must do" first.

His duty fulfilled, Colt pushed his chair back from the table and started to walk toward the kitchen door when Cade stood and put a hand on his arm.

"Colt…"

Colt met his brother's dark, steady gaze.

"Jackson can wait until the storm is over. Remember, we know where he lives."

Colt set his jaw and clenched his hands into fists. Damn. He knew Cade was right. He always was the calm one in the family. Some even considered him a cold man at times, but Colt knew better. Still waters ran very deep with Cade…always had.

He relaxed and rolled his shoulders. "I suppose the bastard can wait. I need to find Elise anyway. Anyone seen her?"

He looked at May, Nan, Mace and the rest of the ranch hands sitting at the kitchen table. They all shook their heads.

When he turned to go, Cade said, "I think I'll go with you to see Jackson tomorrow. I don't want you to *need* a good homicide attorney."

"There'll be no need for that," Elise called out from behind Colt.

Colt turned and looked at her. Standing in the doorway, her clothes soaked and mud splotches splattered all over her, Elise stood ramrod straight, her expression livid. *Oh shit.* His stomach clenched. What had he done now?

She marched over and slammed something in the middle of the wooden kitchen table.

"You'll do better to look amongst your own, Colt," she said in a cold tone as her gaze locked on May's face.

When she removed her hand and he saw a pair of wire cutters, Colt frowned.

May flipped her hair over her shoulder, then crossed her arms over her ample chest, adopting a belligerent stance. "Don't look at me."

"Really?" Elise's continued sarcasm evident. "Geez, and here I thought that's exactly what I was doing."

Shoving the bolt cutter across the table toward May, she lifted her hand and said, "Imagine my surprise when I found this buried in the hay in Bess's stall."

May gasped in outrage and looked at him to defend her. "Colt, you can't let her talk to me like that...to-to accuse me of something so awful."

Then she narrowed her gaze on Elise. "You're trying to set me up."

"Set you up?" Elise's voice shook, she was so angry. "I was looking for my watch that had flung outside Lightning's stall—"

Cutting herself off, she finished, "Screw it. I don't have to explain myself to you. If Colt chooses to believe your lies, then that's his business."

Turning on her heel, her shoulders squared, her drenched boots made squishing sounds as she walked out the kitchen door.

When Colt looked at May and she couldn't keep eye contact with him, his chest constricted at the knowledge of her betrayal. But anger quickly replaced his disappointment. Stepping forward, he set his hands on the table.

"Why, May?" he barked, his tone so harsh everyone in the room jumped. Everyone but Cade.

Nodding toward the door, Cade said, "Go after her."

Ignoring him, Colt laid into May. "You've been a member of this team for seven years. Does that mean nothing to you?"

May started to stand, but her appealing gaze darted to Cade when he put a restraining hand on her shoulder and forced her back in her seat.

"I'll take care of this, Colt," he said in a calm tone.

Colt met his brother's gaze for a brief moment, then nodded his assent. As he turned to go, he heard Cade say in a sharp tone, "Everybody out. Now!"

* * * * *

Elise drove home, fury making her body tense and stiff. She hoped to God Colt didn't let May spin him some fanciful tale about being a scapegoat. If he did, he sure as hell wasn't the man she thought he was.

The rain was coming down so hard and fast, a couple of times her car hydroplaned toward the side of the road. Her heart raced as she intuitively maneuvered the vehicle in the right direction to stay on the road. All she wanted to do was get home and take a hot bath. Later she'd call Colt.

Colt.

More and more she'd come to care for him. What had started out as a pure sexual attraction for the man had turned into a deep, abiding respect for what he stood for, his very sense of doing the right thing by friends and family and his protective nature for the ones he loved.

Loved. Would he ever let himself love her that way? For some reason, Colt held back a part of himself. Elise gave her all in everything she did. And her relationship with Colt was no exception. Plain and simple, she'd fallen for the man. Hard.

As ballsy as she could be with Colt sexually, when it came to deeper emotions, she still hadn't screwed up enough courage to ask him why he'd never stayed the night with her.

Then May goes and reminds her he'd never once asked her to come home with him or offered to show her his place. Damn that woman! She hoped Colt did something about her or she'd do it for him.

She pulled into the parking space at her apartment and cut the engine. The thunder and lightning came from further away, but rain continued to pour down, pinging off her car's hood and roof above her head.

Glancing at her umbrella in the floorboard, she shrugged. What was the point? She was soaked already.

Elise opened the car door, climbed out and quickly shut it behind her. She started to make a mad dash for the stairs when she heard her name being called.

Turning, she saw Colt come around the front of his truck, his cowboy hat pulled low as he strode purposefully toward her, his expression intense.

Her heart hammering in her chest, Elise pulled herself up to her full height and prepared to argue with him.

Colt bore down on her and didn't stop until the toes of his boots hit hers. She didn't get one word out before he'd speared his fingers through her hair on either side of her face and cupped the back of her head, pulling her against his hard chest as his mouth came down on hers—passionate and determined.

Elise thrilled at the intensity of his kiss as his tongue explored her mouth—dominate, seductive, persuasive. Her insides stirred and melted like warm honey at such a deep, emotionally charged kiss while the rain poured around them.

She put her arms around his neck and pressed against him, returning the kiss with everything she had.

Colt lifted his head, his heated gaze burning a hole right to her soul. "We need to get inside, Lise."

She nodded, groggy from such a bone-jarring, heart-wrenching kiss.

Removing his hat, Colt grinned and ducked. Before she knew his intentions, he'd scooped her up and put her face down across his shoulder as he ran up the steps to her apartment. Once he stood outside her door, Colt grabbed the keys she handed him and unlocked it.

He walked inside, kicked the door closed and flipped the

lock. Tossing the keys and then his hat on the table, he headed straight to her bathroom.

When he reached the room, Colt shut the door behind them then set her on the floor. He didn't bother turning on the light but instead pulled on the cord and opened the blinds in the small bathroom window.

The sky was still dark outside and the main light that shined through the window was from the street lamp that burned twenty-four hours a day.

Pulling back the shower curtain, he turned the faucet on full blast then faced her once more. The look on his face told her just how on the edge he was.

Elise's heart raced at his heated look as he pulled at the zipper on her coat. She tugged on his rain slicker and Colt lifted it off his body then dropped it on the floor.

Once she shrugged out of her jacket, he lifted her shirt over her head. Elise shivered at the cold hitting her wet exposed skin, but thrilled at the dark look in Colt's eyes. Even in the dim light she could sense his intemperate mood. She'd never seen him this intense. She let out a cry of surprise when Colt grabbed the waistline on her jeans and yanked her toward him, his mouth capturing hers, possessing her.

Her hands landed on his hard chest for balance as he slid his tongue into her mouth, encouraging a heated response from her. She teased his tongue with hers while she ripped open the snaps on his shirt and ran her hands over his hard chest, moaning against his mouth.

Colt released the button on her jeans and unzipped her zipper. Sliding his hands against her cold, wet buttocks, he pulled her against his hard erection. The steam in the room from the shower enveloped them in its warmth while they continued to explore each other's bodies as they removed the rest of their clothes.

Her heart rate sped up even more as he held her hand and guided her into the tub under the hard spray. Elise turned and let her head fall back, the warm water hammering down on her. She reveled in the water cascading over her body, bringing her body temperature back up and chasing away the shivers.

When she realized Colt had stopped touching her, she opened her eyes to look at him. The hungry, burning look in his gaze, as it roamed over her body, took her breath away.

His steady regard never wavered as his hand slid over her breast and his thumb grazed her nipple. "Ever since that day you cock-teased me while you were in the shower, I've thought of nothing else but seeing you this way again—wet, aroused..."

He pinched her nipple and she gasped as the erotic sensation.

"...and ready," he rasped as he stepped up to her body and his lips grazed her neck.

Elise smiled at the feeling of his hard, hot erection pressed against her belly. She clasped his hand and laced her fingers with his. Lifting his other hand to do the same, she paused when she saw a dark gash marring his palm.

Turning his hand over, she realized the injury was from the barbed wire he'd stopped from hitting her in the face earlier. Her heart constricted and she placed a soft kiss over his wound before lowering his hand to her hip.

Colt's fingers flexed before they firmly clasped her hip. He let go of her hand and used both hands to pull her close, his fingers digging into her rear as he ran his lips down her neck.

Elise threaded her fingers in his wet hair and let her head fall back once more when his lips found her nipple and sucked. She moaned and her sex contracted at the stimulation his mouth caused.

Releasing her, Colt clasped her hand, kissed her palm, then lowered her hand to her mound.

"Show me, Lise," he encouraged. He stepped out of the spray and leaned against the shower wall, waiting.

Elise gave him a sexy smile. He wanted her to make herself come, did he? Well, she'd make him *want* to do it for her before it was all over with.

Placing her hands on his shoulders, she directed him to sit down on the side of the tub facing her.

When he was seated, she laid her hands on his knees and jerked his legs wide open.

Colt's jaw muscle jumped, but he showed no other emotion as she stepped back to retrieve the bar of scented soap.

Lathering the soap under the water, she set the bar aside then met his gaze as she put her foot on his upper thigh.

Blood rushed to her sex at the intense, aroused look on his face.

Running her hands over her breasts, Elise cupped them before slowly sliding one hand down her belly and her thigh. Licking her lips, she ran her hand back up her thigh and bit her lower lip as her fingers met the wet curls between her legs.

When she slid a finger inside her body, she closed her eyes and moaned at the decadent sensation of having Colt watch her. Her gaze flew open as she felt her knee suddenly jerked to the side, exposing her even more for his view.

Colt reached for the hand buried inside her channel and two of his fingers intertwined with hers as he thrust them deep inside her body, once, twice, three times. Her thighs began to tremble at the passionate onslaught.

Her knees almost buckled when he commanded in a rough, barely controlled tone, "Remove your hand. I want to feel you come."

Elise withdrew her hand and barely had time to place it on his shoulder when Colt slid his fingers deep inside her once more, twisting and pressing in all the right spots.

Oh God. Her legs began to quake as he thrust inside her and withdrew again and again. With a low growl, Colt lifted her leg and slid his shoulder under it as he clasped her rear and leaned down to capture her clit with his lips and teeth. Elise keened her pleasure and thrust her fingers in his hair for balance as much as desire to keep him close. As her lower belly tightened, she bucked against him right before her climax roared through her.

Colt didn't wait for an invitation. He immediately untangled their bodies and stood, clasping her buttocks once more.

As he lifted her, Elise put her arms around his neck and moaned in pleasure when he slid inside her slowly. She thrilled at the stretching of skin as her body allowed him access to every last inch of space.

When he was fully seated inside her, Colt held her in the air with his hands, then leaned her back against the wall and began shafting her, slow and deep.

He kissed her neck then met her gaze as he withdrew and sank back inside her. "I want to stay the night, Lise. I want to wake up with you in my arms."

Elise's rapid heart rate skipped a beat or two at his words. Her breathing turned erratic as her body prepared to come once more. Colt's declaration of his desire to stay totally threw her into mushy, romantic, meltdown mode.

Thankful for the water drenching them, washing her tears away, she muffled her sob of happiness against his chest.

Colt stopped moving and lifted her chin until her gaze met his intense one. "Tell me I can stay."

She didn't know what tomorrow would bring for them, but for now, she'd enjoy what he offered. Threading her fingers through his hair once more, she pulled his mouth down to hers and said, "It's about damn time," right before she kissed him.

Chapter Fourteen

After they'd dried off from the shower, Colt carried Elise to the bedroom and laid her on the bed. As he pulled her into his arms, his gaze captured hers. Varied emotions stirred behind their deep blue depths.

He cared a great deal for her. She felt it in the way he wrapped his arms around her and pulled her back against his chest. Knew it by the tenderness with which he brushed her hair away from her face and took a deep, inhaling breath near her neck before he kissed her temple.

Threading her fingers through his, Elise kissed his hand, then snuggled into his warmth. She thrilled at the feel of his muscular, hard body wrapped around her much softer one, but when his erection brushed against her bottom, she couldn't help the smile that spread across her face. Yeah, they were insatiable for each other. No denying that. Already her body reacted to his stimulus, her sex moistening then throbbing in anticipation.

"May has been taken care of," he stated in a matter-of-fact tone.

Elise rolled over and faced him, laying her hand on his jaw. "I'm sorry, Colt. Regardless of my feelings, I know she's been with the rodeo a long time."

He pulled her close and kissed her mouth, his lips tender, lingering.

She wrapped her arms around his neck and hugged him tight before speaking, "If it's any consolation, I've come up with a plan to expand the offerings of rodeo paraphernalia to the fans."

He leaned back and looked at her, surprised. "You have?"

She nodded. "The idea occurred to me while I was

grooming Lightning."

Sitting up on her knees, she turned on the light on the nightstand and faced him, a smile on her face.

"What about offering a store right on the website? That way when tickets are purchased online, the rodeo knickknack stuff can be sold at the same time. The buyers can either choose to have their purchases sent to their homes or pick them up at the rodeo." Getting into her pitch, she continued, excitement in her voice, "Hey, we can even sell little prepackaged items like a T-shirt, a hat and a toy for the kids. Betcha we'll sell more that way."

Colt watched Elise become more animated as she talked about the online store. He took in her rosy cheeks and the long black hair falling over her shoulder and his heart constricted. She looked so beautiful he couldn't resist reaching up and running his hand through her damp hair. At his touch, she stopped speaking mid-sentence and smiled, tilting her head to the side.

"Are you listening to me?"

He gave her a roguish grin. "Yes, I heard every word you said, darlin'."

She raised her hands in the air. "Well, what do you think of my idea?"

Colt pulled her to his chest and kissed her, nipping at her lower lip before taking his time and exploring her mouth. With every stroke of his tongue against hers, he mimicked what he wanted to do to her the rest of the day. Then he rolled her over and clasped her hands above her head as he laid his chest against hers.

"I think you have many great ideas rambling around in that beautiful head of yours."

Her emerald gaze flashed with desire as he slid his thigh between hers, nudging her soft thighs apart, his cock already throbbing to be inside her as he continued in a gruff tone. "But right now I'd really like to get started on the rest of our day and night together, sweetheart, 'cause I don't think I'll ever get enough of you. I think a marathon with food breaks for energy in between sounds pretty good to me."

Her smile and happy sigh of acceptance as he slid inside her made Colt's heart ache. He needed this night with Elise...to imagine what it'd be like to spend every day waking up with her by his side. He wasn't fooling himself. He knew their relationship wouldn't last forever. They were from different worlds. But for now, he'd live the fantasy as long as he kept his heart intact.

As he thrust deep inside her body and she rocked her hips underneath him, moaning in pleasure, Colt felt a shudder ripple all the way through him at her beauty inside and out. God, she felt good and so damn right wrapped around him.

Ah shit, he was in trouble.

* * * * *

The next morning Elise stood watching the Tanner brothers working together with several other rodeo personnel to ready the trucks. The break was over and the rodeo would be back on the road for another few weeks...well, minus May.

Nan told her Cade had fired her the night before and that May had cleared out her things that very night.

The warm sun beat down on her, burning off the dampness from the day before. The smell of fresh hay rushed toward her as she took a long, deep breath. Within a few hours the heat would suck the moisture right out of the air around her and the ground underneath her feet. Her whole body ached from yesterday morning's drenching and the long afternoon and night with Colt. Elise closed her eyes and lifted her face toward the bright light, enjoying the warmth that came with the early morning sun and the temporary cooler weather the storm left in its wake.

The sound of a car driving down the long, gravel driveway drew her attention. When a woman with salt and pepper hair emerged from her station wagon, Elise smiled and ran over to the car.

Hugging the petite woman tight, she could barely contain her excitement, "Aunt Marie, I hope your vacation was a blast." Pulling back, she continued, "I can't begin to thank you for the Lonestar. I've had the best time working on the website, getting to know the members of the ranch, learning the ropes of running a rodeo ranch," she babbled on in her enthusiasm.

Her aunt kissed her cheek, then leaned back smiling. "I'm thrilled to see you so happy. I knew you needed this, sweetie." She glanced over to Colt and his brothers and finished, "Just as much as I knew they needed you."

Elise replied with a laugh, "Oh, I think the Tanner boys are pretty self-sufficient." Shrugging she continued, "I've just done what I could to help out."

Marie's gaze stayed locked on the men, a general fondness reflected in her expression. "They're good men."

Elise followed her gaze and smiled at the good-natured ribbing going on between the brothers. Mace had thrown some hay on his brothers and with their shirts removed and sweat glistening on their upper bodies, the hay stuck all over them. Cade now had Mace in a headlock and he looked at Colt, his serious gaze taking on a devilish gleam, "I think he deserves a dunk in the water trough, bro. What do ya say?"

Colt scowled at his brothers as he brushed off the hay, then crossed his arms. Elise expected him to berate them, but instead he surprised her as he walked around behind Cade.

Grabbing Mace's legs, he said, "Nah, let's throw him in the mucked hay from this morning's stable cleanin'. Might make 'im smell a little better."

As Colt and Cade carried a struggling, cussing Mace toward the back of the barn, Elise nodded in agreement. "I can't believe how different they each are."

Marie nodded. "Yeah, their mother leaving when they were still growing up really left a mark on each of them." She tilted her head and finished, "They've each handled the loss in their own way."

Elise jerked her gaze back to Marie. "What? I assumed their mother had died abruptly and folks just didn't want to talk about her."

Hooking her arm in Elise's, Marie walked her over to the fence. "No, Sharon left their dad when the oldest was just a teenager. She'd grown tired of the ranching life and missed her socialite days, I suppose," she paused and sighed before continuing, "She went home to her family, back to Washington, D.C. Broke Gil's heart and left the boys with their own issues to deal with." She nodded to the men. "For obvious reasons, Colt doesn't trust many women. Cade? Well, he lives a nomad's life, never really settling, and Mace appears to have taken the opposite approach from Colt," she paused and laughed. "He loves *all* women."

Elise's stomach tensed at Marie's assessment of Colt. It all made sense now...why Colt had called her "Princess", why he avoided any type of deeper emotional connection with her. That's what May had started to say to her the other day before Cade interrupted her—that with her father's money, her privileged upbringing, Colt must've seen her as the same type of person as his mother. She'd come to know Colt pretty well...he'd never let himself go through what his father had.

Her chest constricted at the thought while her heart broke for all the Tanner men, especially for Colt's father. What a devastating way to lose the one person you expected to spend the rest of your life with.

"I had no idea, Aunt Marie. Thank you for telling me. A lot of things, little comments here and there, make sense to me now."

Marie turned twinkling green eyes her way, her grin causing deeper wrinkles to form on her attractive face. "Been giving you a hard time, have they?"

Elise snorted. "Nothing I can't handle."

Marie hugged her tight and whispered in her ear, "That's

my girl."

She turned and walked toward the main ranch house, calling over her shoulder, "I'm going to catch up with Nan. Let's have lunch together later."

"Sounds good," Elise replied as she rubbed her sore neck. Good Lord, just what had she and Colt done last night to make her neck hurt so?

* * * * *

Elise spent the first part of her morning straightening her office. Someone had gone through her filing cabinet, leaving her files in shambles. Upon checking Colt's office and finding it in similar shape, Elise knew it had to have been May because May's employee folder was the only one missing from Colt's Lonestar personnel files. Good riddance was all Elise had to say!

She spent the rest of the morning working on the new storefront for the website. When she had a skeleton framework completed, she sat back and rolled her shoulders, then rubbed her aching neck. Sitting and staring at the computer, working so intensely caused a headache to form right behind her temples. Man, she didn't need a migraine right now. She'd only had one once in her life and that was plenty as far as she was concerned.

She looked up when her aunt entered her office, saying in a cheery voice, "I know it's almost 1:00 p.m. I lost track of time chatting with Nan. Are you still up for lunch, dear?"

Elise glanced at her backup watch—she still needed to get her grandmother's repaired—surprised to discover how late it was. Pushing back her chair, she started to stand, saying, "I'm sorry, Aunt Marie, but I'm not feeling so well. I think I'm getting a migraine. I need to go lay…"

She didn't get to finish her sentence as a thousand black and white lights blocked her vision and her knees started to give out from underneath her. Leaning forward, she quickly put her hands on the desk to steady herself.

"Elise!" she heard her aunt cry out her name as the entire

room spun and then went black.

*****

"Colt, Mace, anyone!"

Colt heard someone's voice shouting as soon as he entered the office. He picked up his pace, his heart racing at the alarm in the woman's tone coming from the direction of Elise's office.

Marie was leaning across the desk, trying desperately to hold onto Elise's arms to keep her from falling to the floor. Elise was slumped over her desk, her eyes closed, her face very pale.

Colt's heart jerked in his chest at the scary sight. He took swift strides around the backside of the desk and pulled Elise up into his arms. In a tone sounding much calmer than he felt, he asked, "What happened, Marie?"

Marie brushed Elise's hair off her forehead as he passed her and walked into the hall.

"I don't know," she responded, following behind him. "She asked me to have lunch with her earlier, so once I'd visited with Nan for a while, I came on over. She mentioned not feeling well, something about a migraine, and when she started to stand up, she suddenly looked very pale. Then she fainted."

Colt stopped at the entryway to the office at the same time Mabel returned from lunch. Upon seeing Elise in his arms, she hovered around him too. "Lord, Colt, what happened to Elise?"

As Marie touched her niece's cheek, a concerned expression on her face, Colt's entire body tensed and his heart raced at the idea of something happening to Elise. When Elise stirred in his arms, he quickly said to Marie, "Call Doc Hanks. Tell him to meet us at the hospital—"

Elise lifted her head from his shoulder and moaned out, "No…hospital. Migraine. Just take me home."

Colt wanted to make sure Elise was okay no matter what she said. He changed his request. "Tell Doc to meet me at my house."

"She'll stay with me," Marie quickly said.

Colt met her steady gaze, his expression resolute. "Marie, your niece and I—" he broke off, took a calming breath then finished in a determined tone. "She's coming home with me."

Marie looked into his eyes for a long moment, assessing him before she nodded in agreement.

As he turned to walk out of the office, Mabel had already picked up the phone.

When they'd been in the car for a few minutes, Elise put her hands to her head, moaning. Colt put a reassuring hand on her thigh and squeezed gently; his fingers on the steering wheel turned white, he gripped it so hard in his worry for her.

"I'm here, Lise," he said in a low tone, while glancing back at the road. His stomach clenched at the sounds of pain she made.

"Stop the car," she mumbled.

As soon as his foot hit the brake, she had the door open and was leaning out throwing up.

Colt felt like someone had kicked him in the gut at the sight. Total helplessness rolled over him as he rubbed her back until she finally stopped retching. When the dry heaves came, she pulled the door shut saying in a pained voice, "I think I'll make it home now."

Elise kept her eyes shut the entire trip. Once he arrived at his home and turned the engine off, she opened her eyes briefly while he lifted her out of the car.

"Go figure it'd take me feeling like death warmed over for you to bring me to your house," she croaked as she closed her eyes once more and laid her head against his neck.

Colt's stomach twisted in guilt at her words. She couldn't be feeling too bad if she could crack a sarcastic joke, right?

"Anything you want, sweetheart," he murmured against her temple, ready to give her the world just to make her better again.

"Now he tells me," came her muffled reply against his chest as he entered his house and climbed the stairs to his bedroom.

As he laid her on his bed and pulled off her boots, Elise threw her arm over her eyes and rasped, "No light, please."

Colt shut the bedroom door, then quickly walked over and pulled the drapes closed on the one window in the room, dousing it in semi-darkness.

Slowly making his way back toward the bed, he sat down beside her and reached for her hand. Giving it a gentle squeeze he started to ask, "Elise, are you sure it's a migr—"

"No talking…peace…quiet," she whispered, her voice sounding hoarse.

"I need to know for sure what's wrong." The doorbell rang downstairs, interrupting his question.

Colt left the room and jogged downstairs. Opening the door, he shook the man's hand standing outside.

"Thanks for coming, Doc," he said in a gruff voice. He glanced upstairs. "She's upstairs. Do what you can for her. She means a great deal to me."

The doctor nodded his gray head and as he proceeded up the stairs, Marie stepped inside.

Her appearance startled Colt. He'd been so focused on getting Elise help he hadn't even seen Marie standing there.

"Sorry, Marie." He gave her a tired smile. "I didn't see you there."

She nodded her understanding. "I told the doc to draw some blood to make sure she doesn't have something else going on that should be treated at a hospital."

Colt nodded his understanding, thankful Marie had thought ahead. Right now his brain wasn't firing on all cylinders. He'd do whatever it took to make Elise well.

"Have a seat," he said, then dropped onto his hunter green sofa and ran his hands over his face.

As she settled into a matching chair and propped her feet

on the ottoman, Marie asked, "Has she been around anyone who was sick lately?"

Colt shook his head. "No. We worked pretty hard yesterday and she was soaked to the bone for a good couple of hours during the storm, but no one I can think of."

They sat in silence for a good ten minutes. The longer the time went on, the more his stomach knotted in worry. Just when he was about to get up and go check on the Doc and Elise, the older man closed the bedroom door and pulled off his stethoscope as he walked down the stairs.

He nodded to Marie first. "I took a vial of blood and will run the limited tests I can to make sure things appear normal."

Glancing at Colt, he continued, "I've given her some painkiller and I'll leave you a couple of samples if she needs more when she wakes up. She'll be out a few hours with what I gave her. If she needs more beyond that, she needs to come see me in my office and we can talk options before I fill out a prescription."

Colt took the samples from him and put them in his pocket as he followed the doctor outside. Once the older man climbed in his car, Colt closed the door, leaned on the frame and put his hand through the open window to shake the doc's hand. "Thanks for coming, Joe, I appreciate it."

Before the man could withdraw his hand, Colt held firm. "Can you give her doctor's orders to stay in bed for a couple of days for me?"

"I can't really do that if all she has in a migraine." He grinned, then winked. "But somehow I'll bet if you worked hard at it, you could convince her to stay in bed for a couple of days." Looking back toward the house he continued, "Elise seems like a fine young woman."

Colt nodded. "She is."

As he turned the key in the ignition, he called out over the rumbling of his car engine, "Take good care of her, Colt."

While Doc drove his utility vehicle down the long drive

and the taillights disappeared as he went over a hill, Colt contemplated the possibility of something happening to Elise.

He'd kept his distance so he'd be prepared when she decided to leave, but the very idea of something happening to her made his stomach clench in fear and left a deep ache in his heart.

When Colt went back inside, he asked Marie, "Would you mind hanging out while I go and collect some things for Elise from her apartment?"

She raised a perfectly arched eyebrow and asked, "Colt Tanner, just how close *are* you and my niece?"

He pulled his hat off the table, set it on his head, and replied in a serious tone, "About as close as two people can get, Marie."

A wide grin crossed her face. "Well then, best you get your butt over to her apartment, young man. It's high time you started livin' life instead of just existing in it."

Thankful for what appeared to be Marie's approval, but knowing the inner turmoil he still fought within himself, Colt resisted the urge to wince at her comment as he headed out the door.

Chapter Fifteen

When Colt arrived back at his house with some necessities for Elise, Marie stood and put her purse on her shoulder saying, "Doc called and said Elise's blood test results were negative for anything abnormal. He said he thinks it probably is just one helluva migraine, but if she didn't feel better by tomorrow to come see him."

Relief shot through him at the knowledge Elise's blood tests didn't show any problems. Setting the duffel bag on the counter, he turned to Marie with a smile. "That's great news."

She smiled then headed for his front door. With her hand on the handle, she looked back at him. "You take care of my niece, ya hear?"

"You're leaving? Aren't you staying until she wakes up?" he asked.

She shook her head. "I trust you'll take excellent care of her. Tell her if she needs me to call me and that I'll be ready for that lunch whenever she is."

After Marie left, Colt quietly entered the room and stood beside the bed, staring at the beautiful woman lying under his quilt. She'd entered his life and turned it upside down before he knew what hit him. No matter what came of his relationship with Elise, one thing he knew for sure...she was his match in every sense of the word, so why did his heart ache and his stomach tense at the knowledge?

Elise stirred and called out in a weak voice, "Colt?"

He answered in a hushed tone, "I'm here, Lise."

She opened her eyes, then closed and opened them again. He could tell she was having trouble focusing on him. The drugs were likely still in her system.

"Lay with me," she whispered.

Colt was already kicking off his boots before she finished her request. God, he wanted to hold her close, to smell her scent, feel her against him—safe and healthy.

He pulled off his shirt, moved the covers and crawled in beside her, tucking her back against his chest. Her sigh of contentment made his heart swell. Damn, he could get used to this.

Running his palm along her hip, he said in a low voice, "Your tests came back fine. Guess you just have a bad migraine."

She mumbled her, "Told you so," and then proceeded to fall back to sleep.

Colt lay there with her pressed against him for an hour, listening to her even breathing, inhaling her scent. She was the best smelling woman. Her innate aroma brought to mind the varied scents of a springtime drive on a lazy Sunday afternoon. Right before sleep overtook him, the realization hit him hard— he'd come to care for Elise very much. This way of life, being a rancher was all he'd ever known—all he ever wanted to do. What would he do when she decided she was tired of ranch living?

* * * * *

Elise awoke, thankful her migraine had faded to a dull headache. She glanced at the red glowing light on the alarm clock on the nightstand. Ten-thirty.

Evening had doused the room into total darkness. A little disappointed she didn't get a chance to "see" Colt's bedroom before nighttime arrived, she rolled over and smiled at the deep breathing sounds he made in his sleep. Sliding quietly out of bed, she took off her fitted button-down shirt and pulled her bra off. Sliding out of her jeans and socks, she made her way around to Colt's side of the bed, looking for something a little less confining.

Smiling, she picked up his discarded white T-shirt and slipped into it, then quietly walked downstairs in the dark. When she spied the French doors along the back side of the house, she opened them wide and strolled out onto the deck.

Frogs croaked and crickets made their own nighttime sounds as she took a deep, inhaling breath and enjoyed the gorgeous view Colt's property allowed of the Lonestar as well as the lights from town off in the distance. Even at night she could still make out the beautiful spread.

Wearing Colt's shirt, his masculine smell surrounding her, Elise wrapped her arms around herself as the cool Texas air blew against her, bringing with it the distinct sound of cows mooing in the distance. Goose bumps formed on her arms and a shiver passed down her spine. She squeezed her eyes shut at the realization that the cold hadn't caused the rush that passed through her...she knew without a shadow of a doubt, she was home.

Warm arms wrapped around her as Colt's bare chest brushed against her back, his heat seeping through the thin cotton of her shirt. The feel of his hard, muscular body pressed against hers, made the sense of completeness and belonging flood through her in waves. Elise couldn't stop the tears that silently rolled down her cheeks.

"Hey there," his deep voice rumbled against her back as he planted a gentle kiss on her neck. "I brought some of your stuff from the apartment. Even remembered your birth control pills. I didn't want you or me to have to worry," he finished with a chuckle. "How's the headache?"

His thoughtfulness pushed her over the emotional edge she'd teetered on. Holding back a sob, she wrapped her arms around his. "It's now down to a dull roar and manageable at least. I'll live."

Colt gave her a gentle squeeze. "You had me really worried."

She laid her head back against his neck. "I'm fine."

He turned her around, cupped her face in his hands, and said, "Hey, I do care—" but he cut himself off when his palms brushed against her wet cheeks.

"Why are you crying? What's wrong, Elise?" His voice sounded urgent, worried.

Why do you cry even harder when someone shows concern? she wondered as she let out the sob she'd been holding back.

Colt swiftly picked her up and walked inside. He sat down on his couch next to the low light on the end table he'd apparently turned on and cradled her in his arms. His body tense, he ran his fingers through her hair and cupped her cheek, rasping, "God, Lise, whatever it is, I'll make it right. Just tell me."

Elise wrapped her arms around his neck and buried her nose under his jaw, giving a watery, embarrassed laugh. "I'm fine, really. I'm just happy the headache is gone, that's all." Now why couldn't she tell him how she really felt? *I just realized how complete my life is here with you. Bock! Bock!* She sniffled at the chicken sounds she heard in her own head.

He smiled and pulled her closer. After a few seconds, he stood with her in his arms and said, "Considering you skipped lunch and dinner, I'll bet you're starving. How about I make you something to eat?"

She looked at him in surprise. "You're cooking for me?"

Colt raised his eyebrow as he lowered her feet to the floor. "What? You don't think I can cook?"

She gave him a doubtful look. "You've never cooked at my place."

"Well, you're at my place now. Have a seat, gorgeous." Colt smacked her on the butt, then gave her a devilish smile as he grabbed her rear before heading off to the kitchen.

As she followed him, Elise winced and drew in a breath when he flipped on several overhead lights. He glanced back at her, apologized and turned them off, then turned on the small light over the stove.

Taking the couple of steps up into the kitchen area, Elise sat down on a tall cushioned barstool behind the counter and put her chin in her hand to watch Colt move around the kitchen.

God, he looked hot with his broad bare chest tapering into a faded pair of jeans that fit his muscular butt to perfection. He'd taken off his boots and socks and was walking around his kitchen barefoot. As her heart raced at the sexy picture he made, Elise's breasts began to swell in response. She pressed her knees together to assuage the throbbing heat that had started between her thighs.

While Colt cracked eggs in a pan, she distracted herself from his stimulating appearance by checking out his home. Scanning past the small oak table and spindle back chairs, she took in the comfy-looking hunter green sofa and matching chair and ottoman that sat in front of a stone fireplace. Her gaze shifted to the large stuffed taupe-colored chair that sat next to the huge picture window. She smiled when she noticed a paperback novel stuck in the side of its seat cushion.

Letting her gaze roam, she followed the wooden stairs upward to a hallway that overlooked the kitchen area. At the top of the stairs she saw two doors. She knew the first bedroom was Colt's, so the other must be a guest room.

Colt had a very nice, cozy home, and neat too, she thought as she realized as she notice there wasn't a bit of trash or discarded clothing laying about.

"Eat up," Colt said, drawing her attention as he set a plate of bacon, eggs and toast in front of her.

While he poured her a glass of juice, she picked up the fork and took a bite. "Wow, I'm impressed."

Colt grinned and came around the bar to sit beside her on another barstool.

"Aren't you going to eat?" she asked, taking another bite.

He shook his dark head and smiled. "Nah, I ate while I was out earlier. Plus, I'm enjoying watching you eat," he finished in a seductive tone.

Elise took another couple of bites and smiled. At the look of pure sexual hunger in his deep blue gaze, she couldn't wait to finish eating. The dull throb in her head competed with the aching throb in her sex as she admired his gorgeous chest and defined abs—obviously her libido won the battle. She wanted Colt to take her to his bed and make love to her.

Setting down her fork, she turned in her seat and faced him. "I think you *are* hungry and you're just being polite on my account." His T-shirt was long on her, but when she sat down the hem had ridden high on her thighs. Hooking her toes on either side of the barstool, she spread her legs and put one elbow on the counter and the other on the back of her chair saying, "See anything you like?" The position pressed her breasts against the cotton fabric, outlining her nipples in the dim light.

His gaze burning, Colt brushed his finger along her inner thigh, past her belly until he reached her nipple. Lightly grazing the nub, his gaze darkened, causing the tip to harden in response. "I was wrong about you in a T-shirt," he murmured.

Elise's heart hammered in her chest at the slightest brush of his finger against her, but his words had her meeting his gaze with a puzzled one.

His lips tilted at the corners in a seductive half smile. "You look best wearing *my* T-shirt."

Liquid heat rushed south and her breathing turned choppy. "I think I'll look best wearing nothing at all, lying in your bed," she bantered with a raised eyebrow.

Colt's nostrils flared and his shoulders tensed, so she knew she'd gotten to him.

He placed his hands on her thighs and quickly pulled them further apart as he stepped off his stool and moved between her legs.

Pulling her shoulders so the tips of her breasts brushed his lower chest, Colt tilted her chin until she met his gaze. "There's nothing I'd rather do than take you to bed and make you moan all night long…"

Elise's heart slammed in her chest at the promise in his words.

"...but it won't be tonight, sweetheart."

She immediately frowned, drawing her brows together. "Huh?"

Colt ran his thumb along her bottom lip, then trailed his fingers down her throat, his deep blue eyes ablaze with suppressed passion.

"I want you to recover first, for that headache to be gone."

Elise stared at him for a long minute, gauging him. He was serious!

Letting her disappointment show, she grumbled, "Only *you* would use the excuse of the 'woman's' headache as a reason to avoid sex."

Grasping her chin, he kept her from turning away as he growled out, "I want to take you right now, right in this chair. But I made a promise to myself to hold back and as much as it's killing me to do so, I *will* wait until you're 100% well, Lise."

She couldn't help the smile on her face as she rode up. "I like when you call me 'Lise'. It's very...intimate."

Colt gave her a sexy grin as he dropped his hand and stepped back. "It's meant to be, darlin'."

He pushed her plate closer to her along with a pill. "Eat and take this so you'll sleep well tonight."

While Elise finished eating, Colt started a fire in the fireplace. When the wood crackled and popped as the fire roared to life, he sat back with one leg bent, his elbow propped on his knee, staring at the fire as if in deep thought.

Elise took her pill then walked over to Colt and touched his shoulder. He immediately pulled her into his arms, settling her between his legs.

"I thought we'd enjoy the fire before we went to bed," he commented softly behind her.

"Oooh, going to bed sounds very nice," she replied with a

grin as she snuggled closer and thrilled at the feeling of his body surrounding hers.

When she felt his erection against her back, she repeated, "Verra nice."

"Don't tempt me," he warned in a strained tone.

"But it's what I do best, according to you." She gave a soft laugh and laid her head against his neck, sighing in contentment.

With everything that had happened, she realized she'd been meaning to ask him about his mother. He seemed relaxed, content. Now would be as good a time as any.

"Why didn't you tell me about your mother?"

Colt's body stiffened behind her and he replied in a curt tone. "There's nothing to tell."

Turning her head, she looked up at him. "But I want to know everything about you."

His hold on her tightened for a brief moment before he ground out, "As far as I'm concerned, my mother is dead. I'll talk about anything you want, Elise, but the subject of my mother isn't something I want to rehash."

Elise returned her gaze to the fire and wrapped her arms around his, giving him a hug. "I understand." But in her heart she knew she had to get Colt to face his demons about his mother's desertion or he'd never look at her any other way. She realized that he saw her as a woman with a similar upbringing as his mother. More than ever she was convinced that was the reason he held back a part of himself from her, that he didn't trust she wouldn't eventually desert him too.

Knowing this about him helped her better understand her own feelings for this complex man. Somehow she had to figure out how to get past the invincible wall he'd built around his heart, because she was the type that gave her all when she finally committed, and she'd be damned if she'd accept anything less from him in return. But that was for another day. For tonight, she'd enjoy their time together.

As she relaxed against Colt and turned her head on his shoulder, the paperback book she'd seen stuck in the chair cushion caught her eye once more.

Leaning to the side, she pulled the fiction book out and discovered to her surprise her lover was a suspense reader.

"As if I don't have enough suspense in my life with a neighbor like Jackson Riley creating havoc from time to time," he said in a dry tone as she thumbed through the paperback.

When she pulled out the newspaper clipping he'd used as a bookmark and unfolded it, Elise couldn't resist chuckling as she glanced up at him in surprise.

"You like crossword puzzles?"

"Doesn't everyone?" he answered with an incredulous expression.

She skimmed the finished crossword puzzle then read some of the questions he'd had to answer. He'd answered questions she wouldn't have known where to start if she'd been working the puzzle.

"And you answered them all, too," she teased.

Colt took the paper and put it back in the book saying with a sheepish expression as he set the book on the floor, "I get a bit compulsive until I get them all."

"Now why doesn't that surprise me." She grinned and put her hand on his neck, kissing his jaw.

Colt looked down at her, his lips hovering over hers, close but not touching. Her heart stopped as his deep blue gaze held hers for a long moment.

As the heat from his warm, naked chest soaked through the thin cotton shirt she wore, her fingers threaded in his hair of their own accord. Their intimate closeness, his masculine smell, and the fire's warmth surrounding her only stoked the heat flaring between them. Elise's breath caught and she closed her eyes, waiting for his kiss.

His five o'clock shadow scraped her cheek when he

whispered in her ear, "If I kiss you, I won't stop until I'm sliding inside your sweet body, darlin'."

The low, husky register of his voice rumbled through her like a seductive growl causing her body to ignite. Elise's eyes flew open and she gasped inwardly at the look of raw hunger reflected in his eyes. She'd never been more turned on in her life at the mere mention of what he wanted but "wouldn't" do to her...at least not tonight. She knew Colt would stand by his word no matter what she told him.

Turning her face back toward the fire, she sighed in disappointment, then said softly, "As long as your arms are around me I'll be happy."

He kissed the top of her head and tightened his hold around her whispering, "Me too, sweetheart."

Elise didn't know how long they sat there in silence, but as her rapid heartbeat settled into a slower rhythm and her eyelids grew heavy from the warmth of the fire, she realized she'd never felt more at peace or in tune with another person in her life.

Chapter Sixteen

Colt awoke the next morning and knew a moment's panic when he reached over to an empty bed beside him. Last night, holding Elise and not touching her the way he'd wanted to was pure torture. He'd wanted to lay her out on the carpet in front of the fire and make love to her until, out of sheer exhaustion, she begged him to stop. When she fell asleep in his arms, he felt a sense of fierce protectiveness steal over him. As he'd carried her to his bed, he knew in his heart...she was his. He realized just how tense he'd been as the end of the summer drew near when he'd taken Elise upstairs and laid her sleeping form on his bed last night.

It was as if a heavy weight lifted off his chest as he undressed her, then stepped out of the rest of his clothes...as if his actions with Elise were a nightly routine. When he'd settled her naked body against his chest and pulled the covers over them, he seemed to breathe easier than he had in a long time.

Now, in the light of morning, he realized that by bringing Elise into his home, into *his* bed, he'd opened up his life and his heart to her. Whether married or not, he knew he'd never let another man touch her, not while he still breathed.

Sitting up, he threw his legs over the side of the bed, ready to go find her when he caught the scent of fresh brewed coffee and bacon wafting through the air. The inviting aroma, the smell of a true "home" made him smile, and he instantly relaxed as he rubbed his hands over his overnight beard and headed for the shower.

After he'd showered and shaved, Colt pulled on a pair of jeans and went looking for his woman. Damn, that sounded good, he thought to himself at the feeling of rightness that settled around him as bit by bit he accepted his feelings for Elise.

* * * * *

Elise stood outside on the deck, cupping a mug of coffee in her hands, enjoying the warmth that seeped from the navy blue ceramic to her skin as she took in the breathtaking view Texas hill country had to offer. Cool moisture still hung in the air and while the wind blew against her damp hair, goose bumps formed on her arms. She smiled when the sun finally broke the horizon. Turning her face to the warm sunshine, she enjoyed the fact that the bright light no longer bothered her and her headache was gone. Running her fingers along the lapel of the navy blue robe she'd donned after finding it buried deep in Colt's closet, she thrilled at the unusual fall-like weather that she knew would dissipate as soon as the sun rose high in the sky.

The matching color of the robe and the mug made her smile. Apparently Colt liked navy. When she awoke early this morning, she'd risen from bed and watched him sleep for a few moments. He'd looked so sexy sprawled across his king-size sleigh bed. The crisp white sheets and navy comforter had slipped down past his slim hips, revealing his gorgeous tanned chest and rock-hard stomach. She'd had to tear her gaze away to finally get a look at his bedroom.

It wasn't a large room with its partially vaulted ceiling and exposed four-by-four wood beams, but he'd decorated well with the space he had. An old rocking chair—an antique she'd bet—sat near the extra wide picture window, a stack of paperback books beside it. The sleigh bed and a matching dresser were made of solid, sturdy oak as well as the chest at the foot of the bed.

With its Spartan feel, it definitely was a man's room, but Elise found she liked the simple style that said so much about Colt.

A sudden tingling sensation zipping down her spine drew her out of her reverie. The sensation that she was being watched felt too strong. Elise turned and her breath caught at the sight of

Colt leaning in the doorway to the house watching her. He had on a pair of faded jeans. The unbuttoned button at the top of his jeans drew her gaze to the sexy line of hair that veed beyond the waistband of his pants.

"How are you feeling?" he asked from across the deck as if he couldn't trust himself to come near her until he heard her answer.

She smiled and said, "Great." Her heart hammered in her chest as he approached, the look in his steel blue eyes intense and dark.

Taking the mug from her hands, he didn't say a word as he set it on the railing. Oh, but his eyes held hers and told her exactly what he wanted. Her stomach clenched as he took her hand and led her to the Adirondack lounge chair behind her. Elise sat down on the chair and leaned back. Colt straddled the chair facing her.

When his long, warm fingers encircled her ankles and set her heels on his hard thighs, her body began to ignite. Elise didn't think she could be more turned on by the sight of Colt's steady regard as he slowly slid his hands up her legs until he reached her inner thighs. He applied pressure and she let her legs fall against the arms of the chair, sighing in anticipation of his next move.

Colt's lips quirked upward in a brief, sexy smirk as he pulled the belt around her waist. But when the knot loosened and the robe parted slightly, exposing her cleavage and a line of creamy flesh down the middle of her body, his smile faded. His gaze darkened and his nostrils flared as he pushed the robe out of the way, exposing her naked flesh to his view.

Elise's body burned as his gaze slid over her exposed skin. The cool air didn't even faze her, she was so caught up in all that was Colt as he laid a warm hand on her stomach and another on her inner thigh.

While his fingers trailed down her thigh to tease her dark curls between her legs, he said in a gravely voice, "Last night, as

I pulled your naked body against mine, it was one of the hardest things I'd ever done—being a gentleman and not touching you the way I wanted to."

The seductive tone of his words made a shiver pass through her. Elise started to speak but her words turned to a gasp of pure pleasure when Colt thrust a finger deep inside her. Rocking her hips as he withdrew and thrust back in, she bit her lower lip before panting out, "Take me. I'm yours."

Rubbing his thumb over her clit while he added another finger to the first one, Colt raised one eyebrow, his expression cocky and self-assured. "You're already mine, darlin'."

Elise couldn't answer as he thrust even deeper, taking her heart rate higher. Instead, she gripped the arms on the chair, closed her eyes in sheer sexual bliss, and pushed against his thighs with her feet as her walls began to contract around his fingers.

Riding the waves of her orgasm as long as she could, she sighed in contentment when he withdrew his hand from her body and put her feet on the chair. Elise opened her eyes to see Colt standing over her, his hand held out to her.

She put her hand in his and stood. Colt slid the robe off her body and laid it down on the deck's floor, making his intentions very clear.

She grinned, then laid down on the floor. But when she turned over on her back, she inhaled sharply at the seductive picture before her.

Colt stood over her, his intense expression raking down her body. He unbuttoned his pants all the way, his movements slow and unhurried. When he slipped his jeans down his muscular thighs and his hard erection sprang forward, her heart rate jumped tenfold. She swallowed the gasp that threatened to escape her lips. No need to give him a big head...one swollen one was enough, she thought with an inward chuckle.

All humor fled from her thoughts as Colt moved over her. She barely had time to put her hands on his shoulders before he spread her thighs and slid inside her body in one swift thrust.

Elise gasped in surprise at his aggressive possession, her lungs taking in the morning breeze blowing around them. Colt thrust deeper and then stayed buried, his gaze locking with hers.

His shoulders and back muscles tensed while he supported his weight above her, then said in a husky, barely controlled tone, "Your body feels so right wrapped around me." He paused and dipped his nose to her neck, inhaling her scent before he continued, "A sweet-smelling, perfect fit."

Her stomach flip-flopped at his sexy comment. Sliding her hands up his muscular shoulders, she ran her fingers through his damp hair at the nape of his neck as he lowered his head to her chest.

When he sucked her nipple into his mouth, she arched her back and moaned, reveling in the feeling of his hard body pressed against hers while the warm sun shined down on them. The completeness she felt with him buried inside her, the surety that he *wanted* her here with him, made her bold.

"I want you to make love to me, Colt," she said in a breathless voice as his teeth grazed the pink tip, then bit down gently.

Colt lifted his head and met her gaze, his own intemperate and raw, the hunger so palpable she could almost feel his desire emanating off his skin in heated waves under her fingers.

She let out a cry of dismay when he withdrew from her body, but she sighed in sheer bliss when his lips brushed against her sex.

Colt used his teeth and lips and tongue in perfect tandem to drive her to the edge, only to let her heart calm before he started the same buildup of arousal within her all over again. As her stomach tensed in anticipation for the third time, Elise grabbed his head and held him close, bucking against him, panting as her heart raced out of control.

"Colt," she begged between rapid breaths. Her sex throbbed and her thighs began to tremble from the physical need to climax.

His sapphire gaze met hers, deep unfathomable emotions churning behind them. "No others, Lise. Only me," he ground out as he slid a finger inside her.

Elise knew what Colt meant. He was committing as much as he emotionally could. She'd take what she could…for now. Her muscles contracted around his finger, but she whimpered with need for the thickness only his body could provide.

With a determined expression, Colt moved and leaned over her as he turned his finger and pressed on her trigger spot deep inside. "Tell me," he demanded, his tone sounding harsh, ragged.

Elise reached between their bodies and wrapped her hand around his erection. "You tell me first," she insisted.

He withdrew his hand and shifted, pressing his erection against her entrance. For a long, agonizing moment he held her gaze as he hovered above her. When he finally slid inside her, the completeness of the act wrung a low, keening moan from her as he seated himself fully inside her.

"There are no others for me." He withdrew and slowly slid back inside, connecting his body with hers.

Elise's heart pounded at his statement. She clasped him to her and whispered in his ear, "No others for me either, Cowboy."

* * * * *

While Colt spent all day on the ranch helping the rodeo crew prepare the animals and equipment for another long stint of rodeo travel, Elise worked in the office with Mace, bringing him up to speed on the online store and her suggestions for bundled merchandise and upgraded rodeo paraphernalia.

They worked for several hours as they bounced thoughts and suggestions back and forth, further refining her business plan. After they ate a quick lunch at their desks, Elise and Mace got back to work until they both agreed on a plan that met his advertising and aesthetic vision for the website and her needs as part owner and web developer. A couple of hours later, she sat back and smiled after she completed the finishing touches on the changes to the website.

"Not bad, Elise," she complimented herself, proud of her work.

"Let me see," Mace called out from the doorway as he proceeded to walk around behind her desk and look at the website.

As she clicked through the purchasing process, Mace nodded his approval with a broad smile.

"What the hell did we ever do without you?" he commented as he sat down on the corner of her desk facing her.

"Limped along," she quipped. "By the way, did you ask George if he'd be willing to man the booth for a couple of hours each rodeo?"

Mace laughed. "Didn't take much convincing when I told him he'd get a raise." Rubbing his chin, he continued, "Good idea on putting a brochure about the online store in each customer's bag. That should get the word out there and help boost future sales."

"Why thank you," she replied. "I do try my best."

"And then some," Mace said as he stood and shoved his hands in his back pockets. "Time to shut down your computer now."

She glanced at her watch then gave him a what-the-heck-are-you-talking-about look. "It's only three-thirty."

Mace leaned over and moved her mouse, clicking the shutdown sequence saying, "Colt asked me to look out for you today since he's not in the office."

"I'm not a baby. I'm fully capable of knowing when I've reached my limit," she replied, indignant that these Tanner men thought to coddle her.

Laughing, Mace reached for the clip in her hair and opened

it. As her hair fell down her back, he said, "Nah, darlin', we just want you to let your hair down a little earlier today." Handing her the clip, his green eyes twinkled in amusement. "Actually, I thought you might like to help Nan out today."

Elise perked up while she followed Mace out of her office. "Help Nan?"

"Yeah, Nan's preparing the farewell dinner for the entire rodeo crew tonight. The guys usually eat a big meal and then go out to Rockin' Joe's for dancing and carousing before they have to head out on the road again. Marie's been in the kitchen with Nan since this morning."

She grinned as they walked outside. "Guess you talked me into it. It'll be good to catch up with my aunt while I help Nan."

Elise pulled open the kitchen screen door. Inviting smells wafted toward her. *Mmmm, smoked…something*, she thought as she walked inside with Mace right behind her. Nan and Marie sat at the table, breaking the ends off string beans.

"Hi sweetie," her aunt called out, patting the chair next to her. "I'm glad to see you're feeling better today."

Elise sat down and picked up a handful of green beans. Snapping the ends off of a couple, she threw the beans in the pot in the center of the table and answered, "Yes, thank goodness my migraine went away. That was just miserable. I haven't had a migraine like that since I was a teenager."

"Mace," Nan called out. She got up from the table and whacked him on the butt, as he bent over her pot of beans, then put the spoon to his mouth for a taste. "Unless you plan on stayin' and helpin' cook, get your rear out of here."

Mace grinned and put the spoon down in the spoon rest on the stove. "Guess that's my cue to leave. Colt'll be chasin' me down soon enough to help out."

After Mace left, Marie glanced up from snapping beans. "Just how hot and heavy are you and Colt, Elise?"

Elise laughed. "Going straight to the point, aren't ya, Aunt Marie."

Her aunt gave an unapologetic shrug. "When you get to be my age, dear, you learn the value of being direct."

Elise sighed while Nan stirred the beans and added more pepper to them. "Let's just say Colt and I...well, we care for each other. To be honest, I'm not sure where we're going, but I just wish he didn't have such a bad history with his mom. I believe that's one of the reasons why he's still holding a part of himself back."

Nan sat back down at the table with a paring knife and began peeling an apple. "He had to grow up faster than most young men when his momma left his daddy. Stuff like that can stick with you for a very long time," she finished in a philosophical voice. "Not only did he have to become a man quickly, but when his father died, he gave up his career in the rodeo and took on the role of a second father to his brothers too." Her chocolate brown eyes met Elise's across the table. "He's a good man. If anyone can help him get over his past, you can."

Elise shook her head. "I don't know, Nan. His feelings run pretty deep about his mom. I think with my background, he sees me as a woman just like her. He seems to fight a constant internal battle to trust his heart and me."

"There's a saying, 'Time heals all wounds.' What I say is, 'What time doesn't heal, the need to survive, to move on and be happy, will take care of the rest.'"

"Very well put, Nan," Marie agreed with a nod. "Colt will come around."

"I hope you're both right—that Colt will eventually let go of his past. I'd really like to be a part of his future, but I won't settle for anything less than his total trust in me and us."

* * * * *

Dinner was a complete success. Nan had set the meal up in the formal dining room, taking advantage of the bigger table. The fancier digs didn't stop the rodeo crew from being on their rowdiest behavior. Elise *loved* it! They were in high spirits as they passed around the bowls of food and told rodeo stories about Cade and even some about Colt.

She sat next to Colt and, near the end of the meal, while he ate his apple pie and ice cream, he laid his hand on her thigh under the table. It was a thoroughly intimate gesture, meant to be private, but the warmth of his hand, the feel of his fingers cupping her inner thigh affected her.

As she'd taken a bite of her own dessert and some of the ice cream dripped from the spoon to her lip, Colt surprised her when he ran his finger along her bottom lip, then sucked the ice cream off his finger. She'd been so caught up in his smoldering, deep blue eyes staring at her mouth that it took a moment for her to realize the entire table had gone quiet as they watched her and Colt.

Embarrassed to return her gaze to Colt and with heat rising up her cheeks, Elise picked up their empty plates and carried them into the kitchen.

While she scraped off their plates, she smiled when she heard Colt giving a send-off speech for the crew. He was a *good* man. One she was proud to know.

"He's a good man," a deep voice came from behind her, echoing her thoughts and startling her from her reverie.

She turned to look into Cade's indigo blue eyes. "I couldn't agree more."

His dark gaze narrowed for a moment as if he were assessing her again. She could tell trust didn't come easily for him either.

"I wanted to say goodbye before I headed out," he said in a gruff voice.

Awww, these *tough* Tanner men made her want to take care of them all. With her emotions running high, Elise impulsively reached over and hugged Cade. His body stiffened when her arms encircled his neck, making her realize she must have made him uncomfortable. As she started to pull away, Cade's arms came around her and he gave her a tight hug, pulling her full against his body. He whispered in her ear, "He's a tough sonofabitch at times, but my brother's got a heart of gold. I hope you're here permanently when I return at the end of rodeo season."

Elise didn't know what to say. She pulled back with tears in her eyes and a tremulous smile on her lips. Cade gave her one of his rare, devastating smiles and said, as he chucked her gently on the chin, "I've always wanted a sister." Turning on his booted heel, he walked out of the kitchen, leaving her thoroughly speechless.

Nan and Marie joined her in the kitchen to help clean up while Colt said goodbye to everyone. When Colt came in the kitchen twenty minutes later, he took the dishtowel from Marie and said, "I'll take over. Why don't you stay the night? Nan will make up a room for you."

"Thanks Colt, but I like to sleep in my own bed," Marie said as she walked up to hug Elise goodbye.

"Where's Mace?" Elise asked Colt with a grin, knowing Mace would do anything to avoid kitchen duty.

Colt snorted. "Where do you think? He's gone over to Rockin' Joe's with the rest of the boys to send everyone off with 'a proper goodbye,' so he says."

"I'm heading out since the reinforcements have come. Take care, sweetie," her aunt said. She hugged Elise and kissed her on the cheek. "I'll come visit again in a couple of days and I'll bring my cruise pictures with me next time."

"You do that," she encouraged then walked her aunt to the door.

After Marie left, Elise joined Colt at the sink. The sight of him rolling up his chambray shirtsleeves, revealing his tanned arms, the veins and muscles in them, drew her attention and appreciation. She smiled and turned to the sink when Nan added another pot to the suds. While they worked, Elise teased Colt about several of the rodeo stories the crew had told about him. Colt tried to distract her with whispered suggestions of what he wanted but still hadn't had a chance to do to her.

A knock at the screened back door had Nan, Colt and Elise looking at each other in surprise. It was eight-thirty at night.

Colt set down the towel and moved to the door. When his entire framed stiffened, Elise knew something was wrong.

"Hello, Colt. You look a lot like your daddy," a woman spoke through the screen.

Colt's face turned to stone and he replied in a cold voice, "What are you doing here, Sharon?"

Chapter Seventeen

Whoa! Elise thought, her heart jerking in her chest. *Colt's long-lost mother showing up out of the blue?*

"I tried to knock on the front door, but no one answered, so I came around to the kitchen door." She gave a soft laugh. "Some things never change."

Colt folded his arms over his chest, an impassive expression on his face. "Why are you here?"

She gave an exasperated sound. "Aren't you at least going to invite me in?"

"No—" Colt started to answer, but Elise decided she'd better intervene.

"Of course he is," she replied brushing past Colt and pushing the screen door open.

As the tall, elegant woman with dark hair showing the beginnings of gray walked inside, Elise put out her hand, "I'm Elise Hamilton."

"Sharon Tanner," the woman replied, her expression wary as she assessed Elise.

Nodding to Nan she said, "Hello again, Nan."

"*Harumph*," Nan snorted and turned to put a pot in the cabinet.

"You didn't answer my question, Sharon." Colt's voice sounded cold, emotionless.

When Sharon smoothed her hand over her bob haircut, the gesture told Elise just how nervous she was despite her aloof appearance.

"I received a phone call the other day from a woman who told me the ranch was being sold."

Who the heck called? Elise wondered, but when she met Colt's gaze, she realized they both knew the answer. *May.*

Sharon continued, "The woman said if I had anything I wanted to keep, I'd better come claim it."

Elise's heart jumped at Sharon's words and her spirits soared for Colt.

"I have some things…a couple of family antiques I left behind I wanted to collect," Sharon continued, dashing Elise's hopes that she'd come back to see her boys…to make amends for deserting her family.

"Get your stuff," Colt ground out, turning away from her as he dropped his arms.

"I was hoping…that is…well, I just flew in and I drove all the way out here. My flight out isn't until tomorrow morning. Can I stay here?"

"No," Colt unequivocally replied, turning to face his mother once more.

Elise stepped between them, her back to Colt. "Of course you can stay one night. Colt wouldn't turn you out."

"Like hell I wouldn't," he ground out from behind her.

Elise's temper began to rise. He may resent his mother, but she'd been raised with certain manners and with his emotions riding high, he seemed to have forgotten his…common decency and all.

She turned to face him and said in a calm tone, "Colt, surely she can spend one night before she has to leave tomorrow morning."

Colt's hands were balled into tight fists, his entire body tightly wound. He looked down at her, his expression livid. "No."

Sighing, she turned back to Sharon. "You were misinformed. The ranch is not being sold. As part owner of the Lonestar I say you can stay one night—"

She'd barely gotten the words out of her mouth before she

heard the back door slam behind her. She glanced back to see Colt had walked out.

"Thank you," Sharon said in a quiet voice, drawing her attention.

Elise faced her. "I didn't do that for you. I did it because it was the way I was raised."

A sad, disappointed look crossed the woman's face, making Elise feel guilty. She had no reason to dislike this woman other than the hurt she'd caused her sons and their father.

Tempering her voice to a lighter tone, she responded, "I believe it would be best if you collected your belongings and left before Colt arrives to work on the animals in the morning."

Turning she started to ask, "Nan, would you show—"

"I'll show Sharon to the *guest* bedroom," Nan interrupted in a disgruntled tone.

Oh boy, Elise thought. Not only had she pissed off Colt, she'd also alienated a woman she'd come to respect. She knew Nan thought of the Tanner boys as her very own. Elise hoped Nan would eventually forgive her.

* * * * *

Feeling very sad, Elise walked outside. She felt for Colt, for what he'd been through in his life. How would she feel if the situation was reversed? Yeah, she'd be pissed, but she'd want someone whose emotions weren't so closely involved to keep her from being a complete ass. Noting Colt's truck was missing, she ran to the office, collected her purse and keys, and climbed in her car.

She wondered where he would go as she drove down the ranch's long driveway. More than likely he wouldn't go to the bar because he was in a thunderous mood. Home. He'd go home.

Turning in the direction of his ranch, she stiffened her spine, unsure what kind of reception she'd get from him. Her stomach knotted when she thought of the fact that Colt had just started to open up a bit to her right before this happened.

Sighing, she gripped the wheel and thought of a statement her Aunt Marie had made about relationships. "Every relationship has its ups and downs. It's the weathering the storms that shows the true strength of the relationship in the end." Elise knew that as strong-willed as she and Colt both were, they'd have many storms to weather, but she also believed in their relationship. She hoped Colt did too.

When she pulled up to Colt's house, she turned off her engine and lights. Her heart sank to see the entire place pitch-dark. She got out, peeked in the garage window, and saw it was empty. Where was he?

Feeling depressed, she walked back to her car. As she opened the door, she glanced at the house then let her gaze scan the surrounding property. When she spotted a large shadow out in the field behind Colt's house, her heart leapt. It had to be Colt's truck.

She walked around the house and approached his vehicle, her stomach in knots. Colt sat on the toolbox, leaning against the window inside the back of his truck.

Elise walked up to the truck and put her hand on the side, looking up at him. He didn't turn or even acknowledge her presence. Just when she started to say something, he spoke.

"I've spent all my life forgetting about her, resentful that she left my dad, hurt him the way she did. But the hardest damn thing was having to comfort Mace whenever he got hurt or had a bad nightmare and cried for her, or to try to reason with Cade when he got in fights at school just for fighting's sake." He paused and sighed heavily. "Thank God my brothers weren't here tonight."

The bitterness in his voice conveyed the heavy weight of responsibility he must've carried. It tore at her heart. Guilt swept over her as she swiped silent tears away.

"Colt, I'm sorry for your past. I can't change it, though I

wish I could. You're a good, honorable man and I know you well enough to know that in your heart you would've felt like a heel if you had turned your mother out, no matter what she'd done. So I took the heat. *I* became the bad guy. That's what—" she paused over the word, not knowing best how to categorize their relationship, "partners do. They look out for one another."

When he didn't look at her but kept staring into the woods, Elise took a deep breath and climbed up into the back of the truck until she stood directly in front of him.

Colt didn't look up at her but instead stared at the center of her chest, an impassive expression on his face.

Elise squatted down and put her hands on his knees. Looking up at him, she let her emotions for him pour into her words, "I care what happened to that young teenage boy in the past, but I care more about the man you are today and the person you'll become in the future."

Colt looked down at her, the night shadows hiding the expression in his eyes. Elise's hands felt clammy and her heart rammed in her chest as she awaited his response. Had she totally destroyed the tenuous trust they'd worked so hard to build with one another?

Without a word he swiftly pulled her between his legs and speared his fingers through her hair. She set her knees on the floor of the truck as he cupped the back of her head and pressed her head against his chest, burying his nose in the thick mass of hair between his fingers.

Elise clung to his waist, snuggling as close as their position would allow. Tension flowed from her body as she pressed her nose against his shirt and inhaled his fresh, masculine scent.

Colt reached over and slid one of the windows open to pull out a blanket from the backseat of his truck. Elise helped him spread the soft, thick material out across the truck's bed. When he laid down on it to stare up into the sky, she crawled up beside him and settled her head on his shoulder.

He gathered her in his arms and finally spoke, "Whenever I

felt my lowest, I'd walk to an open pasture and lay down in the grass. While I stared up into the stars, I thought about all the people who had lived and died before me and basically gave myself a pep talk about how my lot in life could be worse. I still had my dad and my brothers. We had our health and we weren't dirt poor."

After that, Colt didn't speak again. She understood. He was sharing his time with her—time he normally sorted things out in his mind, alone. She ran her hand over the hard planes of his chest, giving him the best comfort she could—closeness and companionship.

* * * * *

Colt awoke to the sound of birds chirping, his clothes damp from the overnight dew. The sun was just beginning to peek over the horizon. As he sat up, he rolled his shoulders and pressed his hands against his sore lower back. Sleeping in the back of his truck wasn't the most comfortable bed he'd ever slept on, but holding Elise was certainly the best way he could remember falling asleep when he was troubled.

For a brief moment, seeing the truck bed empty, he felt that old feeling creep into his consciousness, making his stomach pitch. Tensing, he shook off the sense of desertion that threatened to consume him. In his heart he knew he'd find Elise somewhere on the ranch. Rubbing his hands down his face and over his stubble, he thought about the woman he'd come to love.

Last night, as she lay there with him, he admitted to himself just how much he loved Elise. The thought made him almost sick to his stomach—not the idea of loving her but what openly loving her would do to his own vulnerability, when he finally admitted his feelings out loud. Somehow, not admitting to Elise how he felt had given him a sense of control and even now, the thought of telling her still scared him. But he would tell her he loved her. Today.

* * * * *

Elise had slept fitfully because she'd wanted to wake up before Colt. She'd showered and dressed at his house before she headed to the ranch, intending to get there in time to say goodbye to Colt's mother. She had a feeling Sharon wouldn't be receiving a warm send-off from Nan.

Right as she drove up in front of the ranch house, Sharon was walking out to her car. Elise got out of her car and made her way over to the older woman's rental car as she opened the door. "Does your flight leave this early?"

Sharon sighed and turned her blue eyes — the same color as Colt's — her way. "No, but I figure sitting in the airport for a couple of hours is better than the alternative if I wait around here."

Elise nodded her understanding and held the door as Sharon got in the vehicle. Once she closed the door, Colt's mother rolled down the window and leaned out with her hand extended.

When Elise took her hand and the older woman pressed something in her hand, she glanced at his mother in surprise.

"Colt won't accept this from me any time soon and may never."

Elise looked down at the silver antique pocket watch in her hand. She glanced back up as Sharon continued, "Regardless of your motives, you've shown me a kindness I didn't expect to see on this visit, so I feel leaving the watch with you may eventually get it to Colt. I have regrets in my life. Three of them live right here in Texas, but the one thing I wish I had done was try harder to see them."

Elise's heart raced at Sharon's words. Gripping the watch tight, she asked, "You tried to see your sons?"

Sharon nodded slowly. "Several times, but their father forbade me. Technically, I could have gotten a court order, but in the end I realized he spoke the truth, at least while they were young and my leaving was so new. He told me I'd be doing more harm than good, unless I planned on coming back to stay."

She frowned and brushed her hair away from her face. "After a while I just stopped asking. When several years had passed, I was afraid to ask…afraid of the rejection I would receive."

She glanced at the watch in Elise's hand, a poignant look on her face. "That watch belonged to my father. He passed away two years ago and I know he would want his eldest grandson to have it. Please make sure Colt gets it."

Elise's chest felt tight, her heart breaking as she held back the tears that threatened. To think Colt had carried his emotional baggage around as long as he did when his mother had been out there waiting for him but was too afraid to approach him after all this time. She bit her lip and nodded her agreement.

Sharon gave her a sad smile and started the engine. "Goodbye Elise. It was nice to meet you."

Elise watched the car's taillights going down the driveway as she slipped the pocket watch into her jeans' pocket.

* * * * *

Colt arrived at the ranch, his shoulders tight with pent-up tension. He wanted to find Elise right away to tell her how he felt, but even though it was Saturday, the early morning chores around the ranch still needed to be done first. As he headed for the stables, he admitted to himself he was thankful for the reprieve.

He'd been working for half an hour when Mace walked into the stall. He was carrying a pitchfork full of fresh hay.

"Hey ya, bro," he said in a lighthearted tone as he dumped the hay. "How's it goin'?"

Colt leaned on his own pitchfork and eyed Mace. His little brother never volunteered for stall duty. Too many years of having to do it as a kid had set him against it.

Rubbing the back of his gloved hand across his jaw, Colt said, "Nan talked to you this morning, didn't she?"

Mace glanced up from moving a pitchfork full of hay.

"Yeah, she told me." Setting down his pitchfork, he adopted the same position as Colt. "So, what's going on in that head of yours?"

Mace always was the one willing to talk things out. Drove Colt nuts when *he* was that one who was supposed to be the "dad". Sometimes he thought Mace was much better equipped to deal with his mother's desertion than he was. Then again, he was the one who'd comforted Mace for many years when his mom wasn't there. Life was all about balance, Colt thought.

"Not much to say," he said in a gruff tone as he commenced working.

"And Elise?" Mace prodded, concern lacing his tone.

Colt stopped working and looked at his brother. "Is the best damn thing to happen to me in a very long time."

Mace gave him a broad smile. "That's what I wanted to hear."

When he turned to walk out of the stall, Colt called out, "Hey, get your lazy ass back in here and finish the job. At least let me 'believe' you didn't come in here on a fishing expedition."

He looked down, hiding his grin as Mace sighed heavily and came back in the stall to help.

"Just like old times, eh, little brother?" he looked up, teasing.

Colt chuckled when Mace gave a disgruntled snort in response.

* * * * *

After he finished his chores, Colt's spirits were high. Even if he was still tense, he left the stables to go find Elise. As he exited the stables, his heart lurched and he stopped dead in his tracks at the site before him.

Elise stood leaning on the fence in a similar position she was in the first day he met her. But this time, she wasn't alone. This time a man had his hand on her neck, massaging it as if he'd done it a million times. Then he pulled her close and kissed her temple.

Colt's blood boiled as he took in the city slicker and his red sports car. The man stood a good foot taller than Elise. He had short, dark brown hair and was dressed in tan slacks and a white button-down shirt. Yep, the man definitely looked out of place on his ranch. Colt wondered if he'd break some kind of law if he punched the man for daring to touch his woman before he kicked him off his ranch.

Colt walked up behind Elise and her guest, saying, "Mornin' Lise." He kept his voice calm when all he really wanted to do was yank the man's hand away from her. To be faced with the reality of someone else touching Elise was an experience he wasn't prepared to handle.

"Colt!" Elise said as she jumped at his voice. Shrugging out of the man's hold, she turned to introduce him. "Colt, this is Jason Richardson. He just arrived from D.C. Jason is —"

"Her fiancé," the man supplied with a pleased grin. He held out his hand to Colt.

At the man's statement, Colt felt like his head was going to explode. Anger rolled through him in such relentless waves, he didn't hear what Elise said. Ignoring Jason's hand, he folded his arms over his chest and scowled. "I wasn't aware Elise had a fiancé."

Elise frowned at Jason, then elbowed him in his ribs. "Quit trying to rehash old stuff, Jason."

The man gave her an indulgent smile. "You know as well as I do we're a perfect match. Now that the summer is coming to an end, your rebellious days are over, honey. It's time to come home and take on the responsibilities you've avoided as long as I've known you. Your father planned to announce our engagement at the party next week."

"Rebellious?" she said, anger obvious in her tone.

Why didn't she argue the fact he'd said he was her fiancé? Colt wondered. That's because there's some freakin' truth to it, he realized.

Jason's expression turned skeptical. "Hmmm, let's see. When you graduated from college you took off to Europe instead of joining your father's company. Then, when you finally came back, you disappointed your dad again when you accepted a job with that start-up dot com company—"

"That was my decision to make. It's my life," she interrupted, her voice rising. She didn't give a flip who overheard their argument.

"He wanted you to be the Chief Information Officer," Jason argued, incredulous.

"Then *you* take the position. A piece of my father's business is all you and your father want anyway," she replied, crossing her arms over her chest with a mutinous expression on her face.

"That's bullshit and you know it, Elise," he replied in an angry tone. "We're good together, always have been. It's time you grew up and settled. No more," he paused and swept his gaze over the ranch before finishing in a mocking tone, "pet projects."

"You're as bad as my father," she said as she uncrossed her arms. "I'm not coming home with you."

"Don't forget your financial obligation," he reminded her.

Her cheeks turned hot at the reminder she'd yet to come up with the money she'd promised to the charity. "That's none of your business."

"As your future husband, it's entirely my business," he countered. "Keeping your promise is a reflection on my reputation as well. Mr. Riley's offer was higher for your share of this ranch. I think you should take it. There's your financial solution and then some."

"What the hell are you doing snooping in my personal paperwork?" she raised her voice.

"Hey, since you've apparently turned off your answering machine and you don't answer your cell phone, I needed to find out exactly where this ranch was so I could talk to you. Your dad handed me the paperwork."

"Which I'm sure he was ever so happy to do," she replied in a sarcastic tone.

"Enough," Colt barked. Grasping Elise's upper arm, he said in a cold tone, "We need to talk. Now."

Jason put a restraining hand on her shoulder and cast him an annoyed look. "She's not going anywhere. I came here to talk to her."

Colt's gaze dropped to Jason's hand, his stare emotionless, deadly. "Remove your hand, Yank, or I'll remove it for you."

"Colt!" Elise admonished, shocked at his tone and rude behavior. Her stomach had tightened into a hard knot at the complete change in Colt's demeanor. Granted, Jason was pissing her off and his comments were probably making Colt wonder, but sheesh! What was up with these men?

He released her arm, his expression stony as he turned and walked away. When Colt rounded the barn's corner, she glanced at Jason. "I'll be back in a minute. While I'm gone you'd better come to terms with the fact once and for all I'm not going to marry you."

Her heart raced as she walked at a brisk pace to catch up to Colt. No way was she going to run to find him. He could stew for a minute or two.

When she came around the corner of the barn, Colt stood there, his arms crossed, an impassive look on his face. Her heart lurched as she feigned a relaxed position against the barn. She felt anything but calm, but she didn't want him to know how much his current attitude scared her. "What's got you all riled up?"

Before she could blink, Colt closed the distance between then and pressed his hands against the barn wall on either side of her, caging her in. Stormy blue eyes locked with hers and he demanded, "What the fuck is going on? I knew I should've trusted my instincts to stay away from you. Not only are you pretty much promised to another, but you've been playin' screw the cowboy in more ways than one, haven't you?"

Outrage swept over her, making her cheeks grow hot. Elise balled her hands into fists and before she realized what she was doing, she punched Colt in the gut and hissed out in a low voice, "How dare you accuse me of anything but good intentions, Colt Tanner."

Colt let out a grunt when she punched him, but he still managed to rile her even more as he continued as if he weren't affected by her hit, "I call 'em like I see 'em, Princess. Playtime is over. You can go back to your *fiancé* now."

Princess? If he was back to calling her that, it wasn't a good sign. "What the hell do you mean 'I'm trying to screw you'?" She crossed her arms over her chest, frowning up at him.

"Why didn't you tell me about Riley's offer?"

Understanding dawned and she shrugged. "There was no reason to tell you. He contacted me in Virginia and I just assumed he wanted to buy the land. When I turned him down, I had no idea the large role the Lonestar land played in the history between you and your neighbor until Nan filled me in on the details the day May sabotaged the fence."

"And your fiancé? How'd that tidbit slip your memory while you were sleeping with me?" he bit out, his tone rough, accusing.

"Because there was nothing to tell," she replied with a stubborn tilt of her chin. "Ever since Jason and I were kids, our fathers wanted us to marry, to merge the family businesses. Yes, Jason and I dated several years ago, but that's the past." She paused, then said with conviction, "I don't do something just because I'm expected to. I never have and I never will."

Meeting his gaze head-on, she decided to throw her own question his way. "Not that I had to tell you all that, but what this all boils down to is...you either trust me or you don't. Which is it going to be?"

Colt narrowed his eyes for a second before he turned on his heel and walked toward the stables, leaving her leaning against the barn.

Her heart sank that he could mistrust her so completely. Obviously, she understood where his distrust came from, but she'd be damned if she'd be the brunt of it. Shoving her hands in her pockets, she took deep breaths to calm herself as anger and deep hurt flowed through her.

Chapter Eighteen

Colt strode past Jason and headed straight for the stables. Saddling Scout, he mounted his horse and took off at a fast gallop toward the open pastures. As the hot wind whipped against his face, rage welled inside him, making his chest burn and his stomach tighten painfully.

He'd never felt so frustrated, disillusioned and...scared. Slowing his horse down to a trot, he realized just how terrified he was of the idea of Elise deserting him, leaving him behind. What if she left with Jason? His gut clenched at the idea that she and Jason had a past. He didn't want to think of her making love with anyone else.

Jason had known her for years and had pretty much spelled out her nomadic ways. The longer she'd stayed, the more Colt had held onto the hope she planned to live in Texas permanently. But the knowledge there was a real possibility she'd get bored and want to move on hit him hard.

While he was grappling with that and then heard Jason encourage her to sell her half of the ranch to Riley, he thought for sure he'd lose it right then and there. Not only was the man trying to take his woman, but his livelihood too? Being hit with this all at once was like a one-two punch. Colt's shoulders tensed as he gripped the reins until his knuckles turned white.

When Elise first came to Texas he'd offered her everything he could afford to buy her out. Now that she needed cash, he didn't know if he could compete financially with Riley. Frustration mounted as he gazed up at his house sitting atop the hill. Well, almost everything.

* * * * *

On Monday, Elise sat in her office staring at her computer. She'd had several false starts on putting the final touches to the virtual store she'd created. Her mind was definitely elsewhere. After Colt left her on Saturday, she'd gone back to Jason and told him unequivocally she had no plans to move back to Virginia. He'd tried to give her a guilt trip, but she sent him home, telling him she'd meet her financial obligation for the charity in a few days time. Then she'd spent that evening and the entire next day alone in her apartment. Missing Colt.

Every time the phone rang she jumped to answer it. Poor Josh. He'd called to return her phone call to him that she'd made while he was at his conference. She'd thanked him for calling her back but couldn't muster much energy for lively conversation with him. He'd even tried to get her to go out again, but she'd refused his offer.

After hanging up with a disappointed Josh, she decided to just let the answering machine get it if it wasn't Colt. She'd even avoided her father's phone call that way. Colt had never called.

Elise let out a deep sigh and shook herself out of her sad musings. What a sucky rest of her weekend. She glanced at her watch for the hundredth time, wondering where the heck Colt was. It was almost lunchtime and not at all like Colt to show up on the ranch late. Mace had taken off to travel with the rodeo for a couple of days to make sure George was up to speed on running the paraphernalia stand. She and Mace had agreed to hold off on starting up the online store until right before the last few rodeos so they could use those as beta tests. That way she'd be ready when the rodeo started up again next year.

With the men gone and Mabel taking the morning off to attend her grandson's play, Elise had never felt so lonely.

Her heart jerked when she heard the office front door open. Elise immediately placed her fingers on the keyboard and began typing rapidly. She didn't care what she wrote, so long as she looked busy. It had to be Colt. When his heavy footfalls sounded outside her door, she took a minute to glance up as if engrossed in her work. There was no reason to let Colt know just what a miserable couple of days she'd had without him.

Colt stood there, looking tired, but still sexy as hell. Today he wore dark blue jeans, a white button-down cotton dress shirt, black boots and a black cowboy hat. He was definitely the most dressed up she'd ever seen him and damn if he didn't look good enough to eat. The stark contrast of the white shirt against his tanned skin made him look even more rugged and handsome in her mind.

He didn't say a word but just stared at her for a long moment. The silence between them was finally getting to her. Elise opened her mouth to speak when he walked in the room and set down a manila envelope in front of her on the desk.

"Here's the answer to both our problems. It's more than generous. Read it. Sign it and let's move on with our lives," he finished in a brusque, cold tone before he turned on his booted heel and walked out of her office.

Her heart sank at the finality in his words, but it wasn't until she opened the envelope and pulled out the documents with their official seals, stamps and signatures that her spirits plummeted to deeper depths.

Colt was once again offering to buy her half of the ranch, but what made her stomach feel as if she hadn't eaten in a week—that empty, nausea in the pit-of-the-stomach feeling—was the copy of loan papers he had included to show her just how serious he was. He'd taken out a loan against his personal home and property in order to increase his offer to buy her out.

Elise knew how much Colt's home meant to him, how he'd coveted that property as his and his alone. Knowing that, along with the fact he rarely brought women there, told her he saw his home as his personal haven. Now he'd taken a loan against his property, knowing full well he needed money to replace the entire fence around the Lonestar ranch next year along with other improvements.

Rubbing her temples, she stared at the papers, trying to understand how he could so easily throw away what they had and for what? An assumption, she *might* one day sell her half of the ranch to Jackson Riley?

Elise was so lost in her miserable thoughts she jumped when her phone rang. Grabbing the handset, she put it to her ear. "Hello?"

"G'day, mate. And in just what century did you plan to call me back?"

Elise straightened in her chair at the sound of Alex's upbeat voice. She really needed a friend right now.

"Ah, Alex, you were supposed to call me, but I'm not complaining. You always know just when to call," she sighed into the phone.

"That's not sounding so good," Alex's tone turned serious. "What's wrong?"

"Hold a sec," Elise got up and closed her door, then returned to the phone to tell her friend the entire story.

After listening to Elise talk for forty minutes straight, Alex answered as she always did, to-the-point and full of honesty, "Sounds to me like you need to give Colt exactly what he wants."

Elise's entire body tensed at the advice she didn't want to hear. "But-but, I don't want to sell the ranch. I'd have no reason to stay… I love him, Alex." And she did, damnit, even if that was the first time she admitted it aloud.

"Exactly my point," her friend countered.

Confused, Elise frowned. "Um, I don't get—"

"Give the bloke *what* he wants, Elise," Alex insisted.

Alex always was more like a man in that respect, saying as little as possible to get her point across. Elise listened to the inflection in her friend's voice and she finally got what Alex was trying to say.

She nodded as the hint of a smile tilted the corners of her lips. "Have I told you how much I miss not having you around?"

"Not in a while," came her friend's dry response, though Elise could practically "hear" the pleased smile that spread across her face.

"Then we'll have to remedy that situation soon. Thank you for listening with an unbiased ear."

"Any time, babe. Let's not make it so long between talks next time, okay?"

"Maybe slow down on the world gallivanting then," Elise teased back. Sobering, she promised with a smile, "Agreed," before she hung up the phone.

* * * * *

The next day Colt entered the office exhausted. He hadn't slept a wink last night and the two nights before that, he tossed and turned in bed until he gave up on sleep and got up in the wee hours of the morning.

Damn, he missed Elise. He missed her soft skin, her sighs of contentment when he pulled her close. More than anything he missed her company, her infectious laugh and her sassy smile.

The more he thought about missing her, the angrier he became with himself. He knew walking away now was the best thing for him, but damnit, she was the one woman who almost made him forget the wall he'd spent years building around his heart.

He didn't even know for sure if she'd be in the office on Monday. For all he knew, she'd left with Jason. Yet he couldn't help the skip in his heartbeat when he saw her car sitting outside the office yesterday. She'd stayed.

When he'd handed her the envelope and saw the look of unexpected confusion in her eyes, he'd almost yanked it back and tucked it under his arm. But before he gave in or said something stupid like, "I missed you last night," he forced himself to leave the documents and walk away. And spent an entirely shitty day and night alone.

He hadn't seen her car in its normal parking space outside

the office this morning. Nodding to Mabel as he hung up his hat, he asked, "Have you seen Elise? She's usually here by now."

"She left the office around one-thirty yesterday," she paused and gave him a puzzled look. "She hugged me and said 'goodbye' like...like she wasn't coming back."

Feeling tense, Colt continued into his office. Nothing was on his desk. Not a note. No signed papers. He poked his head back out to ask, "Did Elise leave anything for me? Any paperwork?"

Mabel didn't look up from the letter she was writing. "No, nothing."

Where was she? Had she really left already? he wondered as he turned back into his office. Damn he was tired. The whole lack of sleep over the weekend and then last night was getting to him. He'd been up since two this morning.

Maybe it was because he was going on fumes, but to hear that Elise hadn't been back to work yesterday and then hadn't come in this morning, a sense of panic gripped him. The thought she'd left for good, that he might never see her one last time, made him feel sick to his stomach.

He sat down and rubbed his hands over his jaw to shake himself out of this melancholy mood. He'd tried to prepare himself by pushing her away instead of waiting for the day she might decide to leave on her own, but being faced with the reality of her absence... God, he'd never felt so alone. His house was achingly quiet, his bed too fuckin' big. He missed her touch, her enticing smell, everything.

Crumpling some papers on his desk into a tight ball, he threw them in the trash and pushed thoughts of Elise to the back of his mind in order to concentrate on the office work that needed to be done.

After a frustrating and unproductive two hours, Colt glanced at the clock on his desk for the umpteenth time and finally gave up on the bills he'd been trying to work on. There were chores that still needed to be done around the ranch. He'd get those done and then, when he was too tired for his mind to wander, he'd get back to this paperwork. As he stood up, he realized...if Elise really had left, he'd have to hire a webmaster to keep up with everything she'd done on the website. Another reason to miss her. Well, shit. Couldn't he go more than five minutes without thinking about her?

Colt grabbed his Stetson and put it on his head as he closed the office door behind him. He'd just started to walk toward the stables when he looked up to see an Express carrier truck driving down the driveway leading to the ranch.

The driver pulled the red truck to a stop and hopped out, a friendly smile on his face. "Hi, I'm looking for Colt Tanner. I have an overnight delivery for him."

Colt nodded. "I'm Colt Tanner."

The young man smiled and handed him a clipboard for him to sign the paperwork. Once Colt signed, he passed him a bulky envelope.

Colt stared at the envelope as the driver started his truck and headed back down the driveway. Why did he feel like he was about to open divorce papers? His heart jerked when he saw the return address. Elise had sent the package from Virginia. Damn. She'd gone back home. To Jason.

His chest tightened and his stomach tensed as he leaned against the fence and opened the envelope. When he pulled out the paperwork and saw the counteroffer Elise had made on his original offer, he didn't know what to think. She'd marked through his numbers and changed the sale price to one dollar. She'd sold her half of the Lonestar property back to him for a buck and had already signed over the ownership papers. Attached at the top of the paperwork was a short note from her.

Now that you are the sole owner, Riley will have no one to pit against the other for ownership of the Lonestar. I hope that gives you some peace from his antics.

The realization that the Lonestar was finally his, paled in comparison to his concern for her own financial situation.

Where'd she plan to get the money she needed? The thought that she might have gotten the money from Jason made him clench his fist, crushing the papers in his hand.

Stay calm, he thought. *She's no longer yours. You let her go. Hell, you practically pushed her into Jason's arms*, he berated himself.

When he started to put the paperwork back in the legal-sized envelope, Colt saw a smaller envelope inside it. Putting the documents inside the package, he withdrew the smaller envelope, then tucked the package under his arm.

On the outside of the sealed envelope, Elise had written his name. He felt something bulky inside the envelope and his hands shook as he ripped it open. Pulling out an antique, silver pocket watch, Colt frowned in confusion. Then he saw a folded note inside the envelope. Hoping the note would explain the watch he opened it.

> Colt,
>
> *This silver pocket watch belonged to your mother's father. Your mother gave it to me the day she left. She asked me to make sure you received it. She was afraid if she tried to give it to you, you'd refuse to accept it.*

Damn straight, he thought as he tossed the watch back inside the envelope, annoyed. But he read on, hoping Elise had left him a personal note since they didn't get to say goodbye.

> *There's something else I thought you should know. Your mother told me the one regret she had was that she gave up trying to see you and your brothers. She'd asked to see you several times, but your father had refused her, saying, "It's not fair to the boys to see you unless you plan on staying."*
>
> *Call your mother, Colt.*

Elise

Colt pulled the pocket watch back out of the envelope and opened it. His grandfather's name was inscribed on the inside. Closing the watch, he gripped it in the palm of his hand as he looked out over the rolling hills of the Lonestar ranch.

His emotions ran the full spectrum from anger to resignation as he came to terms with the fact that he'd spent his whole life thinking his mother didn't care a lick. One thing would never change...his mother had hurt his father, badly. He didn't know that he could ever forgive her for that, but to know he and his brothers weren't totally rejected by her for all those years made him feel a little less militant toward her.

He was so engrossed in his thoughts he didn't see Marie drive up in her car until she shut her car door. The sound drew him out of his reverie.

Marie walked over and leaned on the fence. Tilting her head to the side, she glanced at the Express envelope tucked under his arm and said, "Elise came to see me yesterday to tell me what she planned to do with her inheritance. I don't disagree with her decision. You deserve to own the Lonestar outright, Colt. You've paid your dues."

Colt looked at her, confused by her statement. "Then why did you give your half to her in the first place?"

Marie turned to look out into the pastures, a thoughtful expression on her face. "Because she needed it and so did you," she finished as she met his gaze once more.

Colt looked away, not wanting Marie to see the deep emotion in his expression. "Yeah, but she's gone now. Back to Virginia."

"You and my niece are well suited for each other."

Surprised to hear her vying so much for them as a couple after he'd practically pushed Elise away, he gave a heavy sigh. "She went back to Jason, Marie."

"And you're just going to let her go? Give up on the woman you love that easily?"

At her assumption he loved Elise, Colt jerked his gaze back to her, frowning, ready to deny it. But he'd denied his feelings for long enough. Giving her a wry smile he replied, "I do love her."

"Then either you stay here, keep that wall you've built around your heart and be miserable. Or you go get my niece and *tell* her how much you love her. It's your choice, Colt."

"She's never said she loved me," he said absently, not at all sure what kind of reception he could expect from Elise.

"All you had to do was see the way she looked at you," Marie answered with confidence. As she turned to walk toward the ranch house, she finished, "I've been around the ranch long enough to know how to help out while you're gone. Plus, Nan told me Mace is due back today, so between the two of us and Rick, we can hold down the fort. Don't let her slip through your fingers."

Colt's gaze followed Marie as she entered the kitchen. When the door closed behind her, the impact of her words washed over him. Did Elise love him? She'd acted as though he meant a great deal to her. One thing he knew for sure...they *were* right for one another. No way in hell was that Yank getting his woman.

Chapter Nineteen

Elise walked around her father's charity party on the back patio in her full-length, red sequined gown, feeling elegant but so totally out of place. Adjusting the halter-top strap around her neck, she realized all the designer gowned and tuxedoed clad people around her made her want to be back in Texas...to get back to wearing boots and jeans, riding Lightning with Colt by her side and...and... She shook her head to stop herself from thinking of fantasy scenarios with Colt. Right now wasn't the best time.

She'd been able to avoid her father most of the morning since she spent her time prior to the party outside helping coordinate the caterers, the waitstaff, and the violinists who were there to play classical music for the event.

When she saw Jason exit the back of the house and walk down the stone steps, nodding to her as if he planned to make his way toward her, she turned and dodged through the crowd, picking up a glass of champagne on her way. Stopping near a tall potted tree, she sipped her drink and blinked against the bright Virginia afternoon summer sun. She couldn't help but compare it to Texas weather. Yeah, Virginia wasn't quite as hot as Texas, but she missed seeing Boone's rolling hills, missed the fresh outdoor scents the Lonestar offered versus the current smell of expensive perfumes and colognes that wafted her way today.

The three-piece violinists' music trailed off as her father stood up on the stage with the mike.

"Welcome, everyone to our fifth annual Save the Heart charity party," he started off.

He looks older than I remembered even from a few weeks ago, she thought, staring at her father's graying hair.

As he went into his normal spiel about the charity, she let her gaze roam the area around the stage. A tall, dark-haired man stood in front of the stage, looking up at her father, his back to her. She tilted her head and smiled thinking, *Man, I'll bet that's what Colt would look like in a tux. He's about the same height and build. Ha! It'll be cold day in hell before I ever see that from Mr. Wranglers.* She chuckled inwardly as the man started up the steps and took the mike from her father's hand.

When he turned around, Elise almost dropped her glass. Colt stood up on the stage with her father.

"Thank you, Fred, for inviting me to emcee the presentation of the donation checks to the Save the Heart charity today," he said in his best Texan drawl. And damn if the man didn't knock her socks off in a tuxedo. He looked every bit as debonair as James Bond and ten times as rugged. What a lethal combination to her libido!

"Where the hell did he come from?" Jason whispered in a disgruntled tone in her ear.

She didn't even look his way, but kept her gaze glued on Colt as she answered, "Texas, born and bred."

When Colt called the head of the Save the Heart charity to come up on stage, Elise handed her glass to Jason and said, "Gotta go" before she made her way over to stand in front of the stage. What *was* Colt doing here? And how in the world did he get her father to invite him to this function?

"I know a little bit about 'saving the heart'," Colt said in a lighthearted manner as Susan Kress, president of the charity, made her way up on the stage.

The crowd laughed and Colt looked right into Elise's eyes when he followed his statement with, "I'm learning more about it everyday." He smiled at her then continued, "I'd like to introduce Save the Heart's first contributor, Elise Hamilton."

Elise walked up on the stage to stand between Colt and Susan. During the crowd's applause, she whispered to him,

"What are you doing here?"

He reached down and clasped her hand, lacing his fingers with hers as he answered in the mike for everyone to hear, "I'm 'saving a heart', darlin'."

She stared at him, dumbfounded, her heart ramming in her chest. Colt's blue eyes twinkled and he winked at her, whispering, "Now's the time to give 'em their check, sweetheart."

Shaking herself out of the surreal dream she seemed to have fallen into, Elise faced Susan and handed her the twenty thousand dollar check she'd had tucked in her hand since the beginning of the party, saying, "I hope your charity can put this to good use, Susan. I'm one hundred percent behind the work you're doing."

"Thank you so much," Susan beamed as she took the check from Elise.

"Why don't you tell everyone just how you're going to spend this money, Ms. Kress," Colt said, handing Susan the mike.

While Susan began to talk about research hospitals and private donations, Colt moved behind Elise and wrapped his arms around her waist.

Elise's heart rammed in her chest that he'd so publicly staked his claim on her. She glanced at her father who had his gaze on Ms. Kress. But before she looked away, she saw him flick his gaze to Colt's arms around her and then above her head as if he were looking at Colt. When he gave Colt a curt, respectful nod, she let out a breath of relief. She had no idea she'd even been holding it, but apparently deep down she'd hoped her father liked Colt.

Colt leaned close to her ear and said, "Good thing your father can't hear this or I'd lose all the respect I've gained, but holy shit, Lise, I've never wanted you as bad as I do this second. I think I'd be willing to don a monkey suit like this every so often just so I can see you all dressed to the nines like you are now." His voice dropped to a husky rasp as he continued, "And do you know why?"

When she didn't answer, but instead squeezed his hand—in truth she was absolutely speechless—he continued, "'Cause I can't wait to peel off the fancy clothes to get to my woman...the woman who looks so damn right in my bed wearing nothing at all but the sweet flesh God gave her. I'm here to convince you to come home with me where you belong, Lise."

Elise clamped her hand over her mouth to stifle her shocked gasp, but her happiness radiated through as she turned in Colt's arms and faced him. Looking over at Susan, she said, "Please excuse us, Susan. My father will present the other checks to your charity now."

Susan nodded her assent, but Colt was already pulling her off the stage. "Colt," she started to say to slow him down as she reached the last step, but he didn't listen. Instead, he scooped her up in his arms and strode off the patio and up the stone stairs into the house. They entered the house among the cheering of the crowd behind them and Elise's heart soared. She tightened her arms around his neck feeling very much like the Princess with her very own Knight in Shining Armor, make that a "Cowboy" knight who had come to sweep her away.

When Jason's voice called her name from outside, sounding close as if he were following them inside, Colt's arms tightened around her and he picked up his pace, opening the first door he came to.

He shut the door behind him and locked it, then let her slide down his body until her high-heeled sandals touched the tile floor. Elise kept her arms wrapped around his neck and whispered in his ear with a soft laugh, "What is it with you and me and bathrooms?"

"It seems to be where we do our best communicating, darlin'," he replied, his tone lowering to a deeper baritone. He placed his large hands against her exposed bare back and clasped her against him as he leaned against the door. His deep blue gaze, full of desire and promise, held hers. "I won't be an easy man to be with, Lise, but one thing I can guarantee you, you'll always come first in my life."

Her breath escaped in a surprised sob and she threaded her fingers in his thick, dark hair. "I think that's the best offer I've heard in a long time, Colt Tanner."

"Nah, sweetheart, I hope the best offer you'll hear is this one…" he said. Dipping his head, he trailed hot, blazing kisses from the hollow at the base of her throat all the way up until he reached her jaw. Sliding his hands further up her back, he pressed her chest against his at the same time his hard erection rubbed against her lower belly.

The feel of his hard, muscular chest pressed against hers, the faint, yet masculine scent of his cologne, coupled with his warm hands on her bare flesh made her go weak in the knees and her heart ram in her chest. As his mouth hovered close to hers, tempting her, taunting her, reminding her of the night by the fire and how they'd denied themselves even one kiss, she closed her eyes, waiting in tense anticipation for his lips to claim hers.

When he said, "Marry me," her eyes flew open at his unexpected proposal, shock slamming through her in waves. She started to speak, but the look of tender love shining in his eyes took her breath away, rendering her speechless.

"I want you to be my wife. I want to fall asleep with you in my arms, to see you pregnant and holding our babies. I want to hear your input on running the ranch, to have you by my side when I'm out on the range, but more than anything…" he paused, and his gaze searched hers as he cupped her face in his big hands and rubbed his thumbs slowly down her cheeks. "I want to grow old with you. I love you, Lise," he finished in a rough voice as if admitting his deepest desires was one of the hardest things he'd ever done.

Elise put her hands on his wrists and sobbed. She'd never thought she'd hear Colt tell her he loved her. It was the sweetest sound she'd ever heard. She didn't bother stopping the tears that gathered in her eyes. As they spilled out, she finally gained the ability to smile.

He rubbed her tears away and gave her a sexy, half-smile. "Does that mean yes you'll marry me, darlin', 'cause right now hearing you say 'I love you' back would do a world of good to my ego."

Her spirits bolstered, she gave him a sassy grin. Unbuttoning his tux jacket, she slid her hands around his waist to press her body close to his once more. "Now what made you think I'd left Texas for good, Colt Tanner? I was coming back. I was nowhere *near* done with you. I just thought you might need a break for a bit—"

She didn't get to finish her cheeky response before Colt's mouth landed on hers, his tongue thrusting inside her mouth. He speared his fingers through her French twist, knocking out the comb holding it in place as he cupped the back of her head.

Colt growled, a low, sexually charged sound at the same time he stepped into her, pushing her back against the sink's cabinet. "I want to hear it, Lise," he said, his voice a low rumble against her mouth. Her stomach flip-flopped at the ferocity in his tone while her lower body began to throb, when he clasped the flesh of her rear through her dress and started to lift her up on the counter. Between kisses, she said, "I love you, Colt Tanner. Yes, I'll marry you…my life is with you, no matter where we live." She clasped his neck tight as he'd placed her on the countertop.

When Colt's hands landed on her thighs, exposed by the two long slits up the side of her gown, tiny shivers made their way up her body. The shivers quickly turned into tingling awareness as he slid his hands up the bare skin until his thumbs rubbed against her silk underwear.

"Now this is where fancy duds gets to be a pain in the ass," he ground out as he flipped the center piece of her long sequined skirt lying between her legs to the outside of one of her thighs to give him better access to her body.

The sensation of his fingers pressed against her damp

underwear caused her chuckle to die on her lips. Desire darkened his blue gaze. One dark eyebrow rose and his expression turned arrogant then seductive as he pulled her underwear down her legs and tossed it on the floor.

She glanced down at the obvious bulge between his legs and as he followed her gaze, he demanded, his voice turning serious, "Look at me, Lise."

She looked up and her heart melted at the intense look in his eyes and the raw hunger she saw reflected in his gaze as he unbuttoned and unzipped his pants. Knowing he wanted her and planned to have her right then left her breathless and her heart galloping in her chest.

Reaching up, she pushed the jacket down his shoulders until it fell to the floor, then quickly pulled his tie apart. With a few seconds, she'd flown through undoing the buttons on his shirt until it fell open, exposing his hard chest. When he dropped his pants and silk boxers, she grinned. "Hmmm, you even wore silk boxers for the occasion." Wrapping her fingers around his hard erection, she enjoyed the heat and smooth feel of his skin.

Colt sucked in his breath at her touch. He wrapped his hand around hers and held her gaze while he guided her hand up and down his shaft, groaning his pleasure.

After a few more stokes, he shook his head, his expression even more focused. "It's not enough, baby. I won't be happy until you're surrounding me from all sides and I'm in as deep as I can get."

To hear the conviction in his voice, to see the deep, emotional fires burning in his gaze, and to know he loved her with all his heart—the whole package was a total turn-on. She ran her tongue along her lower lip, then bit the plump flesh just to let him know how much she wanted him.

Colt's nostrils flared and he stepped closer, his gaze raking down her body. "Unfasten your top," he commanded in a rough-edged tone.

The barely controlled, rasping sound of his voice sent her libido into full throttle. Elise's breathing turned choppy as she reached up and unclasped her gown's halter-top, letting the straps fall down to expose her breasts to his hungry gaze.

She'd barely let go of the straps when Colt's hand came around her back, pulling her close as his mouth captured her nipple and sucked hard on the tightened bud. Burning desire shot straight to her sex at his primal response, making her throb for his touch. Sliding her hands underneath his shirt, she clasped his hard shoulders and felt his muscles flex beneath the warm skin.

"Colt," she managed to sigh out between gasps of pleasure as he sucked hard, using his tongue to rub her nipple against the roof of his mouth before he bit down lightly on the tip. Her body was so in tune with him, she felt tiny tremors in her channel when he moved to the other breast and lavished it with the same attention.

The countertop's extra-tall height wouldn't allow him to enter her from her position, but Colt didn't let that to stop him. He clasped his erection and rubbed the tip of his hot, soft skin along her inner thigh, his actions telling her what he wanted to do to her, teasing her beyond distraction.

"Colt," she said his name again, her tone pleading. She slid closer to him, desperate to have him inside her. Now!

The combination of her impatience and the sequined gown against the slick countertop caused her to slip off the edge. Gasping in surprise, she grabbed his shoulders for support. Colt caught her as a deep chuckle rumbled through his chest.

"Impatient are ya, sweetheart?"

Lifting her rear, he pressed her body high against his. He nipped at her nipple for a brief second before he let her sex slide against his washboard abs and lower. Elise moaned at the delicious sensation of being pressed against his hard warmth as he lowered her body until his cock nudged against her sex.

When he slid inside her, she clutched him close and locked

her legs behind his back, keening her pleasure and enjoying her body's slow adjustment to his width. Once he was fully seated within her, Colt's shoulder muscles bunched and rippled as he lifted her off him and quickly shafted her body, hard and deep. Elise gasped at the pleasure-pain the quick movement caused and screamed at the orgasm his action initiated.

"Damn, Lise," he whispered in a hoarse tone. His body tensed, while she vibrated around him. When her spasms subsided, he carefully turned, then sat down on the closed toilet seat and leaned against the back of the tank.

Elise gave him a sexy smile. Leaning forward she rolled her hips and rubbed her nipples against his chest.

The tactile sensations, inside and out, nearly rocked his world, but Colt held on. He wanted to enjoy the ride a little longer. He wanted to feel Elise come around him at least once more.

Sliding his hands up her skin, under the slits on the sides of her dress, he cupped her sweet ass and rocked his hips, pressing as deep as he could until he touched her womb. She jumped at his movements, gasping in discomfort before she adjusted to his length.

"Better?" he asked. He knew his voice sounded scratchy, but damn he was ready to explode and her tiny sighs of pleasure, combined with her pelvic muscles clasping his cock tight, while her beautiful breasts danced in his face, was more stimulation than any man could take.

When she nodded, he slid his hands down the outside of her silky smooth thighs, past her tight calf muscles until he reached her high-heeled sandals. Guiding his hands under the arches of her shoes, he cupped her shoes' soles and ground out, "You know what I want. Ride me."

Elise stopped rocking her hips and opened her eyes, starring directly into his. God, he could get lost in those beautiful green pools, so full of desire and love.

As she clasped his shoulders, she gave him a seductive

fuck-me smile before she bit her lower lip and raised her hips, pulling off him and slamming back down on his shaft hard and fast.

Colt locked his jaw, determined not to come yet despite the jolts of pleasure shooting through his cock and radiating to his lower belly and thighs.

Elise smiled again as if she knew what it took for him to hold back. Then she leaned close and rubbed her nipples against his chest once more. A shudder ran through him when she ran her tongue up his neck before she nipped at his jaw.

"Elise," he warned, but she paid him no heed. Rolling her hips, she clenched her lower muscles at the same time she pushed against his hands and slowly rose to the tip of his erection. His arm muscles tightened to support the full weight of her body on his hands while she held herself above him. But when he heard her unsteady intake of breath, he knew she was almost there.

As she started to lower herself, he rasped, "That's it, baby, come for me," and thrust upwards just as she came down on him.

She muffled her scream against his shoulder at the same time he felt the tremors ripple through her walls and that's all it took. Colt let go of her feet and clasped her hips, holding her still. Pinning her hips to his, he thrust deeper and deeper into her warm, soft body until he groaned through his own thoroughly satisfying release.

When their breathing slowed, Elise sat up and smiled at him. "You give a whole new meaning to the expression, 'Ride 'em, cowboy'."

Colt laughed out loud at her statement. God, he loved this woman! Leaning forward, he kissed the hollow at the base of her throat then met her gaze. "When are you coming home?"

She laughed and threaded her fingers through his hair. "As soon as I can hitch a ride."

At his confused expression, she grinned. "I sold my car in

order to meet my pledge to the charity."

"Bet your dad thought for sure you'd be staying now with no car. Well, 'til I waltzed in and told him I loved his daughter and planned to ask her to marry me," he finished with a chuckle.

She raised her eyebrows in surprise. "Ah, I wondered what you'd said to my father to not only get yourself invited to the party, but to be asked to help emcee. Very impressive."

Colt winked. "I had to promise your dad you'd come home often — that his grandkids would know your family just as well as their Texan one."

"Oh no, he's going after my children now — recruiting them for the company before they're even born," she groaned.

Colt shook his head. "No, Elise. He just wants you and yours to be a part of his life. That's all he ever wanted."

His suddenly serious tone surprised her. "Really?"

Colt nodded. "You should talk to your dad before we leave."

Elise smiled, knowing she was going to go home with Colt for good. "Hey, speaking of talking to parents...did you call your mother?"

His brows drew together in a frown. "One step at a time, Lise."

"But—"

"I kept the watch," he interrupted in a gruff voice.

Elise smiled and hugged his neck tight. "That's a start, at least."

Colt wrapped his arms around her and whispered, "Thank you for being my partner in every respect."

Swatting her rear, he said, "We'd best get back to the party before your father sends someone after us."

As they cleaned up and rearranged their clothes, they laughed about how well tumbled they both looked. While Elise stood in front of the mirror fixing her hair, Colt stood behind her tying his bowtie. When they both finally looked presentable, he asked, "You think maybe we could loosen the party up a bit? I wonder if the fiddlers out there know how to play Charlie Daniels', 'The Devil Went Down to Georgia'?" he asked with a grin and a wicked gleam in his eyes.

Loving this man's sense of humor more and more, Elise winked at him in the mirror and replied, "Let's go find out."

About the author:

Born and raised in the southeast, Patrice has been a fan of romance novels since she was thirteen years old. While she reads many types of books, romance novels will always be her mainstay, saying, "I guess it's the idea of a happy ever after that draws me in."

Patrice welcomes mail from readers. You can write to her c/o Ellora's Cave Publishing at 1337 Commerce Drive, #13, Stow, Ohio 44224.

Why an electronic book?

We live in the Information Age—an exciting time in the history of human civilization in which technology rules supreme and continues to progress in leaps and bounds every minute of every hour of every day. For a multitude of reasons, more and more avid literary fans are opting to purchase e-books instead of paperbacks. The question to those not yet initiated to the world of electronic reading is simply: *why*?

1. *Price.* An electronic title at Ellora's Cave Publishing runs anywhere from 40-75% less than the cover price of the <u>exact same title</u> in paperback format. Why? Cold mathematics. It is less expensive to publish an e-book than it is to publish a paperback, so the savings are passed along to the consumer.
2. *Space.* Running out of room to house your paperback books? That is one worry you will never have with electronic novels. For a low one-time cost, you can purchase a handheld computer designed specifically for e-reading purposes. Many e-readers are larger than the average handheld, giving you plenty of screen room. Better yet, hundreds of titles can be stored within your new library—a single microchip. (Please note that Ellora's Cave does not endorse any specific brands. You can check our website at www.ellorascave.com for customer recommendations we make available to new consumers.)

3. *Mobility.* Because your new library now consists of only a microchip, your entire cache of books can be taken with you wherever you go.
4. *Personal preferences are accounted for.* Are the words you are currently reading too small? Too large? Too…**ANNOYING**? Paperback books cannot be modified according to personal preferences, but e-books can.
5. *Innovation.* The way you read a book is not the only advancement the Information Age has gifted the literary community with. There is also the factor of what you can read. Ellora's Cave Publishing will be introducing a new line of interactive titles that are available in e-book format only.
6. *Instant gratification.* Is it the middle of the night and all the bookstores are closed? Are you tired of waiting days—sometimes weeks—for online and offline bookstores to ship the novels you bought? Ellora's Cave Publishing sells instantaneous downloads 24 hours a day, 7 days a week, 365 days a year. Our e-book delivery system is 100% automated, meaning your order is filled as soon as you pay for it.

Those are a few of the top reasons why electronic novels are displacing paperbacks for many an avid reader. As always, Ellora's Cave Publishing welcomes your questions and comments. We invite you to email us at service@ellorascave.com or write to us directly at: 1337 Commerce Drive, Suite 13, Stow OH 44224.

Discover for yourself why readers can't get enough of the multiple award-winning publisher Ellora's Cave. Whether you prefer e-books or paperbacks, be sure to visit EC on the web at www.ellorascave.com for an erotic reading experience that will leave you breathless.

WWW.ELLORASCAVE.COM